Praise for Shari Lapena:

'Shari expertly traps you, confounds you and leaves
you gasping at the end. More, please!'
FIONA BARTON

'Meticulously crafted and razor sharp.'
HARLAN COBEN

'A twisty, utterly riveting tale that will send readers on
a wild rollercoaster of emotions. Shocking revelations
kept me turning the pages like a madwoman.'
TESS GERRITSEN

'Creeping sense of dread throughout . . .
A firecracker of a plot twist.'
Metro

'Entirely compelling, utterly realistic and told in a
wonderfully effective spare narrative. You will
not see the twists coming.'
Daily Mail

'Provocative and shocking.'
LISA GARDNER

'I thought the read-it-in-one-sitting thing was
a cliché. Not anymore.'
LINWOOD BARCLAY

www.pengui

D0280863

Shari Lapena worked as a lawyer and as an English teacher before writing fiction. Her debut thriller, *The Couple Next Door*, was a global bestseller. Her second thriller, *A Stranger in the House,* has been a *Sunday Times* and *New York Times* bestseller. Her third novel is *An Unwanted Guest*.

For more information on Shari Lapena and her books, see her website at www.sharilapena.com

Also by Shari Lapena

THE COUPLE NEXT DOOR
A STRANGER IN THE HOUSE
AN UNWANTED GUEST

A STRANGER IN THE HOUSE

Shari Lapena

CORGI BOOKS

TRANSWORLD PUBLISHERS

61–63 Uxbridge Road, London W5 5SA

www.penguin.co.uk

Transworld is part of the Penguin Random House group of companies
whose addresses can be found at global.penguinrandomhouse.com

First published in Great Britain in 2017 by Bantam Press
an imprint of Transworld Publishers
Corgi edition published 2018

A CIP catalogue record for this book
is available from the British Library.

ISBN
9780552173155 (B format)
9780552174978 (A format)

Typeset in 11.5/15.5 pt Sabon by Jouve (UK), Milton Keynes
Printed and bound in Great Britain by Clays Ltd, Elcograf S.p.A.

Penguin Random House is committed to a sustainable
future for our business, our readers and our planet. This book is made
from Forest Stewardship Council® certified paper.

To Manuel, Christopher and Julia, always

Prologue

SHE DOESN'T BELONG here.

She bolts out the back door of the abandoned restaurant, stumbling in the dark – most of the lights are burned out, or broken – her breath coming in loud rasps. She runs like a panicked animal to where she parked the car, hardly aware of what she's doing. Somehow she gets the car door open. She buckles up without thinking, wheels the car around in a screeching two-point turn, and peels out of the parking lot, swerving recklessly onto the road without even slowing down. Something in the strip mall across the street catches her eye – but she has no time to register what she sees, because she's already at an intersection. She runs the red light, picking up speed. She can't think.

Another crossroads – she guns through it. She's driving way over the speed limit, but she doesn't care. She has to get away.

Another intersection, another red light. Cars are already crossing the other way. She doesn't stop. She bursts through it, weaving around a car in her path, leaving chaos in her wake. She hears the shriek of brakes and violent honking behind her. She's dangerously close to losing control of the car. And then she does – she has one moment of clarity, of disbelief, as she frantically pumps the brakes and the skidding car leaps the kerb and plunges headfirst into a utility pole.

Chapter One

ON THIS HOT August night, Tom Krupp parks his car – a leased Lexus – in the driveway of his handsome two-storey home. The house, complete with a two-car garage, is set behind a generous lawn and framed with beautiful old trees. To the right of the driveway, a flagstone path crosses in front of the porch, with steps leading up to a solid wooden door in the middle of the house. To the right of the front door is a large picture window the width of the living room.

The house sits on a gently curving street that ends in a cul-de-sac. The surrounding houses are all equally attractive and well maintained, and relatively similar. People who live here are successful and settled; everyone's a little bit smug.

This quiet, prosperous suburb in upstate New York, populated with mostly professional couples and their families, seems oblivious to the problems of the small city that surrounds it, oblivious to the problems of the larger world, as if the American dream has continued to live on here, smooth and unruffled.

But the untroubled setting does not match Tom's current state of mind. He cuts the lights and the engine and sits uneasily for a moment in the dark, despising himself.

Then, with a start, he notices that his wife's car is not in its usual place in the driveway. He automatically checks his watch: 9:20. He wonders if he's forgotten something. *Was she going out?* He can't remember her mentioning anything, but he's been so busy lately. *Maybe she just went out to run an errand and will be back any minute.* She's left the lights on; they give the house a welcoming glow.

He gets out of the car into the summer night – it smells of freshly mown grass – swallowing his disappointment. He wanted, rather fervently, to see his wife. He stands for a moment, his hand on the roof of the car, and looks across the street. Then he grabs his briefcase and suit jacket from the passenger seat and tiredly closes the car door. He walks along the path, up the front steps, and opens the door. Something is wrong. He holds his breath.

Tom stands completely still in the doorway, his hand resting on the knob. At first he doesn't know what's bothering him. Then he realizes what it is. The door isn't locked. That in itself isn't unusual – most nights he comes home and opens the door and walks right in, because most nights Karen's home, waiting for him. But she's gone out with her car and forgotten to lock the door. That's very odd for his wife, who's a stickler about locking the doors. He slowly lets out his breath. *Maybe she was in a rush and forgot.*

His eyes quickly take in the living room, a serene rectangle of pale gray and white. It's perfectly quiet; there's obviously no one home. She left the lights on, so she can't have gone out for long. *Maybe she went to get some milk.* There will probably be a note for him. He tosses his keys onto the small table by the front door and heads straight for the kitchen at the back of the house. He's starving. He wonders if she's already eaten or whether she's been waiting for him.

It's obvious that she's been preparing their supper. A salad is almost finished; she has stopped slicing mid-tomato. He looks at the wooden cutting board, at the tomato and the sharp knife lying beside it. There's pasta on the granite counter, ready to be cooked, a large pot of water on the stainless steel gas stove. The stove is off and the water in the pot is cold; he dips a finger in to check. He scans the refrigerator door for a note – there's nothing written on the whiteboard for him. He frowns. He pulls his cell phone out of his pants pocket and checks to see if there's any message from her that he might have missed. Nothing. Now he's mildly annoyed. She might have told him.

Tom opens the door to the refrigerator and stands there for a minute, staring sightlessly at its contents, then grabs an imported beer and decides to start the pasta. He's sure she'll be home any minute. He looks around curiously to see what they might have run out of. They have milk, bread, pasta sauce, wine, Parmesan cheese. He checks the bathroom – there's plenty of toilet paper. He can't think of anything else that might be urgent. While he waits for the water to come to a boil, he calls her cell, but she doesn't pick up.

Fifteen minutes later, the pasta is ready, but there is no sign of his wife. Tom leaves the pasta in the strainer in the sink, turns off the burner under the pot of tomato sauce, and wanders restlessly into the living room, his hunger forgotten. He looks out the large picture window across the lawn to the street beyond. *Where the hell is she?* He's starting to get anxious now. He calls her cell again and hears a faint vibration coming from behind him. He whips his head toward the sound and sees her cell phone, vibrating against the back of the sofa. *Shit. She forgot her phone. How can he reach her now?*

He starts looking around the house for clues as to where she might have gone. Upstairs, in their bedroom, he's surprised to find her bag sitting on her bedside table. He opens it with clumsy fingers, faintly guilty about going through his wife's purse. It feels private. But this is an emergency. He dumps the contents onto the middle of their neatly made bed. Her wallet is there, her change purse, lipstick, pen, a tissue packet – it's all there. *Not an errand then. Maybe she stepped out to help a friend? An emergency of some kind?* Still, she would have taken her purse with her if she was driving the car. And wouldn't she have called him by now if she could? She could borrow someone else's phone. It's not like her to be thoughtless.

Tom sits on the edge of the bed, quietly unravelling. His heart is beating too fast. Something is wrong. He thinks that maybe he should call the police. He considers how that might go. *My wife went out and I don't know where she is. She left without her phone and her purse. She forgot to lock the door. It's completely unlike her.* They probably won't take him seriously if she's been gone such a short time. He hasn't seen any sign of a struggle. Nothing is out of place.

Suddenly he gets up off the bed and rapidly searches the entire house. But he finds nothing alarming – no phone knocked off the hook, no broken window, no smear of blood on the floor. Even so, he's breathing as anxiously as if he had.

7

He hesitates. Perhaps the police will think they've had an argument. It won't matter if he tells them there was no argument, if he tells them they almost never argue. That theirs is an almost perfect marriage.

Instead of calling the police, he runs back into the kitchen, where Karen keeps a list of phone numbers, and starts calling her friends.

Looking at the wreckage in front of him, Officer Kirton shakes his head in resignation. People and cars. He's seen things to make his stomach empty itself on the spot. It wasn't that bad this time.

There'd been no identification on the crash victim, a woman, probably early thirties. No purse, no wallet. But the vehicle registration and insurance had been in the glove compartment. The car is registered to a Karen Krupp, at 24 Dogwood Drive. She'll have some explaining to do. And some charges to face. For now, she's been taken by ambulance to the nearest hospital.

As far as he can figure, and according to witnesses, she was travelling like a bat out of hell. She ran a red light and smashed the red Honda Civic right into a pole. It's a miracle no one else was hurt.

She was probably high, Kirton thinks. They would get a tox screen on her.

He wonders if the car was stolen. Easy enough to find out.

Thing was, she didn't look like a car thief or a druggie. She looked like a housewife. As far as he could tell through all that blood.

Tom Krupp has called the people he knows Karen sees most often. If they don't know where she might be, then he isn't waiting any longer. He's calling the police.

His hand trembles as he picks up the phone again. He feels sick with fear.

A voice comes on the line, '911. Where's your emergency?'

As soon as he opens the door and sees the cop on his doorstep, his face serious, Tom knows something very bad has happened. He is filled with a nauseating dread.

'I'm Officer Fleming,' the cop says, showing his badge. 'May I come in?' he asks respectfully, in a low voice.

'You got here fast,' Tom says. 'I just called 911 a few minutes ago.' He feels as if he might be going into shock.

'I'm not here because of a 911 call,' the officer says.

Tom leads him into the living room and collapses onto the large white sofa as if his legs have given out, not looking at the officer's face. He wants to delay the moment of truth for as long as possible.

But that moment has come. He finds that he can hardly breathe.

'Put your head down,' Officer Fleming says, and places his hand gently on Tom's shoulder.

Tom leans his head toward his lap, feeling like he's going to pass out. He fears that his world is coming to an end. After a moment he looks up. He has no idea what's coming next, but he knows it can't be good.

Chapter Two

THE THREE BOYS – two thirteen-year-olds, and one fourteen, just beginning to sprout hair on his upper lip – are accustomed to running wild. Kids grow up fast in this part of town. They're not home late at night, hovered over computer screens doing homework or tucked in their beds. They're out looking for trouble. And it looks like they've found it.

'Yo,' says one, stopping suddenly inside the door of the abandoned restaurant where they sometimes go to smoke a joint, if they have one. The other two spill around him, then stop, peering into the dark.

'What's that?'

'I think it's a dead guy.'

'No shit, Sherlock.'

Senses suddenly on alert, each of the boys freezes, afraid that someone else might be there. But they realize they're alone.

One of the younger boys laughs nervously in relief.

They move forward curiously, looking at the body on the floor. It's a man, sprawled on his back, with obvious gunshots to his face and chest. There's a lot of blood soaking the man's light-coloured shirt. None of them is the least bit squeamish.

'I wonder if he's got anything on him,' says the oldest boy.

'I doubt it,' one of the others answers.

But the fourteen-year-old slips his hand expertly into a pocket of the dead man's pants, pulling out a wallet. He rifles through it. 'Looks like we got lucky,' he says with a grin, holding the open wallet up for them to see. It's full of bills, but in the dark it's too hard to tell how much is there. He pulls a cell phone from the dead man's other pocket.

'Get his watch and stuff,' he tells the others, as he scans the floor hopefully, looking for a gun. It would be great to find a weapon, but he doesn't see one.

One boy removes the watch. The other struggles a bit with a heavy gold ring but eventually tugs it from the corpse's finger and slips it into the pocket of his jeans. Then he feels around the man's neck to see if there's a necklace. There isn't.

'Take his belt,' the older boy, obviously the leader, orders. 'And his shoes, too.'

They've stolen things before, although never from

12

a dead body. They're caught up in the thrill of it, breathing rapidly. They've crossed some kind of line.

Then the older boy says, 'We've got to get out of here. And you can't tell anybody.'

The other two look up at the taller boy and nod silently.

'No bragging to anybody about what we did. You got that?' the bigger one says.

They nod again firmly.

'If anybody asks, we were never here. Let's go.'

The three boys slip out of the abandoned restaurant quickly, taking the dead man's things with them.

Tom can tell by the cop's voice, by his facial expression, that the news is very bad. The police must break tragic news to people every day. Now it's his turn. But Tom doesn't want to know. He wants to start this whole evening over again – get out of his car, walk in the front door, and find Karen in the kitchen preparing supper. He wants to put his arms around her and breathe her in and hold her tight. He wants everything to be the way it used to be. If he hadn't gotten home so late, maybe it would be. Maybe this is his fault.

'I'm afraid there's been an accident,' Officer Fleming says, his voice grave, his eyes filled with sympathy.

He knew it. Tom feels numb.

'Your wife drives a red Honda Civic?' the officer asks.

Tom doesn't respond. This can't be happening.

The officer reads off a licence plate number.

'Yes,' Tom says. 'That's her car.' His voice sounds strange, like it's coming from somewhere else. He looks at the police officer. Time seems to have slowed down. He's going to tell him now. He's going to tell him that Karen is dead.

Officer Fleming says gently, 'The driver is hurt. I don't know how badly. She's in the hospital.'

Tom covers his face with his hands. She's not dead! She's hurt, but he feels a surge of desperate hope that maybe it's not that bad. Maybe it's going to be okay. He removes his hands from his face, takes a deep, shaky breath, and asks, 'What the hell happened?'

'It was a single-vehicle accident,' Officer Fleming says quietly. 'The car went into a utility pole, head-on.'

'What?' Tom asks. 'How can a car go into a pole for no reason? Karen's an excellent driver. She's never had an accident. Someone else must have caused it.' Tom notices the guarded expression on the officer's face. What is he not telling him?

'There was no identification on the driver,' Fleming says.

'She left her purse here. And her phone.' Tom rubs his hands over his face, trying to hold himself together.

14

Fleming tilts his head to the side. 'Is everything okay between you and your wife, Mr Krupp?'

Tom looks at him in dismay. 'Yes, of course.'

'You haven't had a fight, things got a bit out of hand?'

'No! I wasn't even home.'

Officer Fleming sits down in the armchair across from Tom, leans forward. 'The circumstances – well, there's a slight possibility that the woman driving the car, the one who had the accident, may not be your wife.'

'What?' Tom says, startled. 'Why? What do you mean?'

'Since there was no identification on her, we don't actually know for sure at this point that it was your wife driving the car, just that it's her car.'

Tom stares back at him, speechless.

'The accident happened in the south end of the city, at Prospect and Davis Drive,' Officer Fleming says, looking at him meaningfully.

'No way,' Tom says. That was one of the worst parts of the city. Karen wouldn't be caught there in broad daylight, much less be there by herself after dark.

'Do you know of any reason why your wife, Karen, would be driving recklessly – speeding and running red lights – in that part of town?'

'What? What are you saying?' Tom looks at the

15

police officer in disbelief. 'Karen wouldn't *be* in that part of town. And she *never* goes above the speed limit – she would *never* run a red light.' He slumps back against the sofa. He feels relief flood through him. 'It's not my wife,' he says with certainty. He knows his wife, and she would never do something like that. He almost smiles. 'That's someone else. Someone must have stolen her car. Thank God!'

He looks back at the police officer, who continues to observe him with deep concern. And then he realizes, the panic instantly returning. 'So where's my wife?'

Chapter Three

'I NEED YOU to come with me to the hospital,' Officer Fleming says.

Tom can't quite follow what's happening. He looks up at the officer. 'I'm sorry, what did you say?'

'I need you to come to the hospital with me now. We need to get an identification, one way or another. We need to know if the woman at the hospital is your wife. And if it isn't, we need to find her.' He adds, 'You told me you made a 911 call. She's not home and her car has been in an accident.'

Tom nods rapidly, understanding now. 'Yes.'

He quickly gathers his wallet and keys – his hands are trembling – and follows the officer out of the house, where he gets into the backseat of the black-and-white cruiser parked on the street. Tom wonders if any of his neighbours are watching. He thinks fleetingly of how it must look, him in the backseat of a police car.

When they arrive at Mercy Hospital, Tom and Officer Fleming enter through Emergency into the noisy, crowded waiting area. Tom paces nervously back and forth across the smooth, polished floor while Officer Fleming tries to find someone who can tell them where the accident victim is. As he waits, Tom's anxiety climbs. Almost every seat is full, and there are patients on gurneys lining the hall. Police officers and ambulance attendants come and go. Hospital staff work steadily behind Plexiglas. Large TV screens hang from the ceiling playing a series of mind-numbing videos about public health.

Tom doesn't know what to hope for. He doesn't want the injured woman to be Karen. She may be very badly hurt. He can't bear to think about it. On the other hand, to not know where she is, to fear the worst . . . *What the hell happened tonight? Where is she?*

Finally Fleming beckons to him across the crowded waiting room. Tom hurries over. There's a harried-looking nurse by Fleming's side. She says gently, looking at Tom, and then back at the officer, 'I'm sorry. They're doing an MRI on her now. You'll have to wait. It shouldn't be too long.'

'We need to make an ID on this woman,' Fleming presses.

'I'm not going to interrupt an MRI,' the nurse says firmly. She glances sympathetically in Tom's direction. 'I tell you what,' she says, 'I have the clothing and personal effects she was wearing when she came in. I can show them to you if you like.'

'That would be helpful,' Fleming says, looking at Tom. Tom nods.

'Come with me.' She leads them down a long corridor to a locked room, which she opens with a key. She then rummages through several overstuffed cupboards until she pulls out a clear plastic bag with a tag on it and rests it on a steel table. Tom's eyes are immediately glued to the contents of the bag. Inside, there's a patterned blouse that he instantly recognizes. A wave of nausea overwhelms him. Karen had been wearing it that morning when he left for work.

'I need to sit down,' Tom says, and swallows.

Officer Fleming pulls out a chair and Tom sits down heavily, staring at the transparent bag containing his wife's effects. The nurse, now wearing latex gloves, gently pulls the items out onto the table – the patterned blouse, jeans, running shoes. There is blood splattered all over the blouse and jeans. Tom throws up a bit into his mouth, swallows it back down. His wife's bra and panties, similarly bloodstained. A separate ziplock baggie holds her wedding band and engagement ring, and a gold necklace with a single diamond that he'd bought her for their first wedding anniversary.

He looks up in disbelief at the police officer by his side, and says, his voice breaking, 'Those are hers.'

Officer Fleming returns to the police station and meets up with Officer Kirton in the lunchroom a short time later. They grab coffees and find a place to sit.

Kirton says, 'So the car wasn't stolen. That woman was driving her own car like that. What the hell?'

'It doesn't make a lot of sense.'

'She must have been high as a kite.'

Fleming sips his coffee. 'The husband's in shock. As soon as he heard where the accident occurred and how it happened, he didn't believe it was his wife. He almost had me convinced it had to be someone else.' Fleming shakes his head. 'He looked stunned when he recognized her clothes.'

'Yeah, well, lots of housewives have a secret drug habit that hubby knows nothing about,' Kirton says. 'Maybe that's why she was in that part of town – then she got high and freaked out in the car.'

'Maybe.' Fleming pauses and takes another sip of his coffee. 'You never know with people.' He feels bad for the husband, who looked like he'd taken a punch to the stomach. Fleming's seen a lot in his years on the force, and he knows that some of the people you'd least expect are hiding serious drug problems. And hiding seriously sketchy behaviour to support their habits. Lots of people have ugly secrets. Fleming shrugs. 'When we can see her, maybe she'll tell us what the hell she was up to.' He takes a last gulp and finishes his coffee. 'I'm sure her husband would like to know, too.'

Still in the Emergency waiting area, Tom paces fretfully and waits. He tries to remember if there was anything different, anything unusual, about his wife in the last few days. He can't think of anything, but he's been so busy at work. Had he missed something?

What the hell was she doing in that part of town? *And speeding?* What the cop had told him about what she did tonight is so out of character that he can't bring himself to believe it. And yet . . . that's her in there with the doctors. As soon as he can talk to her, he will ask her. Right after he tells her how much he loves her.

He can't help thinking that if he'd been home earlier, like he should have been, instead of—

'Tom!'

Hearing his name, Tom turns around. He'd called his brother, Dan, when he got to the hospital, and now Dan is walking toward him, his boyish face etched with concern. Tom has never been so grateful to see anybody in his entire life. 'Dan,' Tom says with relief.

The brothers hug briefly and then sit on the hard plastic seats across from one another, away from the crowd. Tom fills him in. It feels odd to Tom to be leaning on his younger brother for support; usually it's the other way around.

'Tom Krupp,' a voice calls out loudly across the bedlam of the waiting area.

He stands up immediately and hurries over to the man in the white coat, Dan right behind him.

'I'm Tom Krupp,' Tom says anxiously.

'I'm Dr Fulton. I've been treating your wife,' the doctor says, sounding more matter of fact than friendly. 'She suffered trauma to her head in the accident. We did an MRI. She has a serious concussion, but fortunately, there's no bleeding in the brain. She's very lucky. Her other injuries are relatively minor. A broken nose. Bruising and lacerations. But she'll recover.'

'Thank God,' Tom says, and sags with relief. His eyes well up with tears as he looks at his brother. He only now realizes how tightly he's been holding himself.

The doctor nods. 'The seat belt and the air bag saved her life. She's going to be sore for a while, and she'll have a hell of a headache, but she should be fine, in time. She'll have to take it easy. The nurse will go over with you how to manage the concussion.'

Tom nods. 'When can I see her?'

'You can see her now,' the doctor says, 'just you, for now, but not for too long. We've moved her to the fourth floor.'

'I'll wait here,' Dan says.

At the thought of seeing Karen, Tom feels a new prickle of anxiety.

Chapter Four

KAREN CAN'T MOVE. She's been drifting in and out of consciousness. With her increasing awareness of the pain, she moans.

She tries hard – it seems to take a tremendous effort – and forces her eyes to flutter open. There are tubes going into her arm. She is propped up slightly, and the bed has metal rails on the sides. The sheets are institutional, white. She knows immediately that she's in a hospital bed and is filled with alarm. She turns her head ever so slightly and feels a painful thudding. She winces and the room begins to spin. A woman who is obviously a nurse enters her blurry field of vision and hovers there, indistinct.

Karen tries to focus, but finds she can't. She tries to speak, but she can't seem to move her lips. Everything feels leaden, like there's something heavy weighing her down. She blinks. Now there are two nurses. No, it's just one; she's seeing double.

'You've been in a car accident,' the nurse says quietly. 'Your husband's outside. I'll get him. He's going to be so happy to see you.' The nurse leaves the room.

Tom, she thinks gratefully. She runs her tongue clumsily around the inside of her mouth. She's so thirsty. She needs water. Her tongue feels swollen. She wonders how long she's been here, and how long she will be here, immobilized like this. Her entire body hurts, but her head is the worst.

The nurse comes back into the room, delivering her husband to her as if she's brought her a present. Her vision is growing less blurry now. She can see that Tom looks anxious and exhausted, unshaven, like he's been up all night. But his eyes make her feel safe. She wants to smile at him, but she can't quite manage it.

He leans over her, gazing at her with love. 'Karen!' he whispers, and takes her hand. 'Thank God you're okay.'

She tries to speak, but nothing comes out, only a kind of hoarse whimper. The nurse promptly holds a plastic glass of water with a bent surgical straw to her mouth so that she can drink. She sips greedily. When she's done, the nurse takes the glass away.

Karen tries once more to speak. It takes far too much effort, and she gives up.

'It's okay,' her husband says. He lifts his hand as if to brush the hair away from her forehead, a familiar gesture, but he drops his hand awkwardly. 'You were in a car accident. But you're going to be okay. I'm here.' He looks deeply into her eyes. 'I love you, Karen.'

She tries to lift her head, just a little, but is rewarded with a sharp, searing pain, dizziness, and a wave of nausea. Then she hears someone else entering the doorway of the small room. Another man, taller and leaner than her husband, almost cadaverous, and wearing a white coat and a stethoscope around his neck, approaches her bed and looks down at her as if from a great height. Her husband lets go of her hand and steps aside to give him room.

The doctor bends over her and shines a small light in her eyes, one after the other. He seems satisfied, and puts the light away in a pocket. 'You've sustained a severe concussion,' he says. 'But you're going to be all right.'

Karen finally finds her voice. She looks at the dishevelled, careworn man standing beside the doctor in his white coat and whispers, 'Tom.'

Tom's heart is full, looking at his wife. They've been married just under two years. Those are the lips he kisses every morning and every night. Her hands are as familiar to him as his own. Right now, her lovely blue eyes, surrounded by all the bruising, look full of pain.

'Karen,' he whispers. He leans closer to her and says, 'What happened tonight?'

She looks at him blankly.

He presses her; he must know. His voice takes on a note of urgency. 'Why did you leave the house so quickly? Where were you going?'

She starts to shake her head, but stops and closes her eyes for a moment. She opens them again and manages to whisper, 'I don't know.'

Tom looks back at her in dismay. 'You must know. You had a car accident. You were speeding and hit a pole.'

'I don't remember,' she says slowly, as if it takes every bit of her remaining energy to say it. Her eyes, looking into his, seem alarmed.

'This is important,' Tom says almost desperately, leaning closer. She pulls back, deeper into her pillows.

The doctor intervenes. 'We're going to let you rest now,' he says. He speaks in a low voice to the nurse, and then gestures for Tom to come with him.

Tom follows the doctor out of the room, casting one last glance back at his wife in the hospital bed. It must be the head injury, he thinks, concerned. Maybe it's worse than they thought.

His mind racing, Tom follows Dr Fulton down the

hall. It's eerily quiet – Tom remembers it's the middle of the night. The doctor locates an unused room for them behind the nurses' station.

'Have a seat,' the doctor says, and sits down in an empty chair.

'Why can't she remember what happened?' Tom asks, frantic.

'Sit,' Dr Fulton says firmly. 'Try to calm down.'

'Sure,' Tom says, taking the only other chair in the cramped space. But he's finding it difficult to be calm.

The doctor says, 'It's not unheard of for patients with head trauma to suffer from retrograde amnesia, for a short period.'

'What does that mean?'

'After physical trauma to the head, or even emotional trauma, a patient can temporarily lose memories of what happened right before the trauma occurred. The memory loss can be mild, or more catastrophic. Generally, with a blow to the head, we also see another kind of amnesia – problems with short-term memory after the accident. You'll probably see that for a while, too. But sometimes it can be retrograde as well, and more extensive. I think that's what we're seeing here.'

The doctor doesn't seem too concerned. Tom tries to tell himself that this should be reassuring. 'Is she going to get her memory back?'

'Oh, I certainly think so,' the doctor says. 'Just be patient.'

'Is there anything we can do to help her get it back more quickly?' He's desperate to know what happened to Karen.

'Not really. Rest is what she needs. The brain has to heal. These things happen in their own time.'

The doctor's pager buzzes and he looks at it, excuses himself, and leaves Tom alone with all of his unknowns.

Chapter Five

THE NEXT MORNING, Brigid Cruikshank, a close friend of Karen's from across the street, sits in the lounge on the fourth floor of Mercy Hospital with her knitting on her lap, unspooling the soft yellow yarn from a cloth bag at her feet. The lounge, brightened by large windows that look out over the teeming parking lot, is not far from the bank of elevators. She's working on a baby sweater, but she finds herself dropping stitches and getting angry at the sweater, when really, she knows, it's not the sweater she's angry at.

She spots Tom – in jeans and a plain T-shirt, tall and angular, his hair wild – walking toward the elevators. When he sees her, he seems caught off guard. Perhaps he isn't that happy to see her here. She's not entirely surprised. Maybe he and Karen want their privacy. Some people are like that.

But she needs to know what's going on, so she catches his eye and holds it, and he makes his way slowly over to where she's sitting.

She regards him with concern. 'Tom. I'm so glad to see you. I've been trying to call you. I'm so sorry about—'

'Yeah,' he cuts her off abruptly. He sits down beside her, leans forward, and puts his elbows on his knees. He looks like hell, as if he hasn't slept for the last twenty-four hours. He probably hasn't.

'I've been so worried,' she says. Tom had called her twice the night before – the first time to see if she had any idea where Karen was, and the second time, later, from the hospital to tell her that Karen had been in a car accident. But that call had been brief, and he'd cut it short without giving her any details. Now she's desperate to know. She wants to hear everything. 'Tell me what happened.'

He faces straight ahead, not looking at her. 'She drove her car into a utility pole.'

'What?'

He nods slowly, as if he's unbearably tired. 'The police say she was speeding, that she ran a red light. Somehow she went into a pole.'

Brigid stares at him for a minute. 'What did she say happened?' Brigid asks.

He looks at her now, and she sees a kind of helplessness in his eyes. 'She says she doesn't remember.

Not the accident, or anything leading up to it,' Tom says. 'She doesn't remember last night at all.'

'Really?'

'Yes, really,' Tom says. 'The doctor told me it's normal after an injury like hers.'

Brigid shifts her eyes away from his and back down to her knitting. 'So – will she get her memory back?' Brigid asks.

'They think so. I hope so. Because I'd sure as hell like to know what she was doing.' He hesitates, as if he's not sure he wants to tell her something more. Then he says, 'She left without her purse, and forgot to lock the door. Like she was in a hurry.'

'That's odd,' Brigid says. She's silent for a moment. Finally she adds, 'I'm sure she'll be fine.' It sounds so inadequate. He doesn't seem to notice.

He sighs heavily and says, 'And I have to deal with the police.'

'The police?' Brigid asks quickly, looking up at him again. She notices lines in his face now that she hadn't noticed before.

'They're investigating the accident,' Tom tells her. 'They're probably going to charge her with something.'

'Oh!' Brigid says and puts her knitting aside. 'I'm so sorry, Tom. It's not what you need right now, is it?'

'No.'

Her voice softens. 'If you need a shoulder, you know I'm here for you, right? For both of you.'

'Sure,' he says. 'Thanks.' He stands up. 'I'm going to go get a coffee. Want one?'

She shakes her head. 'No, thanks, I'm good. But can you let Karen know I'm here?'

'Sure. But you might be wasting your time. I don't think she's up to seeing anybody today. She's in a lot of pain so they're giving her heavy-duty pain meds. She's pretty groggy and disoriented. Maybe you should just go home.'

'I'll wait a bit longer. In case she feels up to it,' Brigid says and picks up her knitting again. Once Tom has turned his back to her and is headed toward the elevators, she looks up from her knitting and watches him. She can't believe Karen wouldn't want to see her, just for a minute. She won't stay long. When Tom disappears inside the elevator and she hears the doors slide closed, she gathers up her things and heads for room 421.

Karen shifts her legs restlessly in the white sheets. She's propped up against the pillows. This morning, she already feels somewhat better and is thinking and speaking more clearly. She wonders how long she'll be here.

There's a light tap on her partially open door and she smiles weakly. 'Brigid,' she says. 'Come in.'

'Is it okay?' Brigid says quietly, approaching the bed. 'Tom said you might not want to see me.'

'Why would Tom say that? Of course I'm glad to see you. Come, sit.' She pats the bed feebly.

'Gosh, look at all the flowers,' Brigid says.

'They're all from Tom,' Karen says. 'He's drowning me in roses.'

'I can see that,' Brigid says, sitting lightly on the side of the bed. She studies Karen closely. 'You look awful.'

'Do I?' Karen says. 'They haven't let me near a mirror. I feel like FrankenKaren.' The banter is an attempt to keep at bay the fear she's felt ever since she became aware that she'd been in an accident – an accident that she can't remember anything about. Karen's grateful to see Brigid, her best friend. It's a distraction and a relief from her almost overwhelming anxiety. It feels normal, at a time when very little else does.

She doesn't know what happened last night. But she knows that whatever happened, it was terrifying, and it still threatens her. Not knowing is making her crazy. She doesn't know what to do.

'Thank God you're going to be okay, Karen. I've been worried sick.'

'I know. Sorry.'

'Don't be sorry. You had an accident. It's not your fault.'

Karen wonders how much Brigid knows, what Tom's told her. Probably not much. Tom has never particularly liked Brigid; she has no idea why. They just never seemed to hit it off. It's made things awkward at times.

'It's awful, Brigid,' Karen says hesitantly. 'I don't remember what happened. Tom says I was driving erratically, speeding, and he keeps asking me—'

At that moment, Tom enters the room, carrying two coffees in paper cups. Karen sees him stifle his annoyance at finding Brigid sitting on the bed, but he doesn't fool her. She feels the temperature in the room drop a couple of degrees. Tom hands Karen one of the coffees.

'Hi, Brigid,' Tom says casually.

'Hi,' Brigid answers, glancing at him briefly. She turns back to face Karen. 'I just wanted to see you with my own eyes, make sure you're all right,' she says, getting up off the bed. 'I'll go now, leave you two alone.'

'You don't have to go,' Karen protests.

'You need your rest,' Brigid says. 'I'll come back tomorrow, okay?' She smiles at Tom and slips out of the room.

Karen frowns at Tom and says, 'Why do you dislike Brigid so much, anyway?'

'I don't dislike her.'

'Really? You obviously weren't happy to see her here.'

'I'm just being protective,' Tom protests. 'You know what the doctor said. You need quiet.'

She looks at him over her coffee cup, not quite believing him.

Later that afternoon, when Tom has gone home to get some rest, Dr Fulton returns. Karen remembers him from the night before.

'How are you today?' he asks.

He keeps his voice low and quiet, and she's thankful for that. Her headache has been getting worse throughout the day. 'I don't know. You tell me,' she says cautiously.

He gives her a professional smile. 'I think you're going to be okay. Other than the concussion, everything else is pretty minor.' He goes through his routine of looking in her eyes with his little light, while continuing to talk to her softly. 'The only worrying thing is that you can't remember the accident, but that's not too uncommon. Your memory will most likely come back in a bit.'

'So you've seen this before,' she says slowly, 'where people lose their memory?'

'Yes, I have.'

'And does it always come back?'

'Not always, no.' He's taking her pulse now.

'But usually?'

'Yes.'

'How long does it take?' she asks anxiously. It must be soon. She must know exactly what happened.

'Depends. Could be days, weeks. Everybody's different.' He checks something on a chart and says,
'How's the pain?'

'Bearable.'

He nods. 'It'll get better. We'll keep you in for
observation for another day or two. You're going to
have to take it easy when you get home. I'll give you
a prescription that you can get filled here at the phar-
macy before you go. And I've given your husband
instructions on how to manage a concussion like
yours.'

'Is there anything I can do to help me get my memory back?' she asks.

'Not really.' He smiles at her. 'Just give it time.' And
then he leaves her alone with her simmering panic.

Later, a new nurse comes in, calm and pleasant,
acting as if everything is all right. But everything is
not all right.

'Can I have a mirror?' Karen asks.

'Sure, let me go fetch one,' the nurse says.

She returns with a hand mirror. 'Don't be too
shocked by what you see,' she says. 'There's some
superficial damage, but nothing that won't heal. It's
not as bad as it looks.'

Karen takes the mirror with trepidation. She's
stunned to see that she is almost unrecognizable –
her normally fine features and good skin are
disguised by horrific swelling and deep black bruises.

But it's her own confused, frightened eyes that bother her most. She hands the mirror back to the nurse without saying a word.

Late that night, two teenagers walk home hand in hand from the movie theatre. It's a long walk, but it's a beautiful night; they want to be together, but they have nowhere they can go. Finally he pulls her up against a wall in the dark at the back of a plaza and kisses her. He's older than her, and he's going slow – not like the boys who fumble and rush and have no idea what they're doing. She kisses him back.

There's a loud clatter over by the dumpster and they break apart. A man emptying garbage from a restaurant stares at them. Her date puts his arm around her protectively, sheltering her. 'Come on,' he says. 'I know a place.'

Her body pounds with excitement. She could have gone on kissing him like that forever. She wants to be alone with him, but— She stops. 'Where are we going?'

'Somewhere we can have some privacy.' He pulls her closer. 'If that's what you want.' He kisses her again. 'Or I can walk you home.'

Right now she would follow him anywhere. She gives him her hand and they cross the street, but she hardly notices where they're going. She's only conscious of the feel of his hand in hers, of what she wants. They arrive at a door. He pushes it open. He tilts his head at her. 'Come on. It's okay. There's nobody here.'

She crosses the threshold and he immediately takes her in his arms. He's kissing her again but something's bothering her. There's a smell. She pulls away from him and he seems to notice it, too. They both see it at the same time. There's a body sprawled on the floor, stained with blood.

She screams. He puts his hand gently against her mouth, shushing her. 'Shhhhhh, shhhhhh, you have to be quiet!'

She stops screaming and stares, horrified, at the man on the floor. He drops his hand from her mouth, and she whispers, 'Is he dead?'

'He must be.' He approaches the man and looks down at him. She doesn't dare come any closer. She's afraid she might be sick.

She turns and bolts out of the building and stops in the street, gasping for air. He's right behind her. She looks up at him in anguish and says, 'We have to call the police.' It's the last thing she wants to do. She told her mother she was at a girlfriend's tonight.

'No,' he says. 'Let someone else find him and call the police. It doesn't have to be us.'

She knows what he's afraid of. She's only fifteen. He's eighteen.

'Look,' he says urgently, 'it would be different if the guy were still alive, but there's nothing we can do for him. Let's go. Someone else will find him.'

She thinks it's wrong, but she's relieved to hear him say it. She nods. She just wants to go home.

Chapter Six

JUST AS SHE does every morning, Brigid sits in her favourite chair by the large picture window in her living room, looking out. Brigid's house is directly across the street from Tom and Karen's house. Brigid waits at the window with her cup of coffee watching to see Tom leave for the hospital.

Brigid's husband, Bob, steps into the living room to say goodbye on his way out the door to work.

'I'm going to be late tonight,' he says. 'Might not make it home for dinner. I'll probably just grab something.'

She doesn't answer; she's deep in thought.

'Brigid?' he says.

'What?' she asks, turning to him.

'I said I'll be home late. We have a visitation tonight.'

'Fine,' she says absently.

'What are you up to today?' he asks.

'I'm going to the hospital to see Karen again.' Maybe they will get more time together today.

'Good, that's good,' Bob says. He lingers uncertainly in the doorway for a moment, then leaves.

She knows he worries about her.

He doesn't really care what she does today. He just thinks it isn't good for her to have too much time on her hands. All he's really interested in is if she's keeping her appointments. So she always tells him that she is.

It was a strange enough accident to begin with, Fleming thinks – the driver a supposedly respectable housewife in the wrong part of town, no obvious drugs or alcohol found to explain her behaviour. And now the doctor is telling them that she has amnesia.

You've got to be kidding, Fleming thinks.

'How convenient,' Officer Kirton, standing beside him, says. They stop briefly outside Karen Krupp's door. Fleming puts out a hand to stop the doctor. 'Could she be faking it?' he asks quietly.

Dr Fulton looks at him in surprise, as if it hadn't occurred to him. 'I don't think so,' he says slowly. 'She has a serious concussion.'

Fleming nods thoughtfully. The three of them enter the small private room. Karen Krupp's husband is already sitting in the only chair. It's crowded with all of them there. Karen Krupp, looking bruised and battered, eyes them warily.

'Mrs Krupp,' he begins. 'I'm Officer Fleming and this is Officer Kirton. We hoped you could answer a few questions for us.'

She sits up straighter against the pillows. Tom Krupp shifts nervously.

'Yes, of course,' she says. 'But – I don't know if the doctor has told you, but I can't remember anything about the accident yet.' She frowns apologetically.

'You've been told what happened?' Kirton asks.

She nods uncertainly. 'Yes, but I don't actually remember any of it.'

'That's too bad,' Fleming says. He can tell that their presence here distresses her, although she's trying to hide it. He says, 'The accident occurred at the intersection of Prospect and Davis, in the south end of the city.' He pauses. She looks nervously back at him, but says nothing. 'You live in the north end. Why do you think you might have been in that part of town?'

She shakes her head, winces a little. 'I – I don't know.'

'Can you make a guess?' he asks gently. When she doesn't answer, he says, 'That's a part of town known for drugs, gangs, crime. Not the sort of place a housewife from the suburbs is likely to visit.'

She shrugs helplessly and says in a small voice,

'I'm sorry . . .' Her husband reaches out and squeezes her hand.

Fleming hands her a piece of paper.

'What's this?' she asks nervously.

'I'm afraid it's a ticket for reckless driving, which is a very serious offence in New York.'

She looks at it and bites her lip. 'Do I need to get a lawyer?' she asks uncertainly.

Fleming says, 'That would be a good idea. It's considered a crime. If convicted, you will have a criminal record, and might have to do some jail time.' He sees the shock register on her face. Tom Krupp looks as if he's going to be sick. Fleming glances at Kirton, and the two of them nod goodbye and leave the room.

Dr Fulton follows Fleming and Kirton out. As hectic as his life as an emergency physician is, he's had enough time to wonder what his patient was doing racing red lights in the worst part of the city. She seems like a nice woman. Educated, well spoken – not the kind you'd expect to do that sort of thing. Clearly, her husband is at a loss, too.

He looks at the officers walking away from him down the hall – two solid figures in black uniforms standing out among a sea of the nurses' pastels. He wonders briefly if he should summon them back. But the moment has passed, and he lets them go.

Karen Krupp had been disoriented when they brought her in two nights ago, slipping in and out of consciousness. She hadn't seemed to know who she was, hadn't been able to give them her own name. She'd been agitated, and kept repeating something, he thinks it was a man's name. He can't remember what it was – it had been a crazy night in the ER – but he's pretty sure it wasn't Tom. It's been bothering him. Maybe one of the nurses will remember.

He doesn't think she's faking the amnesia. He suspects she wants to know what happened that night as much as her husband does.

In the evening – it's now almost forty-eight hours since the accident – Tom leaves the hospital and makes his way to his car at the far end of the parking lot. Karen had seemed distracted and upset during his time with her. The visit from the police officers earlier in the day has them both worried. The thought of Karen ending up with a criminal record, the thought of her possibly going to jail, even if only briefly – he's been googling reckless driving in New York – he can't bear to think about it. He takes a deep breath. Perhaps they will be lenient. He has to be strong; he tries to put the police charges out of his mind for now.

As he drives home, Tom thinks about Karen, and about their life together. They'd been so happy, so settled. And now this . . .

When they met, she was temping at his firm, where he's an accountant. There had been an immediate attraction. He could hardly wait for her two-week assignment to be over so that he could ask her out. Still, he was wary, because he'd misjudged before. So he promised himself he would take his time getting to know her. That seemed to suit her as well. She was reserved in the beginning. He thought perhaps she'd misjudged before, too.

But she wasn't like some other women he'd known. She didn't play games. She didn't mess with his head. There was nothing about her to set off alarm bells. There never has been.

There has to be a reason for what she's done. She must have been lured there by someone under false pretenses. She will get her memory back, and then she'll be able to explain everything.

He can tell Karen's scared. He's scared, too.

He parks the car in the driveway and walks heavily up the front steps. Once inside, he looks around the house wearily. The place is a bit of a mess. There are dirty dishes in the kitchen – in the sink, on the table. He's been grabbing a bite at odd times, going back and forth to the hospital.

He'd better clean up. He can't have Karen coming home to a messy house – she would hate that. He starts in the living room, tidying up, putting things away, bringing dirty coffee cups to the kitchen. He runs a vacuum over the large area rug, cleans the glass-topped coffee table with glass cleaner and paper towels. Next he tackles the kitchen. He fills the dishwasher, wipes down the counters, and runs hot water and dish soap into the sink to wash the glass coffee carafe by hand. He searches for the rubber gloves that Karen uses to wash the dishes but can't find them. He plunges his hands into the hot soapy water. He wants Karen to focus on getting well when she comes home, not worrying about the house.

Karen's alone when Dr Fulton stops in for the last time before he leaves that night. It's late, the ward is quiet, and Karen is drowsy. The doctor sits down in the empty chair by her bed and says, hesitantly, 'There's something I wanted to mention.'

She sees the uncertainty in his eyes and feels her body tense.

'When they brought you in, you were very disoriented,' he begins. 'Saying things.'

She's anxious now, and wide awake.

'You kept saying someone's name over and over. Do you remember that?'

She goes completely still. 'No.'

'I couldn't remember, but one of the nurses told me you kept mentioning someone called Robert. Does that name mean anything to you?' He looks at her curiously.

47

Her heart is racing now. She slowly shakes her head back and forth, pursing her lips as if thinking hard. 'No,' she says. 'I don't know anyone by that name.'

'Okay,' Dr Fulton says, standing up again. 'Thought it was worth a try.'

'I'm sure it doesn't mean anything,' Karen says. She waits until the doctor is almost at the door, and then adds, at the last moment, 'I don't think you need to mention it to my husband.'

He turns and looks at her. Their eyes lock for a moment. Then he gives one short nod and leaves the room.

Chapter Seven

TOM'S BARELY OUT of the shower the next morning when the doorbell rings. He's thrown on jeans and a T-shirt and his hair is still wet, but combed. He's leaving for the hospital shortly – another day out of the office. He's barefoot, and has just put a pot of coffee on.

Tom can't imagine who would be at his front door this early. It's not even eight o'clock. He pads over and peers out the door's window. Officer Fleming is standing on the porch.

The sight of Fleming standing outside immediately irritates him. Tom has enough to deal with already, and he doesn't know any more than he did yesterday. He can't help the cops. Why the hell doesn't Fleming just go away and leave them alone until Karen's memory comes back?

He opens the door; you can't leave a uniformed cop standing on your doorstep.

'Good morning,' Fleming says.

Tom stares back at him, unsure of what to do. He remembers how kind Fleming was to him the first time he came to Tom's house, with the terrible news of Karen's accident.

'May I come in?' Fleming asks at last. He's professional and respectful, just as he was that night. He has a quiet, relaxed air about him. He's not threatening; he seems like someone who would want to give you a hand.

Tom nods and opens the door. The house is full of the smell of brewing coffee. He supposes he'd better offer him some. 'Coffee?' he asks.

'Sure,' Fleming says, 'that would be great.'

Tom heads to the spacious kitchen at the back of the house, the cop following him across the hardwood floor. Tom can feel Fleming watching him while he pours them each a cup. He turns around, puts the mugs on the table, and grabs the milk and sugar.

The two of them sit down at the kitchen table.

'What can I do for you?' Tom asks. He feels awkward, and he's not completely able to keep the irritation out of his voice.

Fleming helps himself to milk and sugar and stirs his coffee thoughtfully. 'You were there when we spoke to your wife yesterday about the accident,' Fleming reminds him.

'Yes.'

'You understand why we had to press charges.'

'Yes,' Tom says, his voice sharp. He exhales and adds sincerely, 'I'm just glad no one else was hurt.'

There's a long, heavy silence as Tom ponders just how bad it could have been. Karen might have killed someone – what a horror that would be to live with. That's the sort of thing you never get over. Tom tries to tell himself how lucky they are.

Suddenly Tom wants to talk. He doesn't know why he's telling this police officer – a virtual stranger – this, but he can't seem to stop himself. 'She's my wife. I love her.' The cop looks back at him sympathetically. 'But I have questions, too,' Tom says recklessly, 'the same questions as you. What the hell was she doing down there driving crazy like that? That's not my wife. My wife doesn't do things like that.' Tom pushes his chair back and gets up. He takes his cup to the counter and refills it, trying to regain his self-control.

'That's why I'm here,' Fleming says, watching him closely. 'I wanted to see if you'd thought of anything, remembered anything that might shed some light on the circumstances around her accident. Sounds like you haven't.'

'No.' Tom stares moodily at the floor.

The officer pauses for a moment before asking his next question. 'How is your marriage?' Fleming asks quietly.

'My marriage?' Tom says, looking up sharply. This is the second time Fleming has asked him about it. 'Why do you ask?'

'You made a 911 call that night that she was missing.'

'Because I didn't know where she was.'

Fleming says, his expression neutral, 'Your wife seems to have been running from something. I have to ask – was she running from you?'

'What? No! How could you even ask that? I love her!' Tom shakes his head. 'We haven't been married long – our second anniversary is coming up soon. We're very happy.' He hesitates. 'We were thinking of starting a family.' Then he realizes he's just spoken in the past tense.

'Okay,' Fleming says, making an appeasing gesture with both hands. 'I had to ask.'

'Sure,' Tom says. He wants Fleming to leave.

'What about your wife's life before she met you? Has she ever been married before?'

'No.' Tom sets his mug down on the counter behind him and crosses his arms.

'She ever been in trouble with the law?'

'No, of course not,' Tom says dismissively. But even he can see that, given the circumstances, it's not such a ridiculous question.

'What about you?'

'No, I haven't been in trouble with the law either. I'm

sure you can check us both out. I'm a chartered accountant, she's a bookkeeper – we're rather dull.'

'I wonder . . .' Fleming hesitates, as if he's not sure he should say it.

'What?'

'I wonder if she might be in some kind of danger,' Fleming says carefully.

'What?' Tom says, startled.

'Like I said, she was driving like she was trying to get away from something, as if she were frightened. A calm person doesn't drive like that.'

Tom has no answer to that. He stares at Fleming and bites at his lower lip.

Fleming tilts his head to one side and says, 'Would you like me to help you look around the house?'

Tom regards Fleming uneasily. 'Why?'

'To see if we can find anything that might shed some light . . .'

Tom freezes. He doesn't know how to answer. Normal Tom, before all this happened, would have said, *Sure, let's take a look.* But this is post-accident Tom, who doesn't know what his wife was up to when she fled their house and crashed her car. What if there's something she's hiding, something the police shouldn't find?

Fleming is watching him, waiting, to see what he will do.

*

Brigid is having her morning coffee, sunlight streaming in and falling in a slant across the carpet. Bob has already left for work, slipping away with a peck on her cheek. Things have not been good between her and Bob for some time.

Mostly, he stays away, busy at work. He's the owner of Cruikshank Funeral Homes. But when he's home – when he thinks she isn't looking – he watches her, as if he's worried about her, about what she's thinking, about what she might do. But he doesn't genuinely care how she is, Brigid tells herself. He stopped truly caring a while ago. Now he only cares about how her actions might affect him.

They don't talk about it any more, but Brigid knows that their inability – their failure – to have a child together has changed everything. Their infertility has made her depressed and moody, and it has made Bob withdraw from her. She knows she's changed. She used to be fun, even a little reckless. She used to think she could do anything. But now she feels older, more subdued, less attractive, although she is only thirty-two.

Brigid saw the uniformed police officer arrive in his cruiser a few minutes ago, right after Bob left. She wonders what the cop is doing at the Krupps'. Tom is still home. His car is in the driveway.

She lives so much in her head these days. She knows it isn't good for her, but she has no interest in finding a new job, and *adjusting her expectations*, as Bob encourages her to do. She has a lot of time to think about things. She remembers when Karen first moved in. Tom had been single when he bought the house – the only single man in a neighbourhood full of families. (How bitter Brigid feels; she and Bob had chosen this particular suburb as the perfect place for children – children they will never have.) Then Tom started dating Karen. Once they were married, Karen had made the place her own. Painting, decorating, landscaping. Brigid watched the transformation take place; there's no question Karen has a good eye.

Right from the beginning – before Tom and Karen were even married – Brigid made a point of welcoming Karen to the neighbourhood. Brigid was as friendly as it was possible to be. Karen had seemed reserved at first, but quickly began to accept her friendship, as if she were starved of female companionship. Which Brigid supposed she was, having moved recently from out of state, not knowing anyone. They began to spend more and more time together. Karen genuinely seemed to value her as a friend, even if she wasn't quite comfortable sharing confidences.

Brigid learned that Karen had been temping at Tom's firm and that she was looking for permanent employment. Brigid was the one who got her the spot as bookkeeper at Cruikshank Funeral Homes. It's Brigid who's now making sure that Karen's job is held open for her for as long as she may need. They're relying on a temp in the meantime.

No one could accuse her of not being a good friend.

Chapter Eight

TOM DRIVES KAREN home from the hospital in the early evening. It's been three days since she had the accident. He drives slowly, carefully, avoiding potholes and sudden stops, as she watches out the window. She's grateful. She glances at Tom's profile as he drives. She can tell that he's tense by the set of his jaw, although he's trying to pretend that everything's fine.

They finally arrive at their little street, and Tom pulls into the driveway at 24 Dogwood Drive. It's good to be out of the hospital and home again. She loves that trees have had time to grow here. There's none of that crowding you find in the newer, less expensive suburbs, where houses are crammed so closely together, a measly patch of grass for a lawn. She loves the spaciousness here, the green. She's proud of her garden, bursting now with big pink hydrangeas.

The two of them sit quietly for a minute, listening to the ticking of the cooling engine. Tom puts his hand on top of hers, briefly. Then she slowly gets out of the car.

Once inside the house, she's turning to close the door behind her when Tom tosses his keys on the table by the door. She starts. The loud clatter makes her feel a slice of pain in her temples and a sudden sensation of vertigo. She closes her eyes briefly, sways a little, her hand on the wall.

'Sorry! Are you okay?' Tom asks, contrite. 'I shouldn't have done that.'

'I'm okay, just a little dizzy,' she says. Sharp noises bother her, as do bright lights and sudden movements. Her brain *does* need time to recover. After a moment, she walks into the living room, appreciating the soothing pale gray and white colours and the uncluttered decor. The carefully chosen white sofa faces a modern marble fireplace with a smooth, unfussy exterior. In front of the sofa is a large, square, glass-topped coffee table, with her collection of *Elle Decor* and *Art & Antiques* stored on the shelf beneath it. Above the fireplace is an enormous mirror, and on the mantelpiece there are framed photographs of the two of them, Tom and her. Matching gray chairs face the sofa, with plump pillows in soothing pale pinks and greens. The entire space is light and clean and airy and completely familiar to her. It's as if the last few days have never happened. She moves slowly to the oversized picture window at the front of the room and looks out. The houses across the way look perfectly benign.

At last she turns away and follows Tom into the kitchen.

'I cleaned up,' Tom says, smiling.

Everything gleams. The sink, the taps, the countertop, the stainless steel appliances. Even the dark hardwood floor is shiny. 'You've done a great job,' she says appreciatively, smiling back at him. She glances out the sliding glass doors into the backyard. Then, feeling thirsty, she goes over to the cupboard and reaches in for a glass to get herself a drink of water. She turns on the tap and looks down at the sink and quickly grabs the counter to steady herself. 'I think I'd like to lie down,' she says suddenly.

'Of course,' Tom says. He takes the glass from her and fills it from the tap.

Karen follows Tom upstairs. The bedroom is also light and airy, with lots of windows across the back. There's a novel on her bedside table, and more books on the floor beside the bed. She'd signed them out of the library recently; she'd especially been looking forward to reading the new Kate Atkinson, but she can't read much now until her concussion is better. Doctor's orders. Tom is watching her.

She glances at her dresser. On top of it there's a

mirrored tray holding perfume bottles. Beside that is her jewellery box. Her regular jewellery she's wearing again – her diamond engagement ring and matching wedding band, and the necklace Tom bought her for their first anniversary.

Karen sees herself in the familiar mirror above her dresser, still battered and bruised. She remembers how frightened she'd been. All those times she'd come home and found things slightly out of place, subtle signs that someone had been going through her things. It had scared her. And Tom knew nothing about it.

She's been hiding an awful lot from the man she loves. And she's been so anxious, worried that Dr Fulton would share what she'd said in Emergency with Tom, with the police. If only she could remember what happened that night! She feels as if she's blind, trying to navigate dangers she can't see.

All at once, she's very tired. Tom says soothingly, 'Why don't you rest and I'll make supper.'

She nods. She doesn't want to make supper. She doesn't want to do anything but curl into a ball under the covers and hide from the world.

He says carefully, 'Some of your friends have been asking when they can come visit.'

'I'm not ready to see anyone just yet, except for Brigid.' She's been grateful for Brigid, but she doesn't want to see anyone else; she doesn't want to answer their questions.

'I told them that; they want to come anyway.'

'Not yet.'

He nods. 'I'm sure they'll understand. It can wait. You're supposed to have quiet, anyway.' He looks at her, concerned. 'How do you feel?'

She wants to say, *Terrified*. Instead, she says, with a faint smile, 'Glad to be home.'

Tom lights the grill, marinates a steak, and quickly throws together a small salad and garlic bread. It's a relief to have Karen back home again.

But there's still the elephant in the room. The accident – and what led up to it.

He wants to trust her.

That police officer, Fleming, had wanted to look through the house this morning. Tom remembers how taken aback he'd been when the cop had suggested it. The first thing Tom thought was, *What is he looking for?* Then, *What if he finds something? Something bad?* He told the cop no.

After, he watched from behind the curtains as the cop took a long, lingering look at the house and got back into his cruiser and drove away. Then Tom had done two things. He'd searched online for a local criminal lawyer and made an appointment. And then he'd torn the house apart.

It had taken the better part of the day – with a break to visit Karen in the hospital. The kitchen had taken the longest. He felt through all the cereal boxes, the bags of flour, rice, sugar – anything that wasn't sealed. He took everything out of every cupboard and drawer and looked all the way in the back. He felt unseen surfaces for anything that might be affixed to them. He looked at the top shelves of closets, under the rugs and mattresses, inside suitcases and seldom-worn boots and shoes. He went down to the basement, breathing in the musty air and waiting for his eyes to adjust to the dimmer light. There wasn't much down there – just the laundry room and a few boxes of junk. They used it mostly for storage. He went through everything. He even looked behind the furnace. Finally, he went through the garage. The whole time he was searching, he was in a strange state of disbelief about himself and his situation. *What the hell was he doing? What was he looking for?* He found nothing, nothing at all. He felt foolish, frustrated, and ashamed.

And relieved.

When he was finished, he tidied everything up again the way it had been before, so that Karen wouldn't know what he'd done. And then he'd gone to pick her up at the hospital.

When the steak is done, Tom serves it up and runs upstairs to tell Karen that supper's ready.

They settle in at the kitchen table to eat. Tom offers her red wine but she shakes her head gently.

'Oh, right,' he says. 'I forgot – no alcohol while you're on pain meds.' He puts the wine aside, and gets them sparkling water instead.

Tom looks at his wife across the table, her short brown hair cut in a pixie, bangs falling across her forehead, the lopsided, rueful half smile on her face. If it weren't for the bruising, he could almost believe that nothing had changed.

It's almost like it used to be. But it's nothing like it used to be.

Karen wakes very early in the morning, before first light. She gets up quietly and pulls on a robe. She closes the door behind her and makes her way downstairs to the kitchen.

She knows she won't be going back to sleep. She puts on a pot of coffee and stands looking out with her arms folded, comforted by the familiar sound and smell of the coffee brewing, waiting for it to finish.

As dawn breaks, there's a light mist rising from the back lawn. She stands looking out the glass doors for a long time, trying desperately to remember. She feels as if her life might depend on it.

Chapter Nine

'HEY,' TOM SAYS, quietly entering the kitchen and seeing Karen at the kitchen table with a cup in front of her. It looks like her coffee has long gone cold. He wonders how long she's been up.

She raises her eyes to meet his. 'Good morning.'

She looks charmingly dishevelled in her robe. He feels so grateful to have her here, to have her in his life at all, when he'd been so afraid of losing her the night of the accident. But it feels fragile, too, like they're walking on glass. 'How did you sleep?'

'Not great,' she admits. 'You want some coffee?'

'Sure.'

She gets up and kisses him on the mouth, exactly the way she used to. She pulls away from him, leaving his head spinning. She pours him a cup of coffee and starts to make breakfast.

'No, you sit down. Let me do that,' Tom tells her

firmly. He begins toasting bagels and cracking eggs into a frying pan. 'I've got to start going back into the office again soon,' he says apologetically. 'I wish I could stay home with you, but it's really busy at work right now—'

She says, 'No, that's okay, really. I'm fine. I don't need you to be looking after me all the time. I promise I'll take it easy.' She smiles at him reassuringly.

Tom has something else he needs to tell her; there's no avoiding it. 'There's one other thing.' He pauses, looking up from the frying pan at her.

'What?'

'I made an appointment for us to see a lawyer.' He sees the sudden flicker of fear in her eyes.

She bites worriedly at her lower lip. 'When?'

'This morning, at ten.'

She slides her eyes away. 'Oh. So soon?'

'It's a serious charge, Karen,' he says.

'I know that, you don't have to tell me,' she snaps.

Suddenly they are both tense. Tom wishes they didn't have to see a lawyer, that there had never been an accident, that she'd never run out of the house that night – he feels a flash of anger at her – but what's done is done, and now they have to deal with it as best they can. He realizes he's clenching his jaw, and tries to relax. He keeps his feelings to himself.

*

65

The law firm is in a high-rise office building not far from their house. Karen has been silent for the short drive. Tom doesn't say much either.

It's already hot, but there's nowhere to park out of the sun. When they head inside, the cool, air-conditioned building is a relief. They take the elevator to the sixth floor.

When they get there, the waiting room is empty. Tom watches Karen out of the corner of his eye. She doesn't say anything, doesn't reach for any of the magazines on the low table. She sits tightly in her chair, waiting. It doesn't take long.

'Mr and Mrs Krupp, you can go in now,' the receptionist says, and leads them to an office door that she opens for them, then closes behind her.

Inside, the office looks like the office of any other lawyer – not unlike that of the real estate attorney Tom used to purchase the house on Dogwood Drive before he met Karen. There's an enormous desk, with files neatly stacked all over it. Behind the desk, the lawyer – Jack Calvin – a man with curly salt-and-pepper hair whom Tom judges to be in his midforties, rises to shake hands with each of them, then gestures for them to sit.

'What can I do for you?' he asks. The lawyer looks at the two of them curiously. There's a keen intelligence behind his sharp eyes. Tom can almost see him thinking, *What is this nice couple doing here in my office?*

'I called yesterday, about the charge relating to my wife's recent traffic accident,' Tom says when Karen remains silent. Being in a criminal lawyer's office seems to have cowed her.

'Refresh me,' the man says, not unkindly. 'I get a lot of traffic offences. My bread and butter. Especially DWIs. Is that what we have here?' He flashes a quick, appraising glance at Karen.

'No,' Tom says, and begins to explain about the accident. 'There was no alcohol involved at all. But unfortunately, she was going over the speed limit, and—'

The lawyer cuts him off. 'Sorry – maybe let her tell me what happened, in her own words.'

Tom glances at Karen, who seems to tense up. The lawyer watches her expectantly. When neither Tom nor Karen says anything for a moment, the lawyer glances back and forth between them and asks, 'Is there a problem?'

'Yes,' Karen says, finally speaking. 'I don't remember the accident. I don't remember anything about it.' She frowns apologetically.

'Really?' Calvin says.

'I can't remember anything about that entire evening,' she says. 'It's just a blank.'

'It's true,' Tom says. 'She's got a severe concussion. She only came home from the hospital yesterday.'

The lawyer looks at them, as if amazed. 'Is this for

67

real? Or is this a defence you're trying on? Because you don't need to do that. I'm your lawyer. Leave the defence to me.'

'This is not something we're trying on,' Tom says firmly. 'She has amnesia. But the doctors are pretty sure it's temporary, and that she'll get her memory back.' He looks at Karen, sitting pale beside him. She's getting that pinched look that, since the accident, signals the onset of a pounding headache.

'I see,' the lawyer says. He looks at Karen curiously.

Tom hands him the ticket they got from the police. Calvin reads it over quickly. He looks up. 'Pretty sketchy part of town for a woman like you,' he says, looking at Karen.

She sits perfectly still and straight. The lawyer turns to Tom. 'What was she doing there?'

Tom says, 'I don't know.'

'You don't know,' the lawyer repeats. He studies both of them as if he doesn't know what to think. There's a long silence. Finally he says, 'This is pretty serious. Reckless driving – you don't want to mess around.' He thinks for a minute. 'I tell you what. I will need a retainer today. And then I'm going to delay the court appearance until she remembers what she was doing there and why she was driving like that. Because there may be a perfectly good reason for it – or at least a mitigating one. And if there isn't, we need to know that, too.'

68

Tom glances at his wife, but she's now looking down at her lap. He reaches for his chequebook.

'If you do remember anything,' the lawyer says, directing his comment to Karen, 'please write it all down so that when we meet next time it's fresh in your mind.' He adds, 'And call me when you do.'

Karen nods. 'Okay.'

'Or – perhaps you'd like to see me without your husband present?'

She shoots a sharp look at Calvin. She shakes her head, and says, 'Of course not. I have nothing to hide from my husband.'

Tom watches her carefully. *Does she mean it?*

They settle the retainer, and as they get up to leave, Calvin asks Karen, 'You don't have a record, do you?'

She turns and answers him, looking him right in the eye. 'No.'

The lawyer looks back at her, and something in his appraising eye worries Tom. He realizes that the lawyer doesn't believe her – he doesn't believe her at all.

On the drive home from the lawyer's office, the air is thick with the tension of unanswered questions. Tom used to love driving with Karen – some of his happiest memories are of them together, in this car, driving out to the country for a weekend tryst, bags packed in the backseat, her head tilted back, laughing . . .

It's almost a relief when Tom's cell phone rings. He takes the call. Then he turns to her apologetically. 'I need to go into the office for a bit.'

'Of course.'

'You okay?'

'I have a headache.' She closes her eyes and rests her head against the back of the seat.

Tom drops her off at home. He leans over and kisses her before she gets out of the car. 'Take it easy. Have a nap. I'll try to be home early.'

She gets out of the car and waves at him, squinting in the sun, as he reverses out of the driveway. He waves back and drives away down the street, worrying about what the future holds. Wondering about what secrets his wife might be keeping.

Chapter Ten

ONCE HE'S GONE, Karen turns toward the house and lets herself in. The appointment with the lawyer has unnerved her; he obviously thought she was lying. She presses her fingers to her tired eyes. She makes her way to the kitchen and opens the freezer and grabs the ice pack they sent home with her from the hospital. She's been using it off and on, for the swelling on her face. Now, she puts it to her forehead. The cold feels good. She sits down at the kitchen table with her eyes closed and holds the ice pack to her head, moving it around slowly, trying to relieve the thudding pain.

It's such a hot day, sweltering. She can feel herself perspiring in her blouse, even with the air-conditioning on. Maybe she should turn it up. As the pain in her head abates slightly, she opens her eyes. She stares at the kitchen counter, the one she had replaced when she moved in. She still loves looking at it – its smooth, glossy black surface, flecked with silver. But now, what she sees is an empty glass beside the sink.

She stares at the glass, then glances quickly around the kitchen, but nothing else looks other than it should.

The glass on the counter by the sink wasn't there when they left this morning for the lawyer's office, she's certain of it. Because before they left, she and Tom – mostly Tom – had tidied up the kitchen and put the breakfast dishes in the dishwasher and wiped down the counters. She hates when dishes are left out on the counter. She's a bit of a neat freak. And she knows that she had a last look in the kitchen before joining Tom at the front door and leaving to see the lawyer, because she came back to make sure the sliding glass doors were locked. She always checks that the doors are locked – which is why it was so unnerving when Tom told her she hadn't locked the doors behind her on the night of the accident. Or turned off the lights. Or taken her purse. If only she could remember!

She picks up the glass tentatively, looks inside, holds it to her nose and sniffs. It's empty now, but there was water in it, she's sure – as if someone had come in and helped himself to a glass of tap water from the sink before heading back out into the heat.

Her head is pounding, and she suddenly feels dizzy. She tries to grab the counter, and clumsily drops the glass. It shatters loudly on the floor.

She stares down at the broken glass by her feet, breathing in gasps, her entire body trembling. Then she turns quickly and runs to the living room and grabs the phone. She hits the speed dial for Brigid's number.

'Brigid!' she says, when Brigid answers. 'Can you come over? Hurry!' She doesn't even try to tamp down the fear and panic she's feeling. She just wants Brigid here with her, right away. She doesn't want to be alone in the house.

'Sure, I'll be right there,' Brigid says.

Karen stands impatiently outside on the front porch. Within seconds, she sees Brigid rush out of her own door and cross the street. *Thank God for Brigid.*

'Jesus, Karen, what is it?' Brigid says. 'You're white as a sheet.'

'Someone's been in the house,' Karen says.

'What?' Brigid looks taken aback. 'What do you mean?'

Karen urges her inside. 'Someone was in here, while Tom and I were out this morning. I just got back. When I went into the kitchen—' She can't finish what she's saying.

'Did you see someone? Was there someone in the kitchen?' Brigid asks.

Karen shakes her head. 'No.' She's calmer now that Brigid is here. How fortunate she is to have such a good friend right across the street. Karen knows that whatever kind of trouble she might be in, Brigid would drop everything and race to her side. She wishes she could tell her why she's so frightened. But she can't tell her best friend, or her husband, the truth.

She watches Brigid approach the kitchen and stop just inside the doorway, silently looking around. After a moment, she comes quietly back to Karen's side. 'Karen, what happened?'

'I got home and went into the kitchen. There was an empty glass on the counter. It wasn't there when we left this morning. Someone put it there, and it wasn't me or Tom.'

'Are you sure?' Brigid asks.

'Of course I'm sure! Do you think I'd be this upset if I wasn't sure?'

Brigid looks back at her with concern. Then she glances toward the kitchen and back at Karen. 'How did the glass get broken?'

'I picked it up to look at it, and then I got dizzy – and I dropped it.'

Brigid looks at her uneasily. 'Maybe we should call Tom.'

Tom drives home as fast as he reasonably can, his mind racing. When he arrives he gets out of his car in a rush and sprints up the steps to the front door. He bursts into the living room and sees Karen lying down on the sofa with the ice pack on her forehead, Brigid standing nearby.

'Karen, honey, are you all right? What happened?'

She struggles to sit up. She hands the ice pack to Brigid, who automatically takes it from her to put back in the freezer.

'I don't know,' she says. 'I came home and found a glass on the counter. I'm sure it wasn't there when we left this morning. I thought someone had been in the house.'

Tom moves toward the kitchen, stopping outside the doorway when he sees the mess of broken glass. He catches Brigid's eye as she closes the freezer door and walks cautiously around the glittering shards.

Karen comes up and stands beside him. 'I dropped the glass,' she says.

Tom looks at her with concern. 'Are you sure it wasn't there before? It could have been,' Tom says. He tries to recall if he'd helped himself to a glass of water that morning, and left the glass out on the counter, but he can't remember. He's got so much on his mind, details like this are slipping away from him.

'I don't know,' she says, shaking her head. 'I was so sure. I took a last look in here before we left, to check that the back doors were locked. I thought everything was put away . . .'

'Come, sit down,' Tom says, taking her back to the sofa, while Brigid starts sweeping up the broken glass. He leaves Karen on the sofa and searches the entire house. Nothing is missing. Nothing is out of place as far as he can tell.

When he returns to the living room Brigid is sitting in one of the armchairs across from Karen. She's dressed for the heat, in cotton capris and a tank top, her long brown hair flowing to her shoulders. As he watches, she pulls her hair into a knot at the back of her neck. Tom turns to Karen. 'I don't think anyone's been in here,' he says gently.

Karen looks at him and then shifts her eyes away. 'What, you think I'm imagining it?'

'No,' Tom says calmly. 'I don't think you're imagining anything. I think you don't remember clearly whether there was a glass there before or not. We've both been drinking a lot of water in this heat, either one of us could have left the glass on the counter. I might have – I don't remember.' He reminds her gently, 'You're still recovering, Karen. Remember what the doctor said – you could have some problems with short-term memory for a while after the accident, too. Maybe the glass was there before and you don't remember.'

'Maybe,' she says doubtfully.

Tom turns to Brigid. 'I'll take it from here,' he says. 'Thanks for rushing over.'

'Any time,' Brigid says.

'Yes,' Karen says gratefully, as Brigid gets up to leave. 'I don't know what I'd do without you, Brigid.'

Tom watches Brigid give his wife a gentle hug; Karen hugs her warmly back.

'Thanks for cleaning up the broken glass, too,' Tom says.

'No problem.' She smiles at Karen. 'See you soon.'

Brigid heads across the street to her own house, while the two of them stand on the doorstep watching after her. Tom is standing slightly behind Karen. He's watching Brigid, and he's also watching his wife.

Chapter Eleven

DETECTIVE RASBACH PAUSES for a moment to take in his surroundings. There's a run-down plaza across the road, with a convenience store, a coin laundry, a dollar store, and not much else still open for business. Even on a sunny summer day like this one, the neighbourhood is depressing. In front of him is the scene of the crime – an abandoned restaurant. The building has been boarded up, but someone has pried a couple of boards off the window in the front to look inside, or maybe they've just fallen off over time. Rasbach walks around the outside of the derelict building to the back. He nods to a couple of tech people, and steps inside the yellow crime-scene tape.

He enters the restaurant through the grimy back door, which hadn't been boarded up like the front – at least, if it had, it wasn't any longer. Anybody could get in or out. The first thing that hits him is the smell. He tries to ignore it.

There's an old-fashioned dining counter to his left but there are no tables or chairs; the place has been stripped clean – even the overhead lights are missing. But there is an old couch up against the wall with some empty beer cans on the floor around it. There's some sunlight filtering in from the windows, where the boards have fallen away, but most of the light is coming from lamps put in place by the forensics team. The dirty linoleum floor is cracked, the walls are dark and stained with nicotine. And there's a dead man lying on the floor.

The smell is pretty bad. That's what happens when a body isn't discovered for a few days in the heat of summer. This one is pretty ripe.

Rasbach stands perfectly still in the middle of the reeking restaurant in his smart, expensive suit, thinking he will have to have it dry-cleaned, and pulls a pair of latex gloves out of his pocket.

'Someone called it in. Didn't leave a name,' the uniformed officer beside him says.

The detective nods tiredly. He moves toward the bloody, buzzing mess on the floor. He stands for several minutes looking down at the body, studying it. He's a dark-haired man, probably mid- to late thirties, dressed in expensive-looking black trousers and an equally expensive-looking dress shirt – now crusted in dried, dark blood and covered with flies. The victim had taken a couple of shots to the face, another to the chest. His shoes are missing, revealing rather stylish socks. No belt either. 'Any sign of the weapon?' Rasbach asks a technician standing on the other side of the body, also looking down thoughtfully at the corpse.

'No, not yet.'

Rasbach leans over the body carefully, trying not to breathe, noting the pale shadow around the finger where a ring has recently been removed, and a similar pale band around the wrist, where a watch had once been. He'd been robbed, but this was not primarily a robbery, Rasbach thinks. What had the man been doing here? He didn't belong here, in this neighbourhood. This looks more like an execution. Except he'd been shot in the face and chest rather than in the back of the head. The body looks like it's been dead for at least a couple of days, maybe longer. The face is discoloured and bloated.

'Do we know who he is?'

'No. He doesn't have any ID on him. In fact, he doesn't have anything on him, except his clothes.'

'Any witnesses?' Rasbach asks, already knowing the answer.

'Nada. At least so far.'

'Okay.' Rasbach sighs deeply.

The body would be removed soon and sent to the

medical examiner to be autopsied. They'd get finger-prints from the body and see if there was anything matching them on file. If they couldn't ID him through the prints, they'd have to go through missing persons, which would be tedious, but much of police work is tedious. It's often the tedious work that pays off.

They'll keep looking for the murder weapon. Probably a .38-calibre handgun, by the looks of it. Odds are the shooter disposed of it far away from the scene, or someone else picked it up and is keeping quiet. Given the neighbourhood, Rasbach's not surprised that the belt and shoes have been taken, as well as the victim's wallet and jewellery, and no doubt his cell phone as well.

By the time they've finished with the body and completed a wider sweep of the area, all they've found is a pair of pink rubber gloves with a floral print near the elbows, discarded in a small parking lot a short distance away. Rasbach doesn't think they have anything to do with the victim in the restaurant, but he has them bagged anyway. You just never know.

Rasbach and another detective, Jennings, along with a couple of uniformed officers, spend the evening going door-to-door in the area, looking for witnesses.

Not surprisingly, they come up empty-handed.

*

Dr Perriera, the medical examiner, is expecting them the next morning. 'Hello detectives,' he says, obviously pleased to see them.

Rasbach knows the ME enjoys it when the detectives come to visit. Rasbach marvels at the fact that even after almost twenty years, the depressing nature of the doctor's job doesn't ever seem to get him down. Stabbings, gunshots, drownings, car accidents – nothing seems to bother the sanguine and invariably social Dr Perriera.

He holds out a bowl of wrapped mint candies. They help with the smell. Both detectives take one. The wrappers crinkle as the mints are unwrapped. Dr Perriera holds his hand out for the wrappers and drops them in the trash can.

'What can you tell us?' Rasbach asks as they stand around the long, steel table looking down at the cadaver resting upon it. Rasbach is grateful that Jennings has always had a strong stomach, like him. Jennings looks keen and curious and not at all bothered by the butchery on the table, the mint candy making a bulge in his cheek.

'The body's intact,' Dr Perriera begins cheerfully. 'Caucasian male, late thirties, good health. The first shot went into the chest, the second into the cheek, but it was the third shot, which went right into the brain, that killed him. Death was fairly quick. He was shot at close range – from about six to eight feet away – with a thirty-eight-calibre handgun.'

Rasbach nods. 'When did he die, exactly?' he asks.

Dr Perriera turns to Rasbach. 'I know how much you guys love to pin down the time of death, and I do my best, I really do, but if you send me a corpse that's been sitting idle for a few days, it affects my ability to be accurate, you understand.'

The detective knows Dr Perriera is a perfectionist; he always qualifies his findings. 'I appreciate that,' Rasbach says patiently. 'But I would still prefer your best guess over anyone else's.'

The doctor smiles. 'I performed the autopsy last night. Based on the state of decomposition and the larvae found in the body – bearing in mind, of course, the very hot weather we've been having – my guess is he died about four days before that, give or take a day.'

Rasbach calculates. 'So, four days from last night – that would be the evening of August thirteenth.'

Dr Perriera nods. 'But he could have been killed as early as the evening of August twelfth or as late as the evening of August fourteenth. Somewhere in there.'

Rasbach looks down at the body on the steel table. If only he could talk.

*

Back at the station, Rasbach chooses one of the large meeting rooms for their ad hoc command post, and addresses the team he's cobbled together. He and Jennings are the detectives on this, and he has chosen several uniformed officers from the Patrol Division to assist.

'We still don't know who this guy is,' Rasbach says. 'We have no match on his prints anywhere, against known missing persons, or on any other databases. Let's start circulating a description and photos to law enforcement agencies and the media – see if we can find out who he is. He might still be recognizable to somebody.'

Rasbach decides to check all police records for the forty-eight-hour period between the evenings of August twelfth and August fourteenth. He's looking for anything out of the ordinary. There isn't much; nothing shows up but some minor drug busts and a couple of car accidents. One of the car accidents seems straightforward enough – a mid-afternoon fender bender. But the other one. A Honda Civic had been speeding – away from the vicinity of the crime scene – and had hit a utility pole at around 8:45 on the evening of August thirteenth.

The hairs on the back of Rasbach's neck tingle when he sees it.

Chapter Twelve

'WHAT CAN WE do for you?' Fleming asks Rasbach, sipping coffee out of a mug. 'Not every day a homicide detective comes to our end of the building.'

Rasbach places the photographs of his murder victim on the desk.

Fleming and Kirton both lean forward to look. Kirton shakes his head. Fleming takes his time, looking carefully, but says nothing.

'Body wasn't found for several days,' Rasbach says. 'August seventeenth. At least, no one called it in till then. I think it was picked over by locals first.'

'Don't recognize him,' Kirton says.

'I haven't seen him before either.' Fleming looks at Rasbach. 'What's this got to do with us?'

'He was killed in an abandoned restaurant on Hoffman Street around August thirteenth, give or take a day. I understand there was a car accident not far from there on the evening of the thirteenth.'

Fleming and Kirton share a quick glance. Kirton sits up straighter, nodding. 'There was.'

'Tell me what you know about it,' Rasbach says.

'Woman was speeding, ran a red light. Swerved to avoid a car, lost control, and went into a pole,' Kirton says.

'Did she survive?'

'Yes,' Fleming says, leaning closer over his desk. 'She survived, but apparently she has *amnesia*.'

'You're kidding me, right?' Rasbach says.

'Nope. Everyone's buying it – the doctor, the husband,' Fleming says.

'But not you.'

'I don't know. The husband called 911 reporting her missing the same night. She'd left the house in a hurry without her purse and her phone, forgot to lock the door.'

Rasbach turns to Officer Kirton, who is shaking his head.

'I think she's lying,' Kirton says.

'What do you know about this woman?' Rasbach asks.

'Her name is Karen Krupp,' Fleming tells him. 'She's just a regular housewife – if you ignore where she was and what she was doing that night.'

'A housewife.'

'Yup. Early thirties, works as a bookkeeper. Married to an accountant. No kids. Nice home in the suburbs – Henry Park.'

Rasbach suddenly remembers the pink rubber gloves he picked up and had bagged near the murder scene. They'd been run over, and there were tyre tracks on them. 'What happened to the car?' he asks now.

'A Honda Civic. It was totalled,' Kirton offers.

'I'm going to need to see the tyres on that car,' Rasbach says. He feels a little hum of excitement. Wouldn't it be interesting, he thinks, to find a connection between that car – that housewife – and his murder victim?

'I guess you'll be taking it from here, then, Rasbach,' Fleming says.

Tom is tense and unhappy as he leaves the house the next morning. He's put on jeans to go into the office for a few hours to catch up on work at the weekend. He's missed so much with Karen in the hospital. She seemed tired this morning. She was already up again when he woke; her face when he kissed her was pale. The swelling on her face is gone and the bruising has begun to fade, but she doesn't look like the old Karen.

She's been different since she came home. She used to be so warm and uncomplicated. Now she's a bit distant. She's too quiet. Sometimes, if he reaches for her, she flinches. She never did that before. She seems nervous, jumpy. And he finds the episode about the glass disturbing. He's certain that no one has been in the house. Why was she so convinced that someone had? She got herself into a total panic about it.

He's troubled, too. Does she really not remember that night? *Or is she simply not telling him?*

Suspicion is an insidious thing; doubts have started creeping in, things that he'd previously been able to ignore.

Doubts about her past. When she moved in, she brought so little with her. He'd asked her at the time if she had some things in storage. She'd looked him in the eye, and said, 'No, this is it. I don't hang on to things. I don't like clutter.'

He's wondered, once or twice, why she seems to have no old ties at all. When he asked her about her family, she explained that she had no family. He understood. His parents are gone, too, and he has no one left but his brother. But she has no one at all. He has friends from college, but she seems to have none. When he pressed her on it, she told him that she wasn't good at staying in touch with people. She'd acted as if he were making a big deal about nothing.

He loves her, she loves him; they're perfect together. If she didn't want to tell him a lot about her

life before they met, he accepted that. He's never suspected anything disturbing – he just thought she was
private, not prone to sharing.

But now he's not so sure he's okay with it. He realizes he doesn't really know that much about his own
wife.

Detectives Rasbach and Jennings are at the crime
lab. The lab already has the pink gloves and they're
working on them, in spite of the fact that it's a
Sunday.

Now Rasbach offers a fragrant double espresso to
Stan Price, who has agreed to come in this morning
to go over the evidence with them. It's only Star-
bucks, but Rasbach knows that Stan is usually so
busy he doesn't have time to go out.

'Thanks,' Stan says, his face lighting up as he
takes the cup. 'A good coffee goes a long way.' They
have a crappy little coffeemaker in the basement
here, where the forensics lab is, but it makes fam-
ously lousy coffee. It could be because nobody ever
cleans it, but nobody has been willing to test that
theory by giving it a good scrub. Rasbach now makes
a mental note to get a new espresso maker for the
forensics department for Christmas this year.

'What have you got?' Rasbach asks.

'Well, the gloves. I was able to lift a good tyre print
off one of them.' Stan sips his coffee appreciatively.

89

'The tyre tracks on the glove match the make and model of the tyres on the car in question. They're the right type, but we can't match them definitively to the tyres you brought in. We can't say that it was definitely one of the tyres on that car that drove over that glove. But it could well be.'

'Okay,' Rasbach says. It's something. 'What are the chances of getting DNA off the inside of the gloves?'

'I'd say pretty good, but that's going to take longer. There's a waiting list for that.'

'Can you speed it up for me?'

'Can you keep bringing me this excellent coffee?'

'You bet.'

Karen gathers up her purse, her keys, and her cell, and prepares to leave the house. She has to run to the corner store.

When she opens the front door, there's a strange man standing on the front porch.

She's so startled she almost screams. But the man standing on her doorstep, while unexpected, doesn't appear to be threatening. He's nicely dressed, in a well-cut suit. He has sandy hair and intelligent blue eyes. That's when she notices the second man, still making his way up the steps. She looks at him in dismay, and then back at the man directly in front of her.

'Karen Krupp?' he says.

'Yes,' she answers suspiciously. 'Who are you?'

'I'm Detective Rasbach.' He glances at the other man now joining him on the front porch. 'And this is Detective Jennings.'

Chapter Thirteen

KAREN STARES AT the detective, her heart pumping frantically. She hadn't been expecting this.

'Can we speak to you for a few minutes?' Rasbach asks, pulling out his detective badge and holding it up for her to see.

She can feel her pulse in her temples. She doesn't want to speak to them. She has a lawyer now. Why hadn't he given her any advice on what to say to the cops if they came to question her again? Why hadn't she asked?

'I was just on my way out,' she manages to say.

'This won't take long,' Rasbach assures her, not moving.

She hesitates, unsure of what to do. If she sends them away without speaking to them, it might antagonize them. She decides that she'd better let them in. She'll tell them that she remembers nothing. After all, it's the truth. There's nothing she can tell them about that night.

'Okay, I guess a few minutes would be all right,' she says and opens the door wider, closing it behind them once they're inside.

She leads them into the living room. She sits on the sofa; they take the armchairs across from her. She fights the urge to grab one of the pillows on the sofa and hug it to her chest. Instead, she deliberately crosses her legs and leans back into the corner of the sofa, trying to appear unfazed at having two detectives in her living room.

But the obvious intelligence in the first detective's eyes unnerves her, and she says, a little too quickly, 'I'm sure you know this already from the other police officers investigating the accident, but I don't remember anything about it.' She thinks how ridiculous that sounds. She flushes slightly.

'We did hear that, yes,' Detective Rasbach says.

He appears relaxed, but alert. She feels like she can't put anything past this man. She's suddenly very nervous.

'Actually, it isn't the accident, per se, that we're interested in.'

At this, Karen feels all the blood drain from her face. She's sure they can both see it, her sudden, damning pallor.

'No?' she manages to say.

'No. We're investigating something else. Something that happened not far from where you had your accident, we think at around the same time.'

Karen says nothing.

'A man was murdered.'

Murdered. She tries to keep her face neutral, but suspects she has failed miserably. 'What could that possibly have to do with me?' she asks.

'That's what we're trying to find out,' the detective says.

'I don't remember anything about that night,' she protests. 'I'm sorry, but you're probably wasting your time.'

'Nothing?' the detective asks. He obviously doesn't believe her. She looks at the other detective beside him. He doesn't believe her either.

She shakes her head.

'Maybe we can help you remember,' Rasbach says.

She stares back at him, frightened. She's glad Tom isn't here. Then she wishes that he were.

'We believe you were at the murder scene.'

'What?' She feels faint.

'We found a pair of rubber gloves at the scene,' the other detective tells her.

She's dizzy now, and her heart is pounding. She feels herself blinking rapidly.

'Are you perhaps missing a pair of pink rubber

gloves, the kind you might use for washing dishes?' Rasbach asks.

She lifts her head, straightens her back. 'No, I'm not,' she says convincingly. But she knows her gloves are missing, she was looking for them yesterday. She has no idea where they've gone. She'd asked Tom, but he hadn't known either. She has the sudden courage of someone with a very strong survival instinct who is backed into a corner. 'Why would you think they're mine?' she asks coolly.

'It's quite simple, really,' the detective says. 'The gloves were found near the murder scene, in a parking lot close by.'

She says, 'I still don't see what that has to do with me. I've never had any pink gloves.'

The detective says, 'The gloves were run over, in that parking lot, by a car. Tyre track evidence – it's almost like fingerprints. Your car has the same kind of tyres as the ones that made the tracks in that parking lot. I think you ran over those gloves – in that parking lot. And then you fled – and had an accident in that car around the approximate time of the murder.' He pauses, leans forward slightly. 'I think you've got a problem.'

As Tom pulls into the driveway, he wonders whose car that is, sitting in front of his house. A plain, new sedan; nobody he knows. He gets out of his own car and looks at the one in the street uneasily. Who would be visiting his wife? He hates the suspicion that he feels. Apprehensive, Tom hurries up the steps.

He opens the door quickly and immediately sees two men in suits sitting in his living room.

'Tom!' Karen says, turning her head around, clearly startled. Her expression is confusing, a mix of relief and fear. He can't tell if she's happy, or horrified, to see him. Maybe a bit of both.

'What's going on?' Tom asks the room at large.

The two men remain silent, watching from their seats, as if waiting to see what his wife will tell him. Tom is anxious. He wonders if they're insurance people, here about the accident. He doesn't need any more bad news.

'These two men are police detectives,' Karen tells him with a slightly warning look. 'They're here about . . . the other night,' she says.

The two men stand up in unison. 'I'm Detective Rasbach,' says the taller man, flashing his badge. 'This is Detective Jennings.'

'Do we have to do this now?' Tom says a little rudely, coming farther into the living room. He wants his old life back. 'Can't it wait? Our lawyer said he was going to put things off until she got her memory back.'

'I'm afraid we're not here about the car accident,' Detective Rasbach says.

Tom feels a sudden weakness in his legs. His heart revs sharply. He needs to sit down. He sinks onto the sofa next to Karen. He realizes that he's been waiting for something like this to happen. In his heart, he knew there was more to this story. He feels like he's opened a wrong door somewhere and ended up in some other life, one that doesn't make any sense, peopled by impostors.

Tom looks guardedly at the two detectives. He glances nervously at Karen, but she isn't looking at him.

When no one speaks for a moment, Detective Rasbach says, 'We were just telling your wife – we're investigating a murder that occurred not far from where she had her accident.'

A murder.

Karen turns to him abruptly and says, 'They want to know if we're missing any rubber gloves, but I've already told them we aren't.'

Tom looks back at her, his heart lurching. He shakes his head. Time seems to slow down. 'Rubber gloves? No, we're not missing anything like that,' he says. He feels light-headed, and can taste the bile rising in his throat. He turns to the detective. 'Why?' Tom knows he's a terrible actor. The detective's sharp eyes seem to see right through him. The detective knows he's lying.

'We found a pair of pink rubber dishwashing gloves near the murder scene.' Rasbach adds, 'With a flowered pattern up near the elbows.'

Tom hears this almost as if he's hearing it from a distance. He feels very detached. He frowns. Everything seems to be happening in slow motion. 'We've never had any pink rubber gloves,' he says. He watches Karen turn away from him back to the detective. *Jesus. He's just lied to these detectives. What the hell is going on?*

'It doesn't matter too much where the gloves came from, frankly, or whose they were,' the detective says. 'What's important is that the tyre tracks on those gloves and near the scene of the murder match the tyres of your wife's car. Putting her near the murder scene shortly before she had her accident.' He turns to Karen and says, 'You were driving very fast, apparently.' The detective leans forward and adds, 'A little convenient, having amnesia.'

'Don't insult me, detective,' Karen says, and Tom stares at her in shock. He would never have believed she was capable of such sangfroid. It's as if he's looking at a stranger.

'Don't you want to know who was murdered?' Detective Rasbach asks. He's toying with them. 'Or do you know already?' he adds, staring at Karen.

'I have no idea what you're talking about,' Karen says. 'And neither does my husband. So why don't you stop playing games and tell us?'

Rasbach looks back at her, unruffled. 'A man was shot three times – twice in the face and once in the chest, at close range – in a deserted restaurant on Hoffman Street. We know that your car was near the murder scene. We were rather hoping you could fill *us* in,' he says.

Tom feels physically ill. He can't believe they're having this conversation, in his own living room. He was sitting in this very spot just a few days ago when the police came to tell him that there'd been an accident. Given the circumstances of that accident, he hadn't believed the driver could be his wife. But it was. Now this. What is he to believe this time?

'Who was he?' Karen asks. 'The man who was murdered?'

She's very pale, Tom thinks, *but her voice is steady. She's remarkably composed.* It's almost as if he's watching someone else, an actor, playing his wife.

'We don't know,' the detective admits. Then he reaches into an envelope and says, 'Would you like to see a picture?' It's not really a question.

Tom still feels like everything is happening in slow motion. The detective places a photograph on the coffee table and rotates it so that Tom and Karen are looking at it right-side up. It's the distorted face of a man with bullet holes in his forehead and cheek. The dead man's eyes are open, expressing what looks like

99

surprise. Tom instinctively recoils. The detective places a second photo beside the first. This one shows the bloated body with blood splattered all over the chest. The photos are revolting, disturbing. Tom can't help it, he glances at Karen – she is so still she looks like she has stopped breathing – then he quickly looks away. He can't bear to look at his own wife.

'Is that jogging any memories for you?' the detective asks her a little flippantly. 'Do you recognize him?'

She stares at the photos, as if studying them, and slowly shakes her head. 'No. Not at all.'

The detective looks as though he doesn't believe her. 'How do you explain your car being near the scene?' he asks.

'I don't know.' A note of desperation has finally crept into Karen's voice. 'Maybe someone hijacked my car, and made me wait there, as a getaway driver,' she says. 'And . . . maybe I managed to get away and that's why I was driving so fast.'

Detective Rasbach nods, as if he appreciates her creative efforts.

Tom desperately thinks, *It's possible. Isn't it?*

'What other evidence do you have?' Karen asks boldly.

'Ahh,' Detective Rasbach says, 'that I'm not prepared to say.' He gathers up the photographs, glances at his partner, and starts to rise. Karen and Tom stand up. Rasbach takes a business card out of his suit pocket and offers it to Karen. She takes it from him, looks at it, then places it on the glass coffee table.

'Thank you for your time,' the detective says, and the two men leave, Karen shutting the door behind them. Tom, filled with dread, stands shell-shocked near the sofa. Karen comes back into the living room, and their eyes meet.

Chapter Fourteen

RASBACH REFLECTS ON the interview in the passenger seat of the car as Jennings drives them back to the station. Karen Krupp is hiding something. She was admirably self-possessed on the surface, but she was panicking underneath.

He believes she was there, very close to the murder scene, presumably around the time of the murder – although that's a pretty big presumption at this point, as their estimated time of death is necessarily broad. But he's convinced the timing of the two events is the same. What was she doing there?

The husband is a lousy liar, Rasbach thinks, remembering his demeanour during the interview. He's certain the Krupps are missing a pair of pink rubber gloves.

Someone must have seen Karen Krupp leaving the house that night. They need to know whether she was alone. Rasbach decides to return to Henry Park later that evening to talk to the neighbours. And they'll need all the Krupps' phone records, too. Maybe she got a call. They will look very thoroughly into Karen Krupp.

He leans back in the passenger seat, rather pleased. The case has taken an interesting turn. He loves it when that happens.

Tom, horrified, stares accusingly at his wife. He has just lied to the police for her. The woman he loves. *What has she done?* His heart twists painfully.

'Tom,' she says, and then stops, as if she can't think of what to say next. As if she can't possibly explain.

He wonders if she really can't explain, or if she's faking it all. He believed her in the beginning, believed that she couldn't remember. But now he doesn't know. It certainly looks like she has something to hide. 'What the hell's going on, Karen?' Tom asks. His voice sounds cold, but inside he's feeling desperate.

'I don't know,' she says fervently. Her eyes well up with tears.

She's so convincing. He wants to be convinced, but he can't quite believe her.

'I think you know more than you're letting on,' he says. She stands motionless in front of him, straight-backed, as if daring him to say what he really thinks. But he can't. He can't accuse her of . . . of murder.

103

My God, what has she done?

'You lied to the detectives,' he says. 'About the gloves.'

'So did you,' she says sharply.

This shocks him; it's like a slap across the face. He hardly knows how to respond. Then he says, in a fury, 'I did it to protect you! I didn't know what else to do! I don't know what the hell's going on!'

'Exactly!' she snaps back at him. She walks a few steps closer, never taking her eyes off his. They're within arm's reach of each other. 'That's my point,' she says, less confrontational now. 'I don't know what's going on either. I lied about the gloves because I didn't know what else to do – the same as you.'

Tom stares back at her in dumb shock. Finally he says, 'Whether you remember it or not, those are probably your gloves, and we both know it. *At a murder scene.* Why were you at a murder scene, Karen?' When she doesn't answer, he continues, appalled at what's happening. 'They have evidence! That you were at the scene of a horrible crime!' He can't believe that he's saying this, to Karen, the woman he loves. He runs a frantic hand through his hair. 'That detective obviously thinks you did it, he thinks you killed that man. Did you? Did you shoot him?'

'I don't know!' she cries, desperation in her voice. 'That's the best I can do right now, Tom. I'm sorry. I know it isn't good enough. I don't know what happened. You must believe me.'

He glares back at her, not knowing what to think. He feels life as he knows it slipping away from him.

She looks at him, her eyes steadily on his. 'Do you really think I'm capable of killing someone? Do you really think I'm capable of *murder*?'

No. He can't imagine her killing anyone. The idea is . . . ridiculous. Monstrous. And yet—

'He's coming after you, Karen,' Tom says, stricken. 'You saw what he's like, that detective. He's going to dig and dig and he won't quit until he gets to the bottom of this. It won't even matter that you can't remember. You won't have to – the police will find out what happened, and *they'll tell us*!' He's almost shouting now. He's trying to hurt her, because he's scared, and he's angry and he can't trust her any more.

She's even more ashen now than when the detectives were here. 'If you don't believe me, Tom . . .' She leaves it there, hanging in the air, waiting for him to protest, to say that he believes her. The silence drags on, but he doesn't say it. 'Why don't you believe me?' she asks finally.

'What a question,' he says roughly.

'It's a valid question,' she persists. She's angry now, too. 'What have I ever done that would let you believe that I could kill someone in cold blood?' She steps closer. Tom watches her but says nothing. 'You know me! How can you think I'm even *capable* of something like murder? I don't know what happened that night any more than you do.' Now her face is up close, just below his; he can smell the faint perfume of her skin.

She presses. 'Whatever happened to innocent until proven guilty?' She's breathing rapidly, her face close to his. 'You don't know what happened, so why can't you believe that I'm innocent in all this? Tell me, is that any more far-fetched, any more *insane*, than that I shot someone and left him for dead?' Now *she* is almost shouting.

Tom looks back at her, his heart tight. In all the time he's known her, and loved her, he's never had even the slightest reason to doubt her, about anything. It all comes down to that night. What really happened? Doesn't he owe her something for those years of complete trust?

He shakes his head. In a lower voice, he says, 'The police come in here, accusing you . . . you lie in front of them . . . I don't know, Karen.' He pauses. 'I love you. But I'm scared.'

'I know,' she says. 'I'm scared, too.'

Neither of them speaks for a moment. Then Karen says, 'Maybe it's time to go back to Jack Calvin.'

That evening Karen sits quietly in the living room, a magazine lying ignored on her lap. Tomorrow night will be exactly one week since her accident. A week, and she still can't remember anything.

The afternoon had been terrifying. The police – that cold-blooded detective – had practically accused her of murder. And Tom – Tom seems to believe she might have done it.

She's afraid of the police, afraid of what they might find out. Afraid of what Dr Fulton might tell them.

She realizes that she's clenching her teeth and tries to relax. Her jaw aches.

The photographs – Karen can't get the grisly images out of her mind. She thinks of Tom, upstairs in his office, closeted away with some work he brought home. Or is he just pretending, like her? Is he sitting at his desk staring at the wall, unable to get the images of the dead man out of his mind, too? Probably. He looked sick when he saw the photos. And then after, he wouldn't even look at her.

Now she glances out the front window and starts. She sees two men in suits at the door of a house across the street. Even in the near dark she recognizes the two detectives again. With a feeling of encroaching horror, Karen walks across the room, staying close to the wall. When she gets to the window, she stands behind the curtain, looking out.

They're interviewing the neighbours. Of course.

Chapter Fifteen

BRIGID LOOKS OUT at the street. Darkness is falling. She spends a lot of time here, with her knitting, watching what goes on outside her window.

Brigid is a skilful and creative knitter; she's even had some of her own patterns published. She has a knitting blog that she's very proud of, where she showcases some of her work, and she has a lot of followers. On the banner across the top of her blog is written *Knitting isn't just for old ladies!* And there's a picture of Brigid there, too. Brigid's happy with the picture, which she had taken by a professional photographer. She's very attractive in that photo; she photographs well.

She'd once tried to teach Karen how to knit, but Brigid could tell she wasn't really interested in learning. And she didn't have the patience for it. They'd had some laughs and agreed that maybe it wasn't Karen's thing. Karen seemed to want and enjoy Brigid's company anyway, despite their different interests. It's too bad Karen hadn't taken to knitting; knitting with someone is a great way to get them talking, and Karen isn't one to open up easily.

Earlier today Brigid visited her favourite shop, Knit One Purl Too. She was running out of the fabulous purple Shibui yarn she'd bought last time. The minute she walked in the door and saw all the colourful skeins of yarn bundled along the walls, almost up to the ceiling, she felt her spirits lift. So much colour, so much texture – such unlimited possibilities! She walked happily around the shop, admiring, feeling, and gathering up various yarns of different weights and colours until her arms were full. She loves gorging on yarn.

Brigid was stroking a lovely orange merino wool when a woman she vaguely recognized approached her.

'Brigid?' the woman said. 'I'm so glad to run into you! I wanted to tell you how much I loved your last blog post about fixing knitting mistakes.'

Brigid almost blushed with pleasure.

'I missed an increase, and that trick with the crochet hook worked like a charm.'

'I'm so glad you found it helpful,' Brigid said,

smiling. It was gratifying to share her expertise and be appreciated. It made all the hard work of writing the blog worth it.

Sandra, at the cash register, was also happy to see her. 'Brigid! We don't see you much any more. You must come back to our knitting circle.'

Brigid instinctively cast her eyes to the chairs arranged in a circle at the front of the store. She wasn't ready to come back. She couldn't face it. Too many women happily knitting baby things – at least three of the regulars were pregnant. And they talked about it constantly. She couldn't trust herself not to let her hurt and disappointment spill over; she couldn't trust herself not to say something unpleasant. None of them would understand. Better to keep away. 'Soon,' Brigid lied. 'I'm really busy with work these days.' She hadn't told anyone there that she'd quit her job because of the fertility treatments. She didn't want to tell them about her fertility issues. She didn't need their pity.

She picked up the bulging, expensive bag of yarn and quickly left the shop, her mood spoiled.

Now, Brigid watches as two men in suits come down the street, knocking on doors. The men stop at her neighbour's house. She'll be next.

When she hears the doorbell, she puts her knitting aside and answers it. She's alone in the house; Bob is out at a function, as he so often is. The two men

110

stand on her doorstep. The taller one, handsome with striking blue eyes, pulls out a badge and flips it open.

'I'm Detective Rasbach,' he says. 'This is Detective Jennings.'

Brigid tenses. 'Yes?' she says.

'We're conducting a police investigation. Did you happen to see your neighbour Karen Krupp leave her house on the evening of August thirteenth? That's the night she had a car accident.'

'Pardon?' she says, although she heard him perfectly well.

'Did you see Karen Krupp leaving her house on the evening of August thirteenth? She had a car accident that night.'

'Yes, I know about the accident,' Brigid says. 'She's a friend of mine.'

'Did you see her leave the house that night?' the detective presses.

Brigid shakes her head. 'No.'

'Are you sure? You live right across the street. You didn't see her go out?'

'No, I didn't. I was out until later in the evening myself. Why?' She looks back and forth between the two detectives. 'That's kind of a strange question.'

'We're wondering if she was alone.'

'I'm sorry, I have no idea,' Brigid says politely.

'Perhaps your husband was home that evening? Is he here?' the detective queries.

'No, he's not home. He's out most evenings. I think he was out that night, too.'

The detective hands her a card and says, 'If your husband did happen to be home and saw anything, would you please have him give us a call?'

She watches the two detectives stride back down her walkway and go on to the next house.

Neither Karen nor Tom can sleep, although each pretends for the other. Tom lies on his side with his face to the wall, his stomach churning. He keeps replaying the scene of the detectives in their living room that afternoon, over and over. He remembers the ease with which his wife lied to them about the gloves. In contrast, he had lied badly, and they all knew it.

He feels Karen move restlessly on the other side of the bed; finally, she gets up quietly and creeps out of the room. He's used to this now, her getting up in the middle of the night. Tonight, it's a relief. He hears the bedroom door close softly behind her and turns over and lies on his back, his eyes wide open.

Tom had seen the police detectives going up and down the street earlier that evening, from the upstairs office window. Karen must have noticed them. Yet neither of them had mentioned it to the other.

He feels sick when he thinks about the police investigating her, hates himself for the creeping doubt he feels about her. Now he's watching her all the time, wondering about her, about what she's done.

And he can't help worrying: *What will the police find?*

Chapter Sixteen

KAREN HAS TOM drive her to Jack Calvin's office on his way to work the next morning. Luckily Calvin was able to fit her in. Tom has an important meeting that he cannot miss, and cannot stay. Or so he says. Karen wonders if maybe he can't deal with any more of this, or doesn't want to. Or perhaps he thinks she'll be more forthcoming with the lawyer if he's not there. But she's not going to tell the lawyer any more than she's told her husband. She just wants to know what she should do.

Tom leans over and kisses her on the cheek when he drops her off, but he doesn't meet her eyes. She tells him she'll take a cab home. She stands in the parking lot for a moment watching her husband drive away. Then she turns and walks toward the building. Once inside, she hesitates for a moment in front of the elevators, but then she presses the button. When she arrives at the lawyer's office, she swallows her fear, opens the door, and walks in.

She has a longer wait this time, and her nerves begin to get the better of her. When she's finally ushered in to see Jack Calvin, she can feel the tension in her shoulders, her neck.

'You're back!' the lawyer says cheerfully. 'So soon. Does this mean you've remembered something?' He smiles at her.

She doesn't return his smile. She sits down.

'What can I help you with?' Calvin says now, all business.

'I still don't remember anything about that night,' Karen tells him. She imagines what he must think. He probably thinks she's here to tell him something she couldn't tell him in front of her husband – about some sordid affair she's conducting on the rough side of town. She will have to disappoint him. 'Tom has a meeting this morning that he can't miss,' she says.

He nods politely.

'Everything I tell you is protected by attorney–client privilege, correct?' Karen asks, looking him directly in the eye.

'Yes.'

She swallows and says, 'The police paid me a visit yesterday.'

'Okay.'

'I thought it was about the accident.'

'It wasn't?'

'No.' She pauses. 'They're investigating a murder.'

The lawyer's eyebrows go up, his eyes sharpen. He takes a fresh pad of lined yellow paper from his desk drawer, grabs an expensive-looking pen off his blotter, and says calmly, 'You'd better tell me everything.'

'It was horrible.' She chokes on the last word. She feels nauseated, remembering the photographs of the corpse. She can feel her hands trembling in her lap and squeezes them together. 'They showed us photographs, of the body.'

She quickly tells him about the detectives' visit. 'I didn't recognize the dead man,' she says. She watches the lawyer closely, hoping he will somehow be able to save her.

'You were speeding, running red lights, not far from where a murder took place – possibly around the time the murder occurred,' Calvin says. 'I can see why they might want to talk to you.' He leans forward, his chair squeaking at the movement. 'But is there anything else to tie you to that crime? Because unless there's something else, that's nothing to worry about. That's a dicey area. It has nothing to do with you, does it?'

She feels herself swallow again. She looks at him, steadies herself, and tells him the rest. 'They found some gloves.'

He stares at her with his sharp eyes, waiting. 'Go on,' he says.

She takes a deep breath and says, 'They found some rubber gloves, in a parking lot near the murder.' She hesitates, then adds, 'I'm pretty sure they're mine.'

The lawyer stares at her.

'Our rubber gloves are missing.' She pauses. 'I don't know what happened to them. They're quite distinctive, pink, with a flowered pattern near the top.'

'Did you *tell* them you were missing some gloves?' Calvin asks.

She can tell from his tone how incredibly dumb he thinks that would be. 'I'm not that stupid,' she says tartly.

'Good. That's good,' he says, obviously relieved.

'Tom lied for me,' she says. She can feel her mask of composure slipping. 'He told them we weren't missing any rubber gloves. But they could tell he was lying.'

'Rule of thumb,' the lawyer says. 'Don't lie to the police. Don't say anything. Better yet, call me.'

She says, 'They said they don't need to prove those gloves were mine. Because apparently my car ran over them in that parking lot – they have tyre track evidence – so they can put me, or my car, at least, near the murder scene. They have evidence.'

Calvin looks back at her, his face grave. 'Who's the detective on this anyway, who figured that out?'

'His name is Detective Rasbach,' Karen says.

'Rasbach,' Calvin says, looking thoughtful.

'I don't know what to do,' Karen says in a low voice. 'They were all over my street last night, the detectives, talking to the neighbours.'

The lawyer leans forward intently and fixes his eyes on hers. 'You do nothing. You don't talk to them. If they want to talk to you, you call me.' He takes another one of his business cards, turns it over, and writes a number on the back. 'Use this number if you can't get me on the others. You'll always be able to get me on this one.'

She takes the card from him gratefully. 'Do you think they have enough to charge me?' she asks anxiously.

'Not from what you've told me. You were in a parking lot, near a building where a murder was committed, possibly around the time of the murder. You were speeding, and had an accident. You might have seen something. That's all. The question is, what else will they find?'

'I don't know,' she says nervously. 'I still can't remember anything about that night.'

Calvin takes a minute and scribbles some notes. Finally he looks up at her and says, 'I hate to mention this, but I'll need a bigger retainer, just in case.'

Just in case. Just in case she's charged with murder, Karen thinks. She fumbles in her purse for her chequebook.

'I have to ask,' Calvin says quietly. 'Why might you have had a pair of rubber gloves with you?'

She deliberately avoids his gaze, searching in her purse for her chequebook. She says, 'I have no idea.'

Chapter Seventeen

RASBACH RUNS A thorough background check on Karen Krupp. If you don't count the recent high-speed accident, she's a model citizen. Not a single driving offence on her driver's licence. Not even a parking ticket. A fairly solid employment record – temping and then two years at Cruikshank Funeral Homes as a part-time bookkeeper. Her taxes are in order. No criminal record. A nice, quiet, suburban upper New York State housewife.

But then he digs a little deeper. He knows her maiden name is Karen Fairfield, he knows her date and place of birth – Milwaukee, Wisconsin. He starts with some basic searches.

But he doesn't find much on Karen Fairfield from Wisconsin – no record of her ever having graduated, or even attended, either grade school there or high school. She has a birth certificate and a social security number. A New York driver's licence. But other than that, prior to a couple of years ago, there's nothing on Karen Fairfield with the date of birth he's been given. It's as if she rose, fully formed, at the age of thirty, when she moved to New York State.

Rasbach sits back in his chair. He's seen this before. It's not as rare as the average person might think. People 'disappear' all the time, and take up life elsewhere, under new identities. Karen Fairfield is obviously a fiction. She's a segue into a new life. Tom Krupp's wife isn't who she says she is.

So who is she?

He is going to find out; it's only a matter of time. He drops by Jennings's desk to share what he's learned. Jennings lets out a low whistle.

'I've got something, too,' Jennings says. 'She got a call.' He hands a printout of the Krupps' phone records to Rasbach.

Rasbach takes the printout from the other detective and looks over the information carefully. 'She got a call at eight seventeen P.M. on August thirteenth, the night of the accident,' Rasbach notes, looking up at Jennings.

'From an untraceable cell,' Jennings says. 'A burner phone.' He adds, obviously frustrated, 'We don't know who called her, or from where.'

'You don't use an untraceable cell phone without a good reason,' Rasbach says, pursing his lips. 'What

121

the hell was she up to, this housewife of ours?' he murmurs. He's not surprised to learn that she received a call right before she tore out of her house that night. He expected as much. Because the night before, they'd found two witnesses who had seen her leave. One, a mother of three who lived diagonally across the street from the Krupps, had seen Karen Krupp run down the front steps and get into her car, obviously in a hurry. She said Karen had been alone. Another neighbour further down the street remembered her, because she felt that Karen had been driving too fast when there were kids playing. She, too, was certain that Karen had been alone in the car.

Rasbach says, feeling a familiar excitement, 'She gets a call at eight seventeen, runs out of the house in the middle of making supper, doesn't lock the door, and doesn't take her purse or her cell—'

Jennings says, 'The call was to the landline, rather than to her cell. Her husband was very late getting home from work that night. The call could have been meant for either one of them. Maybe they're both involved.'

Rasbach nods thoughtfully. 'We'd better take a closer look at Tom Krupp, too.'

Karen Krupp leaves the lawyer's building and steps outside into the hot sun. Now that she's alone again, not having to pretend for either her husband or her lawyer, what she feels is blind panic. She has just given a lawyer a very large retainer, *in case she's charged with murder.*

She's terrified. What should she do? Her instinct is to run.

She knows how to disappear.

But it's different this time. She doesn't want to leave Tom. She loves him. Even if she's not so sure about his feelings for her any more.

Tom is finally back in his own office, after an unbearably long morning meeting. He closes his office door and sits down in the chair behind his desk. He's finding it impossible to focus on work; he's falling behind with everything. He's grateful that he has an office with a door that closes, one that doesn't have walls made of glass – otherwise everyone would see how little work he's doing, how much time he spends pacing the floor and staring out his window.

Almost immediately, his cell phone buzzes. He snatches it up and looks at the caller ID. Brigid. Shit. Why the hell would Brigid be calling him? 'Brigid. What's up?'

'Is this a good time?' Brigid asks.

Not an emergency then, Tom thinks. He starts to relax a little. 'As good as any. What is it?'

'There's something I need to tell you,' Brigid says.

Something in her voice warns him that he isn't going to like it. Instantly, he feels himself tense. 'What?'

'I wanted to tell you this before,' she says, 'but Karen's accident just kind of pushed everything else out of my mind.'

He wishes she would get to the point.

'The police were here last night, asking questions.'

Tom feels the perspiration start to bloom on his skin. He closes his eyes. He doesn't want to hear what she has to say, whatever it is. He wants to hang up.

Brigid says, 'I didn't tell the detectives this, but I think you should know. The day that Karen had her accident, there was a strange man looking around your house.'

'What do you mean, looking around?' Tom asks sharply.

'This guy – he was looking in your windows and snooping around the back. I was pulling weeds on the front lawn, and I kept an eye on him. I was almost ready to call the police but then he came over and talked to me and said he was an old friend.'

'Of mine?' Tom can't imagine who it could be.

'No, of Karen's.'

Tom feels an escalating dread. His heart is beating loudly in his ears. 'Did he give a name?'

'No. He just said he knew her *from another life*,' Brigid says, emphasizing the words.

Tom says nothing, startled.

'I don't want to freak you out, Tom, and you know how close Karen and I are,' Brigid continues in a concerned voice, 'but that's kind of a strange comment, don't you think?'

From another life. 'What did he look like?' Tom manages to ask.

'Medium height and build, I think. He was rather nice-looking, dark hair. Well dressed.'

Dark hair. There's a long pause, while Tom thinks, his mind racing.

Brigid finally says, 'You know, it's always seemed odd to me that Karen has never shared much about her past – at least, not with me. Maybe she does with you?' When Tom remains silent, she adds cautiously, 'I hate to suggest this – I know what you're going through with the accident and everything – but . . .'

'But what?' Tom asks sharply.

'What if there's something in her past that she's hiding from us?'

Tom wants to hang up, but he can't move. 'What the hell do you mean?'

'This may sound crazy, but I saw a show on TV a little while ago about people who are running from their pasts. They disappear and take on a new identity. Maybe – maybe that's what she's done.'

'That's ridiculous,' Tom protests.

'Is it?' Brigid counters. 'People do it all the time, apparently. There are people online that can help anyone do it, for a fee.'

Tom clutches the phone and listens with growing alarm.

'They get a new ID, then drop out of sight, move somewhere else, start over. Change their appearance. They become perfect citizens. They don't want to be pulled over, they don't want to be noticed.'

Tom remembers, with dawning horror, how lawabiding Karen is – or was – until the night of the accident. What if Brigid's right, and his wife is using a fake identity? Why would she do something like that?

'Tom? I'm sorry, maybe I shouldn't have said anything. It's because of that damn TV show! It just crossed my mind, when that man was asking about her . . .'

He thought nothing could throw him after the events of the last week, but this . . . the suggestion that his wife may be someone else? It's more than he can handle.

'Brigid, I have to go,' Tom says abruptly. He gets up from his chair and starts to pace, trying to process this terrible new possibility. A man with dark

126

hair was at their house the day of the accident, a man who said he knew Karen *from another life*. What if Brigid is right, and Karen isn't who she says she is? The police will find out. That terrible photograph – the dead man had dark hair. Tom feels sick to his stomach remembering.

Maybe he's just being paranoid.

Or maybe he's starting to see things as they really are.

Chapter Eighteen

WHEN TOM ARRIVES home that evening he carries within him a bubbling stew of negative feelings – anger, distrust, fear, heartbreak. He knows Karen can tell that something has changed. But he's not about to tell her about Brigid's call.

'What's wrong?' she says at last, after an almost silent meal.

'That's kind of a silly question, given the circumstances,' Tom says coldly. 'Maybe I don't like living with the fear of the police showing up on my doorstep to arrest my wife.' He hadn't meant to say it. It just slipped out. He watches her face go white. He wants to blame her, tell her that everything is her fault. But instead, he just turns away from her.

'You haven't asked about my appointment with the lawyer this morning,' she says, equally chilly. He hasn't forgotten about it, he just would prefer not to know.

'How did it go?' he asks, dreading what she might say.

'I had to pay him a bigger retainer.'

Tom gives a bitter laugh. 'Why am I not surprised?'

'Would you rather I didn't pay him?' she asks sharply.

How far their marriage has deteriorated in just a week, Tom thinks. He would never have believed it before. Right now he wants to pin her up against the wall and yell at her to stop lying to him and to tell him the truth. But he doesn't. Instead, he turns away from her and leaves the room.

He can't get past the suspicion that she remembers what happened that night. He can't believe how hurt he is, how manipulated he feels.

And yet, he's still in love with her. How much easier all this would be if he wasn't.

Brigid sits alone in the dark, her knitting idle in her lap. She hasn't bothered to turn on the lights. Bob is out at a visitation again tonight. That's the funeral business for you, lots of euphemisms. She knows other women whose husbands are in business, or the professions, who sometimes accompany their husbands to events – they get a new dress, new shoes – but those are dinners and parties and so on. Not visitations for grieving families, with an open casket at one end of the room, and the overpowering scent and sight of flowers everywhere. No, thank you.

She's begun to dislike flowers, especially flower *arrangements*. Particularly *funeral* arrangements. She used to like to get flowers from her husband on their anniversary, but after a few years she told Bob to please not bother. This was because she began to suspect him of recycling flowers from the funeral home. She didn't actually accuse him of it, and she didn't know for sure. But it seemed like the kind of thing he would do. He's a bit of a cheapskate with the little things. He hadn't baulked at the cost of the fertility treatments, though.

What she would have loved was for him to take her away for a few days – to Venice, or Paris, somewhere full of life – away from the funeral business, or whatever it was that kept him so busy. But he'd always insisted that he couldn't stay away for that long. So now she gets an uninspired pair of earrings once a year that she has no occasion to wear.

It's not like they can't afford to travel. Cruikshank Funeral Homes has expanded, and they now have three different funeral homes in upper New York State, and Bob's busier than ever.

But she isn't. She could have worked for Bob in some capacity, but when he suggested it, she said she'd rather stick pins in her eyes. He'd been offended by that.

The arduous fertility treatments for which she'd quit her managerial job hadn't worked – and now, except for her knitting blog, her days are rather empty. She has her hopes pinned on adoption. She worries that Bob's line of work will hurt them in their application, but it's not as if they *live* in the funeral home. They're a normal couple, with a normal home. The business is completely separate. They don't even talk about it much. He knows she hates to hear about it. What really annoys her is that when they were first married, he was selling insurance, which was completely respectable. But he was entrepreneurial and the opportunity came up. It's profitable, she can't deny that. She just wishes Bob was successful at something else.

She looks intently across the street at number 24, Karen and Tom's house. She wonders what Tom's thinking, after her phone call earlier today. Does he believe, as she does, that Karen is hiding something about her past? It has always puzzled her that Karen is so guarded with her, given that Karen tells Brigid that she is her best friend. Brigid's efforts to draw Karen into greater intimacy have always failed.

And Tom – each night Brigid sees the light on in his office upstairs at the front of the house. He works too hard, like Bob, but at least when he works nights he works at home. Karen isn't sitting alone in the house every evening like she is.

Maybe she should take them over a plate of brownies. As it happens, she baked some brownies this afternoon. She doesn't want to eat them all herself. And it's not that late. Her mind made up, she runs upstairs to change.

She brushes her shoulder-length brown hair, parted in the middle, puts on some red lipstick, and looks appraisingly in the mirror. She practises her most charming smile – the one that makes her eyes light up – and then grabs the brownies from the kitchen.

Chapter Nineteen

KAREN'S IN THE kitchen when she hears the doorbell. She freezes. When it rings again, she still doesn't move. She can hear Tom stirring upstairs. He's probably wondering why she's not getting it.

When it rings a third time, she reluctantly leaves the kitchen to answer it. Her eyes meet Tom's as he's coming down the stairs. He stops halfway down. She can sense the uneasiness radiating off him. She feels an uneasiness of her own as she opens the door.

It's Detective Rasbach and his sidekick, the other detective whose name she can't remember. Her mouth has gone dry. She tells herself to be calm. She reminds herself that she has a lawyer. She remembers his card, in her wallet. She can reach him if she has to.

Karen wants to slam the door in the detective's face.

'May we come in, Mrs Krupp?' Rasbach asks politely. She sees him flick a glance toward her husband, who's still standing like a sentry on the stairs.

She thinks about it. She has only a second or two to make the right decision. Calvin has told her not to talk to the police. But she's afraid that if she sends them away, they will come back with an arrest warrant. She hears Tom walk down the rest of the stairs and come up behind her.

'What do you want?' he says to the detective, a little aggressively.

'I'd rather not do this on the doorstep,' Rasbach answers pleasantly.

Karen pulls the door open wide and allows the two detectives to enter the house, avoiding Tom's eye.

They end up in the living room, like before. 'Please, sit down,' Karen says. She steals a glance at Tom now, and is alarmed by what she sees written on his face. He doesn't know how to dissemble. And right now he looks like he's expecting his world to end.

There's a pregnant silence before anyone speaks. Rasbach takes his time. She can't let it get to her. She waits him out.

At last, Rasbach begins. 'Have you remembered anything about the evening of your accident?' he asks Karen.

'No,' she says politely. After a pause, she adds, 'Apparently that's not unusual in these kinds of cases.' And then she thinks that perhaps she shouldn't have said that. It sounds like she's read it out of a book.

'I see,' the detective says mildly. 'Can I ask – just out of curiosity – what efforts you're making to regain your memory?'

'Pardon me?' Karen says at the unexpected question. She shifts in her seat.

'It seems to me that if you couldn't remember what happened that night you'd be making some attempt to do something about it,' Rasbach says.

'Like what?' she says. She crosses her arms. 'I can't just take a pill and get my memory back.'

'Are you seeing anyone about it?'

'No.'

'Why not?'

'Because I don't think it will help. My memory will come back in its own good time.'

'That's what you believe.'

'That's what my doctor said.' She knows she sounds defensive. She takes a deep, quiet breath.

The truth is she hasn't dared to see a specialist, such as a hypnotist, because she can't risk anyone else hearing what might have happened that night. She needs to uncover this on her own.

135

He changes tack. 'We know that you left the house alone the night of the accident. We have witnesses who saw you leave the house.'

'Okay,' she says. She feels Tom glance sharply at her.

Rasbach says, 'We also know that you received a phone call that night. At eight seventeen P.M.'

'Did I?' she says.

'Yes, you did. On your landline. We've looked at your phone records,' Rasbach says.

'Are you allowed to do that?' Tom asks.

'Yes, we are,' Rasbach says. 'Or we wouldn't have done it. We got a subpoena.' He turns his attention back to her. 'Who do you think might have called you at that time?'

'I have no idea.'

'No idea,' Rasbach repeats.

Tom blurts out, as if he can't stand the tension any longer, 'You obviously know who called her, so why don't you stop playing games and tell us.'

Rasbach glances at her husband. 'We don't actually know who called,' he says. 'The call was made from a disposable cell phone. We can't trace that kind of call.' Then Rasbach leans forward in his chair toward her, a little ominously, she thinks. 'But I imagine you know that.'

Karen feels the eyes of the two detectives and her husband on her at this new information. Her heart is beating double time now.

'That's a bit out of the ordinary,' Rasbach continues, 'don't you think?'

She thinks about the card in her wallet. It was a mistake to let them in.

'Interesting that the call came on the home line, rather than on your cell,' the detective says.

She stares at him, but says nothing. What can she possibly say?

'Perhaps the call wasn't meant for you at all,' Rasbach says.

This suggestion surprises her.

Rasbach turns back to Tom, who looks as confused by this as she is.

'What do you mean?' Tom asks.

Rasbach says, 'I mean maybe the call was meant for you, and she took it instead.'

'What?' Tom says, obviously taken aback.

'The call came at eight seventeen – aren't you usually home by that time?' the detective asks.

Karen watches Rasbach, relieved to have the focus shift away from her and who called her from that burner phone, if even for a moment. Let them waste their time on Tom, she thinks; they won't find anything there. She feels herself start to relax, just a little bit. They obviously don't really *know* anything. They're fishing. They'll be leaving soon, with nothing more than what they came with.

'Yes, I'm usually home by eight or earlier. But I've

137

been very busy at work lately,' Tom says defensively. The detective waits. 'What, you think someone called *me* from an untraceable cell phone?'

'It's possible,' Rasbach says.

'That's ridiculous,' Tom protests. When Rasbach remains silent, simply watching him with his sharp blue eyes, Tom says, 'You think someone called *me* from an untraceable cell phone, and my wife took the call and ran out of the house? Why would she do that?'

Karen watches Tom and Rasbach, surprised at where this is going.

'Yes, why?' Rasbach asks, and waits quietly.

Tom loses patience. 'Detectives, I'm afraid you're wasting your time. Not to mention ours. Maybe you should go.'

'Have you got something to hide, Mr Krupp?' Rasbach asks, as if he already knows the answer.

Karen swivels her startled eyes to her husband's face.

Brigid hesitates on her own doorstep, brownies in hand, when she sees the car in the street in front of the Krupps' house. She knows that car. Those two detectives are there again.

Brigid is dying to know what's going on.

She decides to slip around to the back of the house and leave the brownies just inside the back door. She doesn't want to bother anybody. It's a hot night, and as she hoped, the sliding glass doors are open to let in the breeze. Only the screen door is closed. If she stands very still, in the dark, she may be able to hear what they're saying in the living room, especially if she quietly opens the door to set the brownies down, maybe just inside on the kitchen table . . .

Chapter Twenty

TOM FEELS AN ugly red flush creep up his neck to his face. He's angry with the detective, barging into their home with a lot of sly accusations. He doesn't have to put up with it.

'No, detective,' Tom says, 'I don't have anything to hide.'

'If you say so,' Rasbach replies after a moment.

'Why would you even suggest such a thing?' Tom asks, and then immediately wishes he hadn't.

Rasbach regards him carefully. 'Because we've been looking at the timeline for the night of the accident. Your wife had her accident, not far from the scene of the murder, at approximately eight forty-five P.M. You told the 911 operator that night that you drove home from work and arrived at about nine twenty and found your wife missing, the doors unlocked, and the lights on.'

'Yes,' Tom says.

Rasbach pauses for a moment and then says, 'We spoke to security at your office and they said you left at eight twenty. It's only about a fifteen-minute drive from your office to here. So where were you for that hour? That's a rather critical time in this investigation, from eight twenty to nine twenty or thereabouts.'

Tom suddenly feels light-headed. Karen looks at him, clearly shocked, and he looks away. He can feel himself sweating, can feel the moisture staining his shirt beneath his sleeves.

'For that matter,' Rasbach adds, 'we only have your word for it that you were home at nine twenty. You didn't start calling your wife's friends until' – he looks at his notes – 'nine forty, I believe. And then you called 911 shortly after that.' He waits, but Tom says nothing. 'So where were you?'

'I – was driving around,' Tom answers, faltering.

'You were driving around – for an extra forty-five minutes,' Rasbach says, his eyes like steel. 'Why?'

Tom wants to reach for the other man's throat. Instead he takes a deep breath and tries to steady himself. 'I needed to think, to clear my mind. I'd had a long day.'

'You didn't want to get home to your wife?'

Tom looks at the detective, wonders what he knows, and in that moment hates the man's guts – his smoothness, his composure, his sly innuendo.

'Yes, of course I did,' Tom snaps. 'But – driving helps clear my mind. It helps me relax. I have a very stressful job.' It sounds lame, even to him. Tom sees Rasbach's eyebrows go up. It's something the detective does, for effect, and Tom despises him for it.

'Did you stop anywhere? Anyone see you?'

Tom starts to shake his head and then hesitates and says, 'I stopped for a few minutes to sit at one of the picnic tables along the river. For some fresh air. I don't think anyone saw me.'

'You remember where, exactly?'

Tom tries to think. 'Near the foot of Branscombe, I think, the parking lots there.' He can't bring himself to look at Karen.

Rasbach jots it down, gives him a last, penetrating look, and stands up, putting his notebook away.

Finally, Tom thinks, they're leaving. They've done enough damage for one night.

Karen shows the detectives out, while Tom remains sitting in the living room, staring at the floor, preparing to face his wife.

Karen knows Tom doesn't like driving. It doesn't relax him – if anything, it stresses him out. She feels the ground shifting beneath her feet. She has to ask him. 'So why were you driving around for an hour that night?'

142

'Why did you drive your car into a pole?' he flashes back.

She opens her mouth in surprise.

Tom says abruptly, 'I'm going out.'

She watches him leave. She flinches when he slams the door behind him.

What was Tom doing that night? That detective is no fool. Is it possible that Tom's lying to her? That he's hiding something from *her*?

Troubled, she wanders into the kitchen to get some ice water and immediately spots a plate of brownies on the table. She stops in her tracks. She recognizes the plate. It's Brigid's. Brigid was here, and left her signature brownies. The brownies weren't there before the detectives arrived. She must have left them on the kitchen table while the police were talking to Tom and her in the living room. Karen feels a chill. Could she have overheard anything?

She hates how out of control everything is getting. She closes her eyes, takes a deep breath, and forces herself to relax.

She'll call Brigid tomorrow and thank her for the brownies. She can trust Brigid. She'll talk to her and find out how much she heard.

Karen fills her glass with water from the refrigerator and takes the plate of brownies with her into the living room and waits for Tom to return. *What is he hiding?* Tom has always been an open book. She

143

can't believe that he is keeping something from her. Where could he have been for that hour, and why doesn't he want to tell her?

Tom gets into his car and drives to a neighbourhood bar, the kind of place that local teams go to for a beer after a friendly baseball game. He needs to get his head together. He slides into an empty booth, orders a beer, and slumps over it; he doesn't want to talk to anyone.

He's got himself into a bit of a mess. In fact, the more he thinks about it, the messier it looks. He didn't want to tell the detectives what he was doing that night, not in front of Karen. Because he knows how it's going to look. Now it will all come out.

He was supposed to meet Brigid that night, at 8:30, at their spot by the river, at that quiet place between downtown and the suburbs, where the path is less crowded, and trees provide a bit of privacy. It's where they used to sometimes meet, when they were having their short, misguided, and messy affair.

She had called him that day, the day of the accident, at his office, and asked him to meet her – she wouldn't tell him why. But she stood him up that night. He waited over half an hour, in the dark, but she didn't show.

He still doesn't know why Brigid wanted to meet him. When he asked her, in that terse first phone call

144

when he was looking for Karen, what she'd wanted and why she'd stood him up, she'd brushed him off, saying her sister had had some kind of crisis, and that it could wait. He was more worried about finding Karen, anyway.

He knows he should have told Karen about him and Brigid. Now he'll have to tell the detectives, and it will look as if he were meeting Brigid that night because he wanted to, and keeping it a secret from Karen.

He knows he should tell Karen now, tonight – tell her everything – but he's not in a confiding mood. Maybe he'd feel more like telling her the truth if she went first.

When Tom returns home, his wife eyes him cautiously. They're wary of each other now.

'Do you want one?' Karen asks him after a moment, pointing to the brownies on the coffee table.

'Where did those come from?' Tom asks as he sits down.

'They look like Brigid's. They taste like hers, too.'

'Was she just here?' Tom asks.

'She must have been.'

Tom looks at her questioningly. 'What do you mean?'

'When you left, I went into the kitchen and they were sitting on the table.'

'What?' Tom says. 'When did she put them there?'

'I assume when we were in here talking to the detectives,' Karen says.

'Shit,' Tom says uneasily.

'I'll talk to her tomorrow. Try to explain.'

Tom rubs a hand over his face. 'How are you going to explain two detectives in our living room, asking questions about a murder investigation?'

Karen doesn't even look at him. She says, 'I'll tell her the truth. There was a murder that night near where I had my accident. Nothing to do with me. But the police are desperate and they don't have any leads. They'll give up when they don't find anything,' she says.

She seems to be forgetting about the gloves, Tom thinks, and the tyre tracks. And the mysterious phone call. She's pretending to have a confidence that she can't possibly really feel.

There's a long, fraught silence between them. Finally Tom says, 'Maybe you should see a doctor.'

'Why?' Her voice is sharp.

'Like the detective said – it's not like you're actually doing anything to try to get your memory back.' She stares at him now, but he doesn't look away. 'Maybe you should.'

'What's a doctor going to do?' she says coldly.

'I don't know,' Tom answers. 'Maybe you could try hypnosis.' He's pushing her, goading her. *Let's find out what happened that night. I really want to know. Do you?*

She gives a forced laugh. 'I'm not doing hypnosis. That's ridiculous.'

'Is it?' He's challenging her, and he can tell she doesn't like it.

She gets up and leaves the room, taking the plate of brownies back into the kitchen. Tom remains alone on the living-room sofa, crushed by a devastating loneliness. He hears the door in the kitchen slide open and then close again; she's gone out.

Chapter Twenty-one

KAREN CLOSES THE door behind her and stands briefly on the back patio. She has to fight the urge to cry. None of this was supposed to happen. She's losing Tom. She sits down in one of the wicker chairs, hoping Tom will join her. But he doesn't, and she feels sad and lonely and angry and frightened.

And this terrible suspicion she suddenly feels – where was Tom for that hour? What is he not telling her? How she wishes she could remember what happened that night! What had she done?

She wants to escape the tension of the house with her and Tom in it. She rises from the chair, walks across the back of the house and down the driveway. Maybe she should drop in on Brigid.

But she can't face talking to Brigid right now. She

walks briskly down the sidewalk, away from the house. She needs to think.

Karen's gone out, and Tom's home alone. Brigid saw him return just a few minutes ago. Something's definitely up.

Brigid steps outside and quickly crosses the street. She doesn't know how long she has before Karen returns. She climbs the steps and knocks on the front door.

He doesn't answer right away. She knocks again. Finally, Tom yanks open the door, looking tired and distraught. There are hollows in his handsome face that didn't use to be there; he looks ashen.

'Hi,' she says.

'Hi,' Tom says. His left hand remains on the edge of the door, as if he's about to close it again at any moment. 'Karen's not home, she's just gone out for a bit.'

'I know,' Brigid says. 'I saw her go down the street.' She hesitates. 'I was hoping to get you alone, actually, for a minute.'

She slips past him into the living room; now he either has to ask her to leave, or close the door behind her. She doesn't think he's going to ask her to leave.

'I wanted to ask you about Karen,' Brigid says, turning around to face him. 'How's she doing? Is she all right?'

Tom looks back at her coldly. 'She's getting better.'

'She seemed really rattled when I was here the other day,' Brigid says. 'About the glass. That wasn't like her at all.'

Tom nods. 'It's just – there's a lot going on right now.'

'I know,' Brigid says. 'I saw that those detectives were here again a little while ago.' She pauses. When Tom doesn't say anything, she asks, 'What did they want?'

Tom says tightly, 'They wanted to see if she remembers anything about the accident yet. But she doesn't. She says she doesn't know what happened that night.'

'And you believe her,' Brigid says.

'Of course I believe her,' Tom says, bristling.

'But the police don't?'

'I don't know what the police believe. Nothing they say makes any sense.'

Brigid eyes him carefully. Their earlier phone conversation about Karen hangs between them. She can't resist bringing it up. She says, 'The day of the accident – the reason I called you and asked you to meet me – it was to tell you about the man snooping around, hinting about Karen's past. I thought if I tried to tell you over the phone, you'd hang up on me. But then my sister called, and—'

'I don't want to talk about it,' Tom says abruptly. There's an awkward silence. Then Tom says, 'Maybe you should try Karen again in the morning.'

She nods. 'Sure. I'll call on her then.' She adds, 'You look exhausted, Tom.'

He runs a hand through his hair and says, 'That's because I *am* exhausted.'

'If there's anything I can do to help,' Brigid says, and puts her hand lightly on his arm, 'just ask.'

'Thanks,' Tom says stiffly, 'but I'll be fine.'

She can feel the warmth of his bare forearm under her hand. He moves away from her, breaking the contact.

'Good night,' she says, and turns to go back down the steps to go home. She looks across the lawn and the street to her own house, empty and almost entirely in darkness, except for the light over the front door.

Tom closes the door behind Brigid with relief, then rests his body against it and feels himself sag with fatigue. He always feels awkward and tense around Brigid. He dislikes the close friendship that has developed between Brigid and his wife. He knows it's selfish of him. He drifts into the living room wondering what Brigid is thinking. She recognized the detectives. Detectives don't investigate car accidents. She obviously suspects something more is

151

going on. And he knows she has questions about Karen's past. He wishes she hadn't shared her suspicions with him. If what Brigid suspects is true, then Karen's deceptive behaviour started long before the night of the accident.

And yet, it's so hard to believe. He remembers all the happy times they've had together – holding hands walking through the woods in the fall, having coffee together in the backyard in summer, nestled in bed under the covers in winter. He's always felt completely in love with her, always believed that they were completely committed to each other.

But now . . . now he doesn't know what he believes. If she *really* can't remember, why won't she make an effort to get her memory back, like the detective said?

Tom goes into the kitchen and reaches into a cupboard for a bottle of whiskey. There's a lot of liquor left over from their wedding party almost two years ago. He rarely has anything more than a beer or a glass of wine with dinner. Now he pours himself a stiff one, and waits for his wife.

Chapter Twenty-two

KAREN WALKS QUICKLY, as skittish as a cat. She's breathing rapidly, from a combination of exertion and emotion. She feels as if she's about to crack.

She's been living in fear for too long.

Karen thinks about the first time she came home from work and felt that things were not exactly as she'd left them. She noticed that the novel she'd been reading the night before was placed to the *left* of her bedside table lamp; she was sure she'd put it down to the right of the lamp, on the side nearest the bed, just before she'd gone to sleep. She wouldn't have placed it on the other side of the lamp. She stood there staring at it in disbelief. Anxiously, she scanned the rest of the room. At first glance, everything looked the way it should. But when she opened her underwear drawer it was untidy, as if someone had rummaged through her panties and bras. She knew that someone had. She stood perfectly still, looking down at her drawer, holding her breath. She told herself it was impossible that someone had been in the house, going through her dresser. Perhaps she'd been rushed that morning, sloppy. But she knew she hadn't been. It had just been a regular day.

She hadn't mentioned it to Tom.

Then there was the day she came home, not long afterward, and went into the bedroom to change. She'd made the bed in the morning, as she always did. She always made the bed the way she'd learned to do it when she was a young woman working as a chambermaid in a five-star hotel – all tight corners and firm smoothness. She was taking off her earrings, saw the bed reflected in the dresser mirror, and froze. Then she spun around and stared. She could see – faintly – the impression of a body on top of the pale green bedspread. As if someone had lain down on top of the bed and then smoothed it out, carelessly, afterward. It gave her a fright. She knew she wasn't imagining it. Tom left for work every day before she tidied up and made the bed. She was so rattled that she called Tom at the office and asked him if he'd been home during the day. He hadn't. She told him she'd found a window open that she thought she'd closed before she left for work, but that she must have forgotten to shut it. He didn't seem to give it another thought.

154

After that, she started taking pictures in each room of the house on her cell phone before she left for work each day, and comparing them to how she found things when she got home. She always left for work after Tom and got home before him. They had no cleaning lady, no pets. So if things weren't exactly as she'd left them . . .

The last time had been just a few days before the accident. She could sense that someone had been in the house; she could feel it somehow. She went through the house with her cell phone in her hand, comparing the pictures on her phone with what she saw in the rooms in front of her. Everything was as it should be. Still, she felt certain someone had been there. She was starting to relax until she got to the office upstairs. She stared down at Tom's desk. She thumbed through the pictures on her phone till she got to that morning's picture of the office. Tom's open agenda wasn't in the same place on his blotter; it was about six inches higher on the blotter than before. She stared at the photo, and then at the desk. There was no doubt about it. Someone had been here, inside their house.

Someone had been in their house, going through their things. Lying on their bed.

She never told Tom.

And now she knows who it was. It had been him, all along. He'd been in their house, coming and going at will. Watching and waiting. The thought of it makes her ill.

But now he's dead. The hideous pictures of the corpse invade her mind and she tries to push them out again.

That time with the glass on the counter – she must have been mistaken – her raw nerves had made her panic. The glass must have been there before, and she'd just forgotten, probably because of the concussion.

Her fears now are all centered on that damned detective.

Her heart thuds in her chest and she walks faster, toward home.

She enters the house, anxious to get inside. She closes the door firmly behind her and locks it. She turns around and sees Tom watching her intently from the living room. He's standing by the fireplace, holding a whiskey in his right hand.

'Can you pour me one of those?' she says. She's done with the pain meds, and she needs a drink.

'Sure.'

She follows him to the kitchen. As he reaches up in the cupboard for the bottle, she watches him. She wishes they could get past this mistrust, this tension. She wonders if that will ever be possible now.

He turns and hands her a short glass with a shot of whiskey, neat.

'Thanks,' she says. She takes a sip and immediately feels the liquor burn down her throat, steadying her a little.

'Where have you been?' Tom asks.

He's trying so hard now to keep any hint of confrontation out of his voice that he doesn't sound natural at all. Gone is the light-hearted, unthinkingly happy man she married. The man with the quick laugh, the spontaneous hugs and kisses. She's changed him.

'I went for a walk,' she says, her voice neutral.

He nods. As if it's perfectly natural for her to go for a walk alone after dark, without him.

It's like we're perfect strangers, Karen thinks, taking another sip of whiskey.

'Brigid dropped by,' Tom says. He's leaning against the counter, facing her.

Karen's heart tightens. 'She did? What did she say? Did she overhear anything?' she asks.

'She must have,' Tom says irritably.

'But you didn't ask?'

'You can ask her tomorrow,' Tom says. 'Better that you ask her, anyway.'

She nods. She looks at her husband and her heart lurches as his eyes slide away. They both need to know what her mind has blocked out.

'Tom,' she says, hesitantly. 'Do you want to drive me down there, to where they found the body?'

'What, now?' Tom says, caught off guard.

'Why not?' She remembers how he goaded her, how he accused her of not doing anything to get her memory back. She's offering to do something about it now. If he only knew how desperate she was to know what happened that night. 'Maybe it will help me remember.' She knows the address; she clipped it out of the newspaper.

'All right,' Tom says, putting down his drink. He picks up his keys on his way out the door and she follows him.

Chapter Twenty-three

AS THEY LEAVE their own familiar neighbourhood behind and head south, Karen feels more and more uncomfortable. It feels like looking for trouble, driving a Lexus through these decaying streets. *See, I'm trying*, she wants to say to him, but she doesn't. She watches out the window at the depressing view, trying to remember, but nothing is coming back to her.

'I think that's it,' Tom says, pulling into a strip mall's empty parking lot and looking across the street at the derelict restaurant that they've heard so much about.

They sit in the darkness, looking at the ugly, boarded-up building. She doesn't want to get out of the car in this neighbourhood. Now she just wants to go home. Nothing looks familiar. She's never seen this place before. She's never been here. She starts to tremble.

'Let's go take a look, shall we?' Tom says, a little callously.

She'd never intended to get out of the car. She just meant to see the place from a distance. She shrinks back into her seat. 'I don't want to.'

He gets out of the car anyway. She has no choice but to follow him. She doesn't want to sit here alone. She gets out of the car and closes her door angrily. She has to walk quickly to catch up with him as he crosses the street and strides toward the restaurant on the opposite side. She looks around nervously, but there's no one else in sight. Together they stand in front of the building, saying nothing. She can feel his recrimination in the set of his shoulders, the cold expression on his face. He knows she was here, and he can't forgive her for it. Without speaking, Tom heads around the side of the building toward the back. She follows him, stumbling a little in the dark because she feels unsteady on her feet. She's breathing quickly and it's making her light-headed. She feels a terrible fear. But she recognizes nothing. She remembers nothing.

At the back, the yellow police tape is mostly still up, but dragging a bit in places, moving in the breeze.

'Is this helping at all?' Tom asks, turning to her.

She shakes her head. She knows she looks frightened. 'Let's go back, Tom,' she says.

He ignores her. 'Let's go in.'

She hates him for challenging her this way, for not caring how frightened she is. She thinks about turning back and making her own way to the car. If she had her keys with her she'd drive away and leave him here.

Instead, her anger gives her the courage to go after him under the police tape and up to the back door. He pushes it with one elbow. Surprisingly, it opens. She supposes that the police are done here, and have left things as they found them.

Tom walks in ahead of her. There's light coming from the streetlight out front, slanting in through a break in the boarded-up window, enough light to see the interior fairly well. There's a dark stain on the floor where the body must have been, and a lingering, repellent odour – the smell of a rotting animal. She stops, rigid, staring at the stain. Her hand goes involuntarily to her mouth, as if she might gag. Tom looks back at her.

'Anything?' he says.

'I've had enough,' she says, and turns and stumbles out of the restaurant. Once outside she bends forward and gulps deep breaths of fresh air. When she lifts her head again, she's looking at a parking lot a short distance away. Tom comes up beside her, and looks in the same direction.

'I think that's where they found the tyre tracks. And the gloves,' Tom says, and walks toward the parking lot. She watches him. He turns around after a few paces and says, 'Coming?'

'No. I'm going back to the car.' She starts walking without looking at him. All this has done is frighten her. It hasn't helped her remember, and her efforts haven't won her any goodwill or sympathy from Tom either.

Tom watches Karen head back toward the strip mall. She's upset with him, but he doesn't care. It even gives him a nasty sort of satisfaction. After all, this is all her fault. He sees her cross the street and wait beside the car. He has the keys, and she can't get in.

He makes a show of looking around the parking lot, wondering where, exactly, her car had been parked. Where the police had found their gloves. He takes his time. But he keeps an eye on her, to make sure she's all right, standing alone beside an expensive car.

Finally he returns to her, unlocks the car, and drives them silently home. He reflects that all this little excursion has done is further show the fault lines in their already fractured relationship.

When they arrive home, it's late. Tom tosses his keys on the table inside the door and says, 'I'm tired, I think I'll go up to bed.' He turns away from her and heads upstairs. And with each step he takes, his despair deepens.

*

162

Bob lets himself into the house quietly. He peeks into the living room, where he knows he'll find Brigid, sitting in the dark. He knows she isn't waiting up for *him*. She used to, but she's not interested in him any more, all she's interested in is the damn neighbours.

He's hurting, too. He could still love her, if she could only move on from her grief about their childlessness. It's torn them apart, and it's affecting her emotional health. She's always been the emotional one; he's always been the steady one, her rock. But now he doesn't know what to do. He knows how to talk to grieving families, he does it all day long, he's quite good at it, but he has failed miserably at it at home. He can't help his wife deal with her feelings of loss, or deal properly with his own.

'Brigid?' he says softly, seeing the outline of her head dark against the back of the chair. For a moment she is so still that he thinks she might be asleep. He takes a few more steps into the living room. When she speaks, it startles him.

'Hi,' she says.

'Shouldn't you go to bed?' Bob asks, approaching and looking down at her with concern. She doesn't even raise her eyes to look at him; they are fixed on the house across the street.

'Those detectives were back tonight, talking to Karen and Tom,' she says.

Bob doesn't know what the hell's going on with Karen and Tom Krupp. She seems to be in some kind of trouble. He doesn't really know them, but he knows Brigid and Karen are close. 'What's going on, do you think?'

Brigid shakes her head. 'I don't know.'

'Has Karen remembered anything yet?'

'No.' She finally turns to look at him. 'I made brownies. Do you want one?'

Karen watches Tom's retreating back, her heart sinking with each step he takes away from her.

Still trembling, she goes into the kitchen and pours herself another shot of whiskey. Then she carries it into the living room and slumps onto the sofa, cradling it in her unsteady hands. She gulps the alcohol and stares at a blank spot on the wall, for how long she has no idea. It's perfectly quiet. Suddenly she hears the phone ring in the kitchen. Her entire body stiffens. The phone stops on the second ring – Tom must have picked it up in the bedroom – but all at once she's remembering that other phone call . . .

She closes her eyes. She's back in the kitchen, making a salad, slicing a tomato on the cutting board . . . She was expecting Tom home soon. She was looking forward to seeing him. When the phone rang, she thought it might be him, saying he was going to be even later than expected. But it wasn't Tom. It's coming back to her now, and she concentrates. She wants to know.

It was a voice she hadn't heard in almost three years, one she thought she'd never hear again. She'd know that voice anywhere.

'Hello, Georgina.'

Her heart began to pound; her mouth went dry. She considered ending the call without uttering a word, but that would be like a young child crouching and closing her eyes tightly thinking no one could see her. She couldn't hang up the phone; she couldn't just close her eyes. He'd found her. She already knew he'd found her; he'd been in her house. She'd been waiting, in plain view, trying to pretend this wasn't going to happen. And now it was.

She'd fled that life. Begun over as someone else. She'd found unexpected happiness with Tom. And with one phone call, she could feel her new life shattering into a million jagged pieces.

He gave her the address of an abandoned restaurant in a neighbourhood she would never have set foot in otherwise, then Karen hung up the phone. All she could think about was protecting herself, and not letting anyone destroy what she now had with Tom. She saw the pink gloves sitting on the counter and grabbed them. She retrieved her gun from its hiding place in the furnace room – the gun that Tom knew nothing about – putting it with the gloves in a cloth bag. Then she swiped her car keys off the table and flew down the steps, not even thinking about locking the door, or leaving a note for Tom.

She drove, her hands tight around the steering wheel, staying just within the speed limit, her mind blank.

For a moment, everything stops. Karen can't remember what happened next. She takes another gulp of whiskey, tries to relax. And then suddenly she remembers parking the car in that lot. She remembers pulling the gloves out of the cloth bag and slipping them on. They looked absurd. She took the gun out of the bag. She was trembling. She looked around to see if anyone was watching – the place was deserted – and then got out of the car and walked nervously in the dark toward the back of the building, where he'd told her to go. When she got there, the door was already slightly ajar, and she pushed it open with her gloved fingers – but here her memory fails her. She waits, she tries to force it, but nothing will come. She fights tears of frustration. She still doesn't know what happened inside that restaurant. She doesn't know how he was killed. She must know what happened! How can she decide what to do if she doesn't know the truth? But she can see nothing more.

What she saw tonight with Tom – it's all terribly familiar to her now. She can't bear to think about it any more. She finishes her drink in one big gulp, puts the glass down on the coffee table, and buries her face in her hands.

Chapter Twenty-four

THE NEXT MORNING, Tom has gone to work, and Karen's alone in the house. She feels the walls closing in on her. She sits in the kitchen, ignoring the cup of coffee in front of her, her entire body tense.

She's terrified that Rasbach will be back; in the meantime, she imagines him scurrying around, digging, finding out things. Finding out things about her. *Finding out who the dead man is*. Then it's just a matter of time.

Karen hasn't told Tom what she now remembers. She can't. She has to think, figure out a way through this. But her normally sharp mind, so good at planning, isn't working so well right now. Perhaps it's because of the concussion.

She escaped before – she got away from him, away from Las Vegas, started over.

She told him that she was going sightseeing that

day, to the Hoover Dam, just outside of Vegas. The night before, she picked up the secondhand car she'd bought with cash a few weeks earlier. She'd arranged to leave it with the dealer until she needed it. She'd used her new ID – obtained through someone she hired online – to register the vehicle. Then she drove it out to the dam and left it in the parking lot below the Hoover Dam Bypass Bridge. She called a cab using a prepaid cell she'd bought at a drug store with cash, and had the driver take her back to the Strip and drop her at the Bellagio. She also paid him cash. She took another cab home, and got there before he returned. She knew he was going to be out late. She could barely sleep that night – she was too nervous, worried about what might go wrong.

Very early the next morning, she drove back out there, taking US 93 South from Las Vegas, tense behind the wheel, and parked her car in the same lot below the Bypass Bridge. When she saw her getaway car at the other end of the parking lot, waiting for her, it suddenly felt real for the first time. She left her wallet with all her ID in the glove compartment. Then she went to the bridge. There were a few people around, enough to be sure that she was seen. She stood at the guardrail and looked down. It was about a 900-foot drop to the Colorado River below. She felt dizzy at the view. Jumping or falling would mean certain death. She took out her cell phone and snapped a picture. Then she sent the picture, along with a text, to him. *You can't hurt me any more. This is it. And it's on you.* Once the message was sent, she flung the cell phone off the bridge.

After that she had to act quickly. She left the bridge, went down to the parking area, and stepped into one of the portable toilets when nobody was looking. Inside she quickly stripped off everything but her bra and panties. She had a sundress in her pack, which she slipped over her head, then put on the sandals with heels she'd also brought. She bundled her shorts, T-shirt, sneakers, and baseball cap into her pack, then let her hair down and put on big sunglasses. She pulled out a small compact and applied lipstick. Except for the pack she was carrying, she looked completely different.

Farther down the parking lot her secondhand car was waiting, with her expensive new ID as Karen Fairfield in the glove compartment. She had on her whatever cash she'd managed to save. She walked across the lot to her getaway car, the sundress swirling around her bare legs, feeling like she could almost fly.

She got in the car, put the windows down, and started driving. And with every mile, she started to breathe a little easier.

'I saw you coming up the path,' Brigid says, opening her door. 'Come on in.'

Brigid's obviously happy to see her, and for a moment everything seems like it used to. Karen wishes she could confide in Brigid about the mess she's in. How much easier this would be if she could share her burden with someone else, but she must keep her secret, even from her closest friend. And her husband. Because she doesn't know what she might have done the night of the accident.

The two of them head automatically to the kitchen at the back, out of habit.

'I was just putting on a pot of coffee. Do you want some? It's decaf.'

'Sure.' Karen sits down in the seat she usually takes at Brigid's kitchen table, and watches her as she prepares the coffee.

'How are you feeling?' Brigid asks, glancing at her over her shoulder.

'Better,' Karen says.

'You look good, considering,' Brigid says.

Karen smiles ruefully. It feels good to pretend, even briefly, that life is what it used to be. She touches her face gingerly. The swelling has gone and the bruises have faded and yellowed.

'I don't mean to pry, at all' – Brigid looks back at Karen over her shoulder again – 'but if you want to talk about it, I'm here. Or if you don't want to, we don't have to. I'll understand.'

Karen can tell that Brigid is dying to talk about it.

'It's just that – it's the strangest thing – I don't remember anything about that night,' Karen lies, 'from the time I was making supper till I woke up in the hospital, so I don't have much to say.'

'That must be so weird,' Brigid says sympathetically, coming back to the table with two cups of coffee. She puts out milk and sugar and sits down across from Karen. 'I've seen the detectives going in and out of your place. They were here, too, asking questions.'

'They came here?' Karen says, feigning surprise. 'Why would they come here? What did they ask you?'

'They wanted to know if I'd seen you leaving that night, before your accident, whether there was someone with you, that kind of thing.'

'Oh.' Karen nods. That makes sense. They know that she left the house alone, in a hurry, after getting that call at 8:17 P.M. Karen wishes she knew exactly what else the detectives know, or suspect.

'I told them I didn't see anything. I wasn't home.'

Karen takes a sip of her coffee. 'Thanks for the brownies, by the way,' she says. 'They were delicious, as always.'

'Oh, you're welcome. I couldn't eat them all myself, anyway.'

'You must have dropped them off when the police were over,' Karen says.

Brigid nods. 'I didn't want to bother you,' she says, 'so I thought it would be better just to drop them off.'

For the first time it occurs to Karen to wonder why Brigid didn't leave them on the porch, which is the custom around here. That's what neighbours do, if someone's sick, or has a baby, or there's been a death in the family. They leave a plate of something outside the front door. Never the back.

'Why didn't you just leave them on the porch?'

Brigid hesitates. 'I didn't want to interrupt. I thought if I went to the front, you might hear me and come to the door.'

'You must've overheard some things, when you were in the kitchen,' Karen suggests.

'No, I didn't hear anything,' Brigid says. 'I just dropped the brownies and left.' She leans toward Karen, concern on her face. 'But I know detectives don't usually investigate car accidents. What's really going on, Karen?'

Karen looks back at her and makes a quick calculation. She has to tell Brigid *something*. 'They're investigating a murder.'

'A murder!' Brigid looks aghast. 'What's that got to do with you?'

'I don't know.' Karen shakes her head. 'Some man was shot. All they know is that my car was in the area, and because I was driving so fast and had my accident, they think I might know something about what happened. Like probably I was a witness or something. So they keep coming around prodding me to see if they can get me to remember something. They want me to help nail whoever it was that killed that man. But unfortunately, I haven't been much help.' How fluidly the lies come, she thinks.

'Do the doctors have any idea how long it will take for you to remember?'

Karen shakes her head again. 'I may never remember, because of the trauma of it – they think maybe I saw something terrible happen.'

'Well, you've got other things to do than do the cops' jobs for them. Let them figure it out,' Brigid says. She gets up and grabs a box of cookies from the cupboard and brings them back to the table. 'Want one?' Karen takes a cookie out of the package. Brigid takes one, too, has a sip of coffee, and says, 'So you still have no idea why you left the house so quickly?'

Karen hesitates and says, 'Apparently I got a phone call, but I don't remember who from.'

'And the police can't figure it out?' Brigid asks over her coffee cup, her eyes wide.

Karen is now sorry she's told Brigid anything. She doesn't want to tell her about the burner phone. How's she going to explain why the police can't figure out who called her?

'No, they can't,' Karen says rather abruptly, wanting to be done with the conversation. She swallows

174

the last of her cookie and gets up to go. 'I really should be going, I was on my way out for a walk.'

The two of them get up from the table. As they go out through the living room, Brigid asks, 'Do you think you're in any danger?'

Karen turns back abruptly and looks at her. 'Why do you say that?' Perhaps Brigid can see the fear in Karen's eyes.

'Just, you know, if the police think you're a witness, and that you know something ... maybe someone else might think so, too.'

Karen stares at her, saying nothing.

'I'm sorry, I don't want to make you worry,' Brigid says. 'I shouldn't have said anything.'

'No. It's okay. I've thought that myself,' Karen lies.

Brigid nods. They're both standing outside on the front porch now. 'But Tom's not going to let anything happen to you.'

Chapter Twenty-five

TOM'S AGREED TO meet his brother, Dan, at their favourite greasy spoon for lunch. Dan also works downtown; their offices aren't far apart. When Dan called earlier this morning, he sounded worried. Tom's been keeping him pretty much in the dark. Suddenly Tom felt guilty for not staying in better touch.

He also feels the need to talk to someone he can trust. And right now, it feels like his little brother is the only person who fits that description.

When Tom gets to the restaurant, he finds a table in the back corner and waits for his brother. When Dan arrives, Tom waves him over.

'Hey,' Dan says. 'You don't look so great.' There's concern in his eyes.

'Yeah, well . . .' Tom says, looking up at his brother. 'Have a seat.'

'What's going on?' Dan asks, sitting down. 'I haven't heard from you in the last couple of days. How's Karen?'

Tom says, 'She's doing okay.' But his distress must be coming across loud and clear. Dan could always read him pretty well.

'So what are you not telling me, Tom?' Dan says, leaning toward him. 'What the fuck is going on?'

Tom takes a deep breath and leans in closer, pausing while the waiter drops a couple of menus on their table and moves out of earshot. Then he tells Dan everything – about the dead man, the gloves, the call from the burner phone.

Dan looks back at him in disbelief. 'This doesn't make any sense. What would Karen be doing there? And who the hell would be calling *Karen* on a burner phone?'

'We don't know,' Tom says. 'But it made the police suspicious.'

'No kidding,' Dan says. 'So . . . what do *you* think Karen was up to that night?' Dan looks worried.

'I don't know,' Tom says, and shifts his eyes away. 'She still says she doesn't remember.' Tom wonders if Dan can sense his own doubt. There's a long silence between them, and then Tom says, 'Maybe we should order.'

'Sure.'

As they review the menu, Tom tries to decide

whether to tell Dan the rest – that he's starting to wonder about Karen's past, that she might be hiding something from him. What if he's wrong? But first, there's something else he needs to talk to Dan about. The waiter takes their order and Tom sets the menu aside. 'The police are asking questions about me.'

'About you? What the hell are you talking about?' Dan asks. He looks genuinely freaked out now, as if he's afraid of what he's going to hear next.

Tom leans in closer to his brother and lowers his voice further. 'They're asking where I was at the time of Karen's accident – at the time of the murder.'

There's a long, pregnant pause while Dan stares at him. 'Why the hell would they be asking you that?' Dan says.

Tom swallows. 'I never told you this, but . . . you know that neighbour of ours, Brigid, who lives across the street? I think you've met her.'

'Yeah, sure. What about her?'

Tom looks down at the table, ashamed of what he's about to admit. 'I was involved with her, before I met Karen.'

Dan says, rather sharply, 'Isn't she married?'

'Yes, but—' He meets Dan's eyes briefly then shifts his gaze away. 'She misled me – she said her marriage was already over, that they were separating. But she was lying.'

Brigid had tricked him into an affair. He'd only realized it when Bob invited himself over for a beer one evening, obviously unaware of what was going on between Tom and his wife, and it became clear that Bob had no idea that his marriage was in trouble. That she'd lied.

Tom had been easy enough to manipulate. He'd felt an overwhelming attraction to her. There was something terribly exciting about Brigid, about her disregard for boundaries. She was his walk on the wild side.

But as soon as Tom realized that she'd lied to him about the state of her marriage, he broke it off. As he expected, she didn't take it well. She coaxed, she sobbed, she screamed. He was afraid she might do something rash. Tell her husband about them. Slash his tyres. But then she'd calmed down and agreed not to tell Bob. Shortly after that, Tom met Karen. When he became serious about her, he made Brigid promise not to tell Karen about what had happened between them. He was ashamed of sleeping with another man's wife, even though it was only because he'd been deceived. He didn't know then that Brigid and Karen would become close friends. He'd watched it happen with deep dismay. He'd had a few uncomfortable moments – he didn't completely trust Brigid not to say something – but Brigid had kept her side of the bargain. For a long time, his only relationship

179

with Brigid has been as a friend of Karen's. Until she called that day.

'So,' Dan says slowly, 'what are you trying to tell me, Tom? Are you sleeping with her again? Were you with her that night?'

Their food arrives and they abruptly stop talking until they're alone again.

Tom's feeling very uncomfortable with this conversation. He looks earnestly at his brother and says firmly, 'No. I'm not sleeping with her. Like I said, it was over before I even met Karen. And Karen doesn't know about it. She thinks we're just neighbours. We agreed to keep it quiet.'

'Was that wise?' Dan asks.

'In hindsight, no.'

'So why can't you tell the police where you were, Tom? Christ, please don't tell me you're mixed up in anything—' Dan looks distraught.

Tom interrupts him. 'I haven't done anything wrong. I'm not involved in this thing that Karen's tangled up in, whatever the hell it is. I promise you that.' He hesitates. 'But – Brigid called me that day, the day of the accident, and asked me to meet her that evening. She wanted to talk to me about something. She said it was important.' He runs his hands through his hair. 'But she never showed up. I waited for over half an hour. And now the police want to know where I was. I told them I was just driving around for a while, trying to unwind, because work is so stressful. I lied in front of Karen.'

'What a mess,' Dan says.

Tom nods. 'Yes, it is, isn't it?'

'You have to tell the police the truth. And Karen is going to find out.'

Tom frowns unhappily. 'I know.'

'So what did Brigid want to talk to you about?'

Tom looks up uneasily at his brother, and tells him about the dark-haired man snooping around the house that day, and Brigid's suspicions about Karen's past. 'She says she saw some TV show and what that man said made her think that maybe Karen disappeared from another life and is using an alias,' Tom says.

'Seriously?'

Tom nods. 'I know – it sounds ridiculous, right? But she told me she wanted to meet me that night and tell me in person because she thought if she tried to tell me over the phone I'd just hang up on her.'

'Why would you?'

Tom looks away. 'She used to call me – and I'd hang up on her. But that was a long time ago.'

'So, why didn't she show up, then?'

Tom looks Dan in the eye again. 'She said her sister needed her – her sister's always having a crisis.

Anyway, she's got this idea in her head now about how little we know about Karen's past, how she has no relatives and so on.'

'She's right about that,' Dan says slowly.

'And I started to think about it – my God, Dan, *what if Brigid's right*?'

Chapter Twenty-six

TOM RETURNS TO his office after lunch, but he's not back long when the receptionist out front buzzes him and tells him that 'two gentlemen' are here to see him. The two gentlemen can only be those damned detectives. He saw them just last night. Why do they want to talk to him again today? Tom feels sweat start to form down the middle of his back beneath his shirt. He takes a moment to compose himself, straightening his tie a little, and then says, 'Send them in.'

Tom comes out from behind his desk as Detectives Rasbach and Jennings enter his office. 'Good afternoon,' Tom says, closing the door behind them. He remembers how Dan urged him to cooperate with the police. He must tell them about Brigid.

'Good afternoon,' Rasbach says pleasantly.

Tom dislikes Rasbach's pleasantness. From his

experience, it's always hiding something disturbing. Tom returns to his desk and wonders anxiously if they have a bombshell to drop. First it was the gloves at the murder scene. Then the call from the burner phone. What will it be this time?

'We have a few more questions,' Rasbach begins, as they are all seated.

'I'm sure you do,' Tom says.

The detective regards him impassively. 'Where did you meet your wife?' Rasbach asks.

'What difference does it make?' Tom says, surprised.

'Bear with me,' Rasbach says mildly, 'and answer the question.'

'She was a temp, here at the office. She was only here for a couple of weeks. She's a bookkeeper, but she was new in town so she was doing a bit of temping. She wanted to be placed in an accounting firm. She worked on our floor for two weeks. When her assignment was over, I asked her out.'

Rasbach nods and tilts his head to the side. 'Do you know much about your wife?'

'I'm married to her – what do you think?' Tom says testily. His mind is racing. What have they found out? His heart begins to pound. That's why they're here. To tell him who his wife really is.

Rasbach waits a moment, then leans slightly

forward and assumes a more sympathetic expression. 'I don't mean do you know what her favourite toothpaste is. I mean, do you know where she came from? Her past?'

'Of course.'

'Which is what?' Rasbach asks.

Even though he suspects he's walking right into a trap, Tom can't think of anything else to say, so he tells them what Karen has told him. 'She was born and raised in Wisconsin. Her parents are dead. She has no brothers or sisters.'

'Anything else?'

'Yes, lots of things.' Now Tom glares at the detective and says, because he can't bear the tension any longer, 'Why don't you get to the point?'

'All right,' Rasbach says. 'Your wife is not who she says she is.'

Tom looks back at him, deliberately impassive.

'You don't seem surprised,' Rasbach says.

'Nothing you people say surprises me any more,' Tom replies.

'Really?' Rasbach says. 'It doesn't surprise you to learn that you're married to a woman who disappeared and took on a new identity?' The detective leans forward and fixes his eyes on Tom's and Tom finds that he cannot look away. 'Your wife was not born Karen Fairfield.'

Tom sits perfectly still. He doesn't know what to do. Should he admit his suspicions about Karen? Or pretend he has no idea?

Into the silence, Rasbach presses. 'Your wife has been lying to you about who she is.'

'No, she hasn't,' Tom says stubbornly.

'I'm afraid so,' Rasbach says. 'She invented Karen Fairfield and a background for her. It was well done, considering, but not good enough to bear real scrutiny. She would have been fine if she'd kept her nose clean. If she'd stayed out of trouble, no one would probably ever have been the wiser. But showing up at a murder scene was not a smart move.'

'I don't believe it,' Tom protests. He tries to look indignant, but he knows he probably just looks like a desperate man in denial of an ugly truth.

'Come now,' Rasbach says. 'You don't trust your wife much more than I do.'

'What?' Tom snaps. 'What are you talking about? Of course I trust my wife.' Tom feels himself flush up to the roots of his hair. 'If you're so goddamned smart,' Tom says, before he can stop himself, 'who is she, then?' He immediately regrets asking, dreading the answer.

Rasbach sits back in his chair and says, 'We don't know yet. But we'll find out.'

'Well, when you find out, I'm sure you'll let me know,' Tom says bitterly.

'Of course we will,' Rasbach assures him. He gets up to leave and adds, 'By the way, have you had a chance to think any more about where you were that night?'

The son of a bitch. Tom steels himself; he knows this is going to be painful. 'I didn't tell you everything last night,' he says. Rasbach, standing, looks back at him, waiting. 'I didn't want to tell you because you'll twist it into something it isn't.'

Rasbach sits down again. 'We deal in facts, Mr Krupp. Why don't you give us a chance?'

Tom glares at him. 'I was supposed to meet someone. Brigid Cruikshank, a neighbour from across the street.' Rasbach looks at him, waiting for more. 'She called me and wanted to meet at eight thirty. Down by the river. I went there, but she didn't show up.'

Rasbach retrieves his notebook from his suit pocket. 'Why not?'

'She says her sister needed her.'

'Why did she want to meet you?'

'I don't know,' Tom lies. He doesn't want to tell the detective about the dark-haired man Brigid saw around their house that morning. Brigid said she hadn't told the detectives about him.

'You haven't asked her?'

Tom knows he has to tell them. 'If you must know, before I met my wife, Brigid and I had a – well, we had an affair.'

Rasbach looks back at him steadily. 'Go on,' he says.

'It was very brief – I broke it off, just before I met Karen.'

'And does your wife know?'

'No, I never told her.'

'Why's that?'

'Why the hell do you think?'

'And you have no idea why this – Brigid – wanted to meet you that night?'

Tom shakes his head. 'No. Karen's accident put it right out of my mind somehow.'

'You're not sleeping with her now?'

'No. Absolutely not.'

'I see.'

Tom wants more than anything to take a swing at the detective. But he doesn't. As they take their leave, Tom stands up and watches them go. He has to stop himself from slamming the door behind them in fury.

Chapter Twenty-seven

'DO YOU THINK he knows who his wife really is?' Jennings asks as they settle into the car and buckle up.

Rasbach shakes his head. 'I doubt it. He looked terrified that we were going to tell him something about his wife he didn't want to hear.' He pauses, and adds, 'He's got to be going through hell.'

Jennings nods. 'Can you imagine going to bed every night with a woman who might be a murderer? It's got to take a toll.'

Rasbach is frustrated that they haven't been able to find any missing persons who match Karen's profile. 'Who the hell is she?' he wonders out loud. 'I'd like to bring her in for questioning, but I don't want to spook her.' He considers for a moment. 'If we had enough to arrest her, we could get her prints and see if we could get an ID that way. We know she's involved somehow. But the evidence we have against her now isn't enough.'

'Trying to find out who she is is like looking for a needle in a haystack,' Jennings says. 'You know how many people disappear in this country every year?' Rasbach raises his eyebrows at him. 'I was speaking rhetorically, of course,' Jennings adds.

'I think the key to this is the victim,' Rasbach says. 'Unidentified woman possibly kills unidentified man. Who are these people?'

'Organized crime? Witness protection?'

'Could be. I don't know. But if we can ID either one of them, I think we'll be able to ID the other.' He's quiet for a moment. 'She knows,' Rasbach says thoughtfully. As they pull into the station, he adds, 'Let's ask her to come in. We'll be low-key about it.'

Karen gets into the shower, allowing herself to cry while the water pours over her. She doesn't want to flee – she doesn't want to leave Tom – but that might be her only option if things go south really quickly.

After a while she pulls herself together because she has to. She can't just go to pieces. Even if it looks really bad right now, it doesn't necessarily mean the police are going to be able to build a case. She needs to talk to Jack Calvin again, without her husband. She needs to know what her options are.

Because as soon as they identify the victim – as

soon as they realize the dead man is Robert Traynor – then they will look more deeply into his life.

They will see that his wife died rather tragically almost three years ago.

There are photos of Georgina Traynor. She knows that detective will recognize her. He's going to put it together and realize that she faked her suicide to run away from her husband, that he found her, and that he called her on the burner phone that night. And he's going to think she killed him.

She feels sick with fear. It's just a matter of time.

And Tom – what will Tom think when he finds out that she's a fraud, that when he wed her she was already legally married to someone else? What is he going to think when they try to tell him that she's a murderer?

She gets dressed quickly and retrieves Jack Calvin's card from her wallet. She looks at the emergency number on the back. He said she could call him at this number, at any time. She sits down on the living-room sofa and reaches for the phone, but before she can lift the receiver, it rings. Startled, she answers it. 'Yes?'

'It's Detective Rasbach.'

They know.

'Yes, detective?' she manages to say, her chest tight.

'We'd like you to come down to the station and

answer some questions. Completely voluntarily, of course. You're not obligated to do so.'

For a moment, she freezes. What should she do? 'Why?' she asks.

'We have a few more questions,' he repeats.

'Have you identified the man who died?' she asks.

'Not yet,' the detective says.

Her pulse races. She doesn't believe him. 'Fine. When would you like me to come?' She tries to keep her voice casual, so he won't know how terribly frightened she is.

'Anytime this afternoon would be fine. Do you know where the police station is?' He tells her where to find him, but she's not listening.

After she hangs up, she walks briskly to the bedroom and hurriedly starts packing a bag.

Chapter Twenty-eight

TOM GRABS HIS cell phone off his desk and prepares to leave, although it's only early afternoon. He
gives the receptionist a terse, 'I won't be back for the
rest of the day,' without looking at her, and makes
his way out of the building to the parking lot.

He drives down to the river and simply stares at
the water flowing by for a while. It does nothing to
soothe him.

He doesn't know who his wife is. Where did the
lies begin and when will they stop? He feels tears
burning his eyes and rubs them away.

Suddenly he needs to confront her. He can't stand
the tension between them any more, the stress of
being under the scrutiny of the police, the needling
from that horrible detective. Tom gets back into his
car and drives home nursing his anger, so that he has
the courage to confront her. When he pulls into the

driveway he feels a little tug of fear at his heart. What will he find waiting for him this time?

She won't be expecting him now – it's early after-noon. He lets himself in the house quietly. He wants to surprise her, see what she's doing when she doesn't know he's home.

He walks softly around the ground floor; she's not there. Then he walks up the carpeted stairs and down the hall to the bedroom. He stands at the open bedroom door, his heart breaking at what he sees.

Her back is turned to him and she's absorbed in the task of packing an overnight bag. Her move-ments are hurried. *She's running away. Was she even going to tell him?*

He opens his mouth to say her name, but no words come out. He stands there, stricken, watching the woman he loves preparing to leave him without even saying goodbye.

She turns suddenly and sees him. She gives a little jump of surprise and fear. And then they stare at each other for a long moment, saying nothing.

'Tom,' she says, and then falls silent. He sees the tears start in her eyes and spill down her face. She doesn't move to embrace him; he doesn't move toward her either.

'Where are you going?' he asks brusquely, although he realizes it doesn't matter. She's leaving, and it doesn't matter where she goes. She's leaving him to avoid a murder charge. At this moment, he doesn't even know for sure if he wants to stop her.

'Detective Rasbach called a few minutes ago,' she says, her voice shaky. 'He wants me to go down to the police station for questioning.'

Tom stares at her, waiting for more. *Tell me*, he thinks. *Tell me the fucking truth.*

'I don't want to go,' she says, and looks away and down. 'I don't want to leave you.' Tears are streaming down her face now.

'Did you kill that man?' Tom asks in a low, desperate voice. 'Tell me.'

She looks back at him with dread. 'It's not how it looks,' she says.

'*Then tell me how it is*,' Tom says harshly, glancing for a moment at the overnight bag resting on the bed, contents half spilling out, and then fixing his eyes on hers. 'I want to know what happened. I want to hear it from you, *and I want it to be the truth.*'

He wants her to exonerate herself in his eyes. That's all he wants; and then he can take her in his arms and figure out what to do. He wants to stand by her if he can. He loves her, that hasn't changed. He's surprised that he can still love her, when he doesn't trust her. He wants to trust her again. He wants her to be honest with him.

'It's too late,' Karen says, collapsing to the bed and covering her face with her hands. 'They know. They must know!'

'Know what? What do they know? Tell me!' Tom cries.

'He was my husband,' she says, looking dully up at him.

'Who?' Tom says, not understanding at first.

'The dead man. He was my husband.'

No, Tom thinks. *No. This can't be happening.*

She looks up at him, her eyes filled with tears. 'I ran away from him. I was afraid of him,' she says. 'He was abusive. He said if I left him, if I ever *tried* to leave him, he would kill me.'

As Tom listens, he grows numb with horror. His fear is huge. But his heart also fills with a fierce desire to comfort and protect her.

'His name was Robert Traynor,' she tells him in a monotone. 'We were married six years ago, and lived in Las Vegas.'

Las Vegas? He can't imagine Karen in Las Vegas.

'As soon as we were married, he changed. It was like he became someone else.' She looks down at the floor, shoulders slumping. Tom remains standing, looking down at her. After a pause, she continues. 'I realized that I would never be able to get away from him – I couldn't leave him or divorce him. I knew a restraining order wouldn't help. I knew if I ran away

196

he would follow me to the ends of the earth.' She says this bitterly, her voice ragged.

She looks up at him, eyes filled with remorse. 'I'm so sorry,' she whispers. 'I never meant to hurt you. I love you, Tom. I didn't want any of this to touch you.' The tears flow down her face, her hair is tangled. 'After I got away from him, I just wanted to pretend that part of my life had never happened.' She turns away hopelessly. 'I wanted to erase the past.' Then she seems to stall.

Tom looks at her, his heart breaking, but he's also wary. He knows there's more coming.

She gathers her resolve and starts again. 'I faked my death. It was the only way to be sure he wouldn't come after me.'

Tom stands utterly still and listens to her with growing despair. She tells him everything – how she got a new identity and faked her jump off the Hoover Dam Bridge. He's certain now that she's telling him the truth, but more appalled than ever at where this is leading.

'Then, a few weeks ago I began to notice things, things that scared me.'

'What kind of things?'

She raises her head and looks at him. 'Someone had been in the house. Remember when I called you at work that day and asked if you had come home in the middle of the day? I told you I must have left a window open. But that wasn't true. Someone had been through my things, someone had gone through my drawers. I could tell. You know how tidy I am. I knew things had been moved. I was terrified. I thought it was him.'

She looks at him with an expression of abject misery. 'I think he was coming into our house for weeks, sneaking in when we weren't home.' She shudders. 'One time I could tell that someone had lain down on our bed. I started taking pictures on my phone in the morning before I left for work – I could tell that things had been moved sometimes. I didn't know what to do. I couldn't tell you.' She looks at him beseechingly.

'Why couldn't you tell me, Karen?' Tom asks desperately. 'I would've understood. I would've helped you. We could have figured out what to do together.' Did she trust him so little? He would have stood by her, if only she'd been honest with him. 'We could have gone to the police. I wouldn't have let him hurt you.' He thinks, *And then you wouldn't be a murderer, and our lives wouldn't be destroyed.*

'I've started to remember,' she confesses. 'Last night – not when we were down there, where it happened, but later, when the phone rang – it started to come back.' She wipes her eyes with the back of her hand. 'He called me that night.' Her face takes on an additional pallor as she tells him the rest. 'He said,

"Hi, Georgina," and his voice was exactly the same – coaxing and threatening at the same time. It was as if I were right back there, with him.'

Tom notices that her eyes have become glazed and her voice has gone flat.

'I wanted to hang up, but I had to know what he was going to do. I knew he'd found me, that he'd been in our house. I was so scared.' She starts to shake.

Tom sits down on the bed beside her and puts his arm around her shoulders. He can feel her body tremble. His own heart is beating wildly. He has to hear the rest of her story, all of it. He has to know where they stand before he can figure out what to do.

'He said didn't I think I was clever, fooling everybody. But I didn't fool him, he said. He kept on looking for me. I don't know how he found me. He said that if he couldn't have me then nobody could. He told me to meet him at that restaurant.' She looks at Tom with terrible fear in her eyes. 'He said if I didn't come, he would kill you, Tom! He knew all about you! He knew where we lived!'

He believes her now, every word. He folds her into his arms and lets her cry. Her sobs beat against his chest. He kisses the top of her head and thinks furiously about what they should do. Finally she pulls away from him and tells him the rest, staring at the floor.

'I took my gun – I've kept a gun, hidden, in case he ever found me – and I drove there to meet him. I parked in that lot and I went to the back door of the restaurant.' She looks up at him urgently. 'I swear, Tom, I didn't plan to kill him. I took the gun for my own protection. I was going to tell him I would go to the police and tell them everything, that I wasn't afraid of him any more – I wasn't thinking clearly, I should have gone to the police first, I know that now. When I got there, the back door was open. I remember putting my hand on it – but that's all I remember. After that, everything is still just a blank.' She looks up at him. 'I don't know what happened after that, Tom, I swear.'

He looks down at her traumatized face. Does she really not remember?

She collapses exhausted into his arms. He holds her while she cries.

So, now he knows. She had good reason for what she did. He can't condemn her for it. Perhaps she really doesn't remember. Perhaps it's too difficult for her to face. She took the gun. He understands that. But she also took the gloves. It looks like she meant to do it. What the hell do they do now?

She sits up straight again. Her face is blotchy from crying, her eyes swollen. 'I must have panicked. And I drove too fast, and ran those red lights, and went into that pole.'

'What happened to the gun?' Tom asks, thinking rapidly.

'I don't know. I must have left it there. It obviously wasn't in the car. I suppose someone found it and took it.'

Tom's heart beats fast in fear at what she's done, at the terrible uncertainty of their position. What if someone turns in the gun? What then? 'Jesus,' Tom says.

'I'm sorry,' she says, miserably. 'I didn't want to tell you. I didn't want to lose you. And I don't want to get you into trouble, too. This is my problem. I have to fix it. I can't let it touch you.'

'It *has* touched me, Karen.' He takes her by the arms and looks deeply into her tear-filled eyes and speaks urgently. 'It's your lawyer's job to fix it. It's going to be okay. You were afraid for your life. You had good reason for what you did.'

'What are you saying?' she asks, drawing back. 'I still don't think I killed him, Tom. I don't think I could do that.'

He looks at her in disbelief. 'Then who did?'

'I don't know.' She looks at him as if hurt that he doubts her. 'I wasn't the only one who hated him.'

He hugs her close to him so he doesn't have to look in her eyes, and whispers, 'Don't run. Stay and face this. Don't leave me.'

Chapter Twenty-nine

AN HOUR LATER, Karen and Tom present themselves once again at Jack Calvin's office. Karen has washed her face and reapplied her make-up. She now feels calm and detached – almost stoic in the face of disaster. She takes comfort in Tom's support. But she's terrified of what happens next.

'Come in,' Calvin says, brisk and professional. He'd rearranged his calendar for this meeting. There's no chitchat today. 'Have a seat.'

As they sit, Karen thinks of how every time she's in this office, things are worse.

'What's happened?' Calvin asks, studying each of them intently.

She lifts her eyes to his and says, 'Detective Rasbach has asked me to come down to the station this afternoon to answer some questions. I'd like you to be there with me.'

Calvin looks carefully from her to Tom and back to her again. He says, 'Why go at all? You're not obligated to. You're not under arrest.'

'Maybe I will be, soon,' Karen says.

Jack Calvin doesn't look as surprised as he might have, she thinks. He picks up a yellow legal pad and that same expensive pen she recognizes from her last visit, and waits.

'Maybe I'd better start at the beginning,' she says, and takes a deep breath and exhales. 'I staged my suicide and ran away to escape an abusive husband. I've been living under a new identity.'

'Okay,' Calvin says slowly.

'Is that a crime?'

'That depends. It's not a crime, per se, to fake your death, but you may have committed other crimes in doing so. And adopting a false identity is perpetrating a fraud. But let's come back to that later. What was your name before?'

'Georgina Traynor. I was married to Robert Traynor. He's the man they're trying to identify, the one who was killed that night.' She glances at Tom for support, but he's watching the lawyer, not looking at her.

Now Calvin seems worried. She knows how bad it looks.

Tom says, clearly agitated, 'As soon as they identify him, they're going to figure it out. They'll see

203

that his wife died. They already know that Karen took on a new identity, that Karen Krupp isn't who she really is. They've already been to my office to tell me,' Tom says.

Karen looks at him in shock. Tom already knew. The detectives know. 'You didn't tell me that,' she says. But he turns away from her and looks at Calvin.

'What matters is what they can prove,' Calvin says evenly. He leans forward over his desk. 'So, tell me what happened that night,' he says. 'And please remember, I have a duty not to lie to the court, so don't tell me anything that will put me in a difficult position.'

She hesitates. 'I don't remember everything, yet, but I can tell you what I do remember,' she says. She tells Calvin what she told Tom earlier – except she leaves out any mention of the gun. But she tells him everything else, up to when she opened the door of the restaurant.

Calvin stares at her as if trying to decide whether to believe her. An ominous silence fills the office. 'Might you have had a gun with you, hypothetically?'

'There may have been a gun, hypothetically,' she answers carefully.

'Is there any way that this hypothetical gun, should it be found, could be traced back to you?' He looks at her closely, concerned.

The gun was purchased illegally, and not registered to her. They can't trace it to her if it's found. And there are no fingerprints on it, she's sure of that. She never handled it without gloves. 'No,' she says firmly.

Calvin sits back in his chair, which squawks a little, and is quiet, obviously thinking. Then he leans forward again and places both hands on his desk. 'Here's what we're going to do,' Calvin says. 'We're going to see if they come up with enough to charge you. I'm sure they will, once they identify him. The circumstantial evidence is strong – it will be enough. But it's another matter to prove it at trial.'

'But—' Karen blurts out.

Calvin looks at her enquiringly. 'But what?'

'I couldn't have killed him,' she says firmly. 'I couldn't have,' she repeats. 'I don't think I'm capable of it.'

Her lawyer and her husband look at her. Tom quickly glances away, almost as if he's embarrassed. But the lawyer stares at her.

Calvin says, 'Who do you think might have killed him?'

'I don't know.'

'Can you take a guess?'

She glances at Tom and then looks back at the lawyer again. 'He might have had enemies.'

'What kind of enemies?'

'Business enemies.'

'What kind of business was he in?' the lawyer asks.

'He was an antiques dealer.' She adds, 'I'm not sure all of his business dealings were entirely on the up and up, but I knew better than to ask. He knew some shady people.'

There's a silence in the room that seems to stretch on forever. Karen sits completely still in her chair. The thought of going to trial for murder terrifies her. Sitting in the lawyer's office, she realizes it's too late. *I should have run*, she thinks.

Finally she says, 'Detective Rasbach is expecting me at the station.'

'You're not going,' Calvin says. 'When they think they've got enough, then let them arrest you. Now – tell me more about how you got away from Robert Traynor.'

She tells him everything – about the months of planning, how she squirrelled money away, all the while secretly visiting a women's shelter for support, and finally what she did that day at the Hoover Dam Bypass Bridge. She adds in a dull voice, 'In a way it was easy, because I had no family to leave behind. My parents were dead, I had no siblings. We had no life insurance policy on me, so I knew the insurance companies wouldn't be looking into it. I thought I

206

could pull it off, and I was desperate. I didn't think I had anything to lose.'

When she's finished, there's a long silence.

Then Calvin asks, 'What did you do with the pack?'

'Oh yes, that.' She pauses, remembering. 'I had to get rid of it, but I couldn't just toss it out the window. Everything in it could be traced back to me. So I added some heavy rocks to it and dropped it off a bridge into a lake in the middle of the night.'

Tom looks at her as she says this, and then averts his eyes, as if he can't bear to imagine her doing it.

'I know it makes me seem cold-blooded,' Karen says, eyeing each of them almost defiantly. 'But what would you have done in my place?' When neither man answers, she says, 'Right, you would never *be* in my place. How wonderful for you – how easy it must be to be a man.'

Tom shoots her a conciliatory look, as if he personally wants to make up for every lousy male on the planet.

She says to him, 'I kept thinking I would tell you at some point.' She asks him now, ignoring the lawyer, as if he weren't even in the room, 'When should I have told you? Right at the beginning? What would you want with a woman who'd run away from her life and had a fake ID? Later on? You would have felt hurt, lied to – like you do now. The truth is, there was never a good time to tell you.' She's almost matter of fact. She isn't exactly apologizing. She did what she had to do. And this is the result.

Tom squeezes her hand. But he isn't looking at her. He's looking down at her hand, in his.

Chapter Thirty

AS THEY LEAVE Calvin's office, the lawyer tells
them, 'It probably won't be long before they identify
the victim, and then things are going to get tense.
You've got to be prepared for that.' He looks them
both in the eye. His gaze lingers longer on Tom, as if
he can sense that of the two, Tom is the least prepared for what's going to happen.

Tom suspects he's right. His wife is much stronger
than he ever realized. He can't imagine cold-
bloodedly faking his own death to escape a maniac,
and starting over as someone else. She must have
nerves of steel, he thinks. He's not sure he likes
thinking of her that way.

As they make their way back to the car in the
parking lot, Tom is utterly terrified. Their lives are
going to enter a whole new realm of awful. She will
probably be charged with murder. She will have to

go to trial. She may even be convicted. He doesn't know if he's strong enough for this, if their love for each other can survive what's ahead.

Tom drives, focusing on the road in front of him, mostly because he doesn't want to look at his wife. But he can feel her eyes on him.

'I'm so sorry, Tom,' she says. 'I didn't want to do this to you.'

He doesn't trust his voice to answer. He swallows, and keeps his eyes straight ahead.

'I never should have agreed to marry you without telling you everything,' she whispers, distraught.

It dawns on him then – they're not really married. On the day of their wedding, she was already legally married to someone else. The thought makes his head spin. She stood beside him when they were saying their vows – and she knew she was already married to somebody else. Her vows were meaningless. He has to resist the urge to stop the car suddenly and tell her to get out.

Somehow, he keeps driving. 'It's okay,' he says. 'It's going to be okay.' He's saying it automatically; he doesn't believe it.

Maybe if he could just hold her, without looking into her eyes, he would be all right. He needs a moment to ground himself again so that he can go on, but he's driving the car.

They ride in silence. As they reach home, he tells

her, 'I have to go back to the office for a bit, not for long. I'll be home soon, for supper.'

She nods. 'Okay.'

He stops in their driveway, and before she gets out of the car, he leans over and hugs her tight. For that moment, he tries to forget everything that's happened, and to focus on how it feels to have her in his arms. Then he pulls away from her and says, 'Don't run. Promise me.'

'I promise.'

He holds her eyes with his; even now, he doesn't know if he believes her. Is this what life is always going to be like now?

Tom lets her go and then reverses the car and heads back downtown. He has no intention of returning to work. He heads back to his spot by the river, wishing he could wash himself clean of the whole sordid business, but knowing that he cannot – not now, not ever.

Brigid had been making a little baby sweater in pale yellow for a friend who was expecting, but found she couldn't bear it, so she's switched to a colourful striped fall sweater for herself. But now the half-finished garment trails off her lap as she watches the house across the street. Her body tenses, and she leans forward slightly.

She sees Tom and Karen pull into the driveway

and stop, but instead of getting out of the car, they sit there for a moment. Brigid waits expectantly. Now Karen's getting out and Tom isn't. Brigid wonders where they've been. She thinks a lot about Tom and Karen, about where they are and what they're doing, about their life together. It's like she's caught up in a particularly good television show and can't wait to see what happens next.

Bob tells her that she's obsessive. He complains that it's not normal. He tells her she's become obsessed with the Krupps' lives because she's lonely and bored and has nothing to do all day. He tells her she's too smart to be doing nothing.

But he doesn't understand. He doesn't know.

She watches Tom reverse the car and head back down the street – she can see through the open car window that his face is set and grim. She wonders if they've been arguing. She turns her attention to Karen, now unlocking the front door. She can sense discouragement in the way Karen carries her shoulders. Maybe they *have* argued.

Brigid puts her knitting aside, grabs her keys, and locks her own door behind her. She walks over to Karen's house and rings the bell.

When Karen opens the door and sees her, Brigid thinks she looks slightly reserved, even unwelcoming. Why isn't Karen happy to see her?

'Hi, Brigid,' Karen says, not opening the door

wide. 'I just got home. I've got a headache. I was actually just going to lie down for a bit before supper.'

'Oh,' Brigid says. 'I thought you looked like you could use a friend.' She gives Karen the warmest smile she knows how. 'Is everything all right?'

'Yes, everything's fine,' Karen says. Brigid stands her ground until Karen opens the door wider, and then she steps over the threshold.

They settle in the living room. Karen looks exhausted. Her eyes are puffy, as if she's been crying, and her hair has lost its shine. How much she's changed in just a few days, Brigid thinks. 'Why don't you tell me what's going on,' she says. 'It might help.'

'Nothing's going on,' Karen says, running a hand through her lank hair.

But Brigid knows she's lying. She's been watching everything unfold from across the street. And Karen looks far too distressed for nothing to be going on. She's not a fool; she wishes Karen wouldn't take her for one.

'Is everything all right between you and Tom?' Brigid asks bluntly.

'What? What do you mean?' Karen says, clearly taken aback.

'Well, I just saw him drive away, and he looked angry. And you seem upset. This must be hard for him, all of this,' Brigid says delicately, 'the accident,

213

the police.' As Karen stares back at her, she amends, 'For both of you.' Karen shifts her eyes away, toward the window. After a short silence, Brigid asks, 'Have you remembered anything helpful to the police?'

'No,' Karen says, rather sharply. 'How have things been with you?' she asks, trying to change the subject.

'Karen, this is Brigid you're talking to. You can tell me anything.' She means it. It annoys her that Karen's so tight-lipped; she doesn't disclose many of the intimate details of her life. Brigid has told Karen about her difficulties getting pregnant, her failed fertility treatments. But Karen never shares. Even now, when things are far from perfect, and you'd think she'd need a friend. How shocking it must be for Karen, she thinks suddenly, that things aren't absolutely perfect.

Things should be more equal between friends, Brigid believes, and as far as she's concerned, Karen hasn't done as good a job at their friendship as she could have. Brigid has worked very hard at this friendship. Karen has no idea how hard it's been, how much she's had to swallow. Karen doesn't know about her and Tom, how difficult it's been for her, all this time, watching Karen and Tom together. Having to pretend it doesn't bother her. So many times she's been tempted to blurt it out, but she's always bitten her tongue.

Karen's never taken that great an interest in Brigid's life, really, Brigid thinks now. Not as great an interest as Brigid has taken in hers. For instance, Karen has never shown much curiosity about her knitting blog, something that has always bugged her. Brigid Cruikshank is a goddess among online knitters. But Karen doesn't knit, and she doesn't care.

Karen looks at her now and says, 'I appreciate your concern, Brigid, I really do. You're a good friend.' She smiles at Brigid. Brigid smiles back mechanically. 'You know, my headache's getting worse. I should probably lie down,' Karen says. She gets up off the sofa and walks Brigid to the door.

'I hope you feel better soon,' Brigid says, and gives Karen a brief hug.

Then she walks back across the street to her own empty house, and takes up her position at the window with her knitting, to wait for Tom to come home.

It's grown late in the afternoon, and it seems clear that Karen Krupp isn't going to show up voluntarily. Rasbach is pondering next steps when Jennings enters his office and says, 'We might have something.' Rasbach lifts his eyes. 'I just got a call from a pawnbroker I spoke to after we found the body. He says a boy just pawned a watch and a ring.'

'Does he know the boy?'

215

'Yup.'

'Let's go,' Rasbach says, grabbing his shoulder harness and his jacket.

When they arrive at Gus's Pawn Shop, the place is empty except for the owner standing behind a grimy counter. The man nods at Jennings, recognizing him, and chews the inside of his cheek.

'This is Gus,' Jennings says, introducing him to Rasbach. The man nods. 'Want to show us what you've got?' Jennings asks.

The man dips below the counter and brings out a man's watch and lays it on the glass counter. Beside it he places a heavy gold ring.

The detectives take a look. 'Looks expensive,' Rasbach says.

'Yup. Genuine Rolex.'

Rasbach pulls on a pair of latex gloves and examines first the watch and then the ring for any identifying marks or engraving, but there's nothing. He puts the items back down on the counter, disappointed.

'How did the boy say he came by these?' Rasbach asks.

'He said he found them.'

'What's his name?' Rasbach asks.

'Here's the thing,' Gus says. 'I know the kid. He's only fourteen years old. I don't want him to get into a lot of trouble.'

'I understand,' Rasbach says. 'But we need to know if he found anything else, any ID along with the jewellery. Something that will help us with our investigation. We don't think this boy had anything to do with the murder.'

'I just want you to scare him,' Gus says. 'Like, scare him straight, you know? Too many kids get into crime around here. I don't want to see him go down that road.'

'Sure. I get that,' Rasbach says, nodding. 'What's his name?'

'Duncan Mackie. Lives over on Fenton. Number 153. I know the family. Go easy on him. But not too easy.'

Rasbach and Jennings drive to the address Gus gave them. Rasbach's hoping that this is the lead they've been waiting for. He knocks on the front door of the shabby house. He's relieved when a woman answers, because he can't talk to the boy without a responsible adult present. Rasbach says, 'Are you Duncan Mackie's mother?' The woman immediately looks alarmed. When he shows his badge, she looks worse.

'What's he done?' the woman asks, dismayed.

'We just want to talk to him,' Rasbach says. 'Is he home?'

She steps back from the door and lets the detectives in. 'Duncan!' she hollers up the stairs. Rasbach and Jennings sit in the tiny kitchen and wait.

The boy comes down the stairs, sees the detectives sitting in his kitchen, and stops dead. He looks at his mom nervously.

'Sit down, Duncan,' the woman says sternly.

The boy sits and stares at the table. His face is flushed and sullen.

Rasbach says, 'Duncan, we're police detectives. You don't have to talk to us. You can ask us to leave if you want. You're not in custody.' The boy says nothing, but looks up at him cautiously. Rasbach says, 'We're interested in the watch and the ring that you left with Gus.'

The boy squirms and says nothing, while his mother glares at him.

'We just want to know if you found a wallet, too. Something with identification in it.'

'Fucking Gus,' the boy mutters.

'Duncan!' his mother says harshly.

Rasbach says, 'If you have the wallet, maybe we can let this go.'

It seems to dawn on the mother then why they're here. 'This isn't about that dead man that was found near here, is it?' Her face is stricken.

The boy looks nervously at his mother, and then at the detectives. 'He was already dead when we got there. I can get the wallet.'

His mother covers her mouth with her hand.

'I think that would be a good idea,' Rasbach says.

'Because this is making your mother very upset, Duncan. And I think it would be better to come clean and turn over a new leaf before it's too late. You don't want to be arrested, do you?'

The boy shakes his head. 'I'll get it.' He looks at his mother. 'You stay here.' Then he bolts back upstairs, where he obviously has a hiding place he doesn't want his mother to know about.

After a strained moment, they hear him pounding down the stairs and he reappears in the kitchen. He hands a leather wallet over to Rasbach. It still has a few bills in it.

Rasbach takes the wallet from him and opens it. Pulls out a driver's licence. 'Thanks, Duncan.' He gets up.

Jennings turns to the boy on their way out and gives him a friendly look. 'Stay in school,' he says.

As they walk to the car, Rasbach says with satisfaction, 'We've got him. Robert Traynor, of Las Vegas, Nevada.' He feels the familiar adrenaline surge he gets when a case begins to move. They get into the car and head back to the police station.

Soon Rasbach is reviewing some very interesting material. The dead man, Robert J. Traynor, was thirty-nine years old, a successful dealer in antiques. No children. His wife, Georgina Traynor, had predeceased him about three years earlier. Rasbach looks at a photo of Georgina. He leans forward, examines it more closely. Imagines her with shorter, darker hair. He looks again at the dates.

Bingo. Georgina Traynor isn't dead. She's alive and well, and living at 24 Dogwood Drive.

Chapter Thirty-one

KAREN CLIMBS UPSTAIRS and lies down on the bed, relieved to be alone. Brigid had made her feel uncomfortable. Maybe a nap before Tom gets home will help get rid of her pounding headache.

She is rigid on top of the covers, staring at the ceiling. She's going to be charged with murder.

Everything would still be perfect, she thinks bitterly, tears leaking down the sides of her face, if it weren't for Robert finding her. She wonders how he did it, three years later. How was he able to track her down?

Finally, she crawls under the covers and falls into a brief, exhausted sleep.

Rasbach sits at his desk and rubs his tired eyes. He picks up the picture of Georgina Traynor again, and thinks about Karen Krupp, in her comfortable suburban home. She's probably frightened out of her wits, he thinks.

His next thought – she's been frightened before, and found a way out. She's a survivor.

He looks at the facts, the way he's been trained to do: married woman fakes death, turns up somewhere else with a new identity. Three years later, the husband she left behind turns up dead, and it looks like she was there. He knows what it looks like, but he mustn't jump to conclusions.

If she was a battered wife, trying to escape an unbearable situation, then truth be told, he's sympathetic to her. He's sympathetic to any woman who's ever been driven to take such extreme measures to protect herself. These things shouldn't happen. But he knows they do, every day. The system does a rather poor job of protecting these women, and he knows it. It's a damaged, messed-up world.

He's feeling very negative tonight; it's not like him. He wants to solve the case; he always wants to solve the case. He thinks he knows what happened here, and he thinks he knows why. But then it will go out of his hands into the hands of the lawyers, and there's no predicting what will happen. The whole thing depresses him.

He thinks about Tom Krupp. He tries to imagine what he must be going through, but he can't, quite. Rasbach has never been married. The right woman has eluded him all these years. Perhaps it's because of the job. Maybe he will still meet her, someday. And when he does, he tells himself, taking another look at the photo of Georgina Traynor, he'll do a thorough background check on her himself.

Tom has come home again, and they've had a quiet dinner together, with only the scrape of cutlery on plates to break the silence. Now Karen stares out the living room window into the darkness, unwilling to go to bed. She'll only stare at the ceiling again. She tells herself that there's no one out there. Robert is dead. There's no one to be afraid of now.

Except for that detective. And she's terrified of him.

Tom's upstairs in his office, working late. She doesn't know how he can work at a time like this. Perhaps it's his way of avoiding thinking about things. He'd rather stare at lines of numbers than into his own appalling future. She doesn't blame him; her own thoughts are driving her crazy.

Rasbach is going to be back. She's sure of it. She's wound up tight, as if poised for flight. But she's made Tom a promise. She has to place her faith in Jack Calvin.

She decides to go upstairs and have a long, hot bath. Maybe it will help her relax. She puts her head in the upstairs office and tells Tom. He looks up briefly, nods, and looks back at his computer screen. She turns away and goes into the bathroom and starts filling the tub, trying to decide between bubble bath and Epsom salts. But what does it matter? Rasbach is still going to arrest her.

As her eyes fall briefly on the vanity, she freezes. Something's wrong. Her pulse begins to race. Her heart knocks painfully against her ribs and she feels slightly dizzy. She scans the vanity quickly, trying to take in details. It's her perfume. Someone has taken the stopper off her perfume.

She knows it wasn't her.

Karen stares at the perfume bottle, paralysed with fear, as if she's found a snake curled on the vanity. She didn't use that perfume today, she's certain of it. And she would never leave the stopper off. 'Tom!' She calls his name frantically. But he doesn't seem to hear her over the rushing water of the taps. She runs down the hall to his office, screaming his name.

She collides with him in the office doorway.

'What is it?' Tom asks her, his eyes wild. Before she can find the words to tell him, he rushes past her into the bathroom. She comes up behind him. 'What? What is it?' he asks. He can't see what's scaring her so badly, but he's infected by her panic.

Karen points at the perfume bottle, with the stopper lying on the vanity behind it. 'My perfume. Someone took the stopper off. It wasn't me.'

Tom looks at the perfume bottle, then back at her, relieved, but irritated. 'Is that all? Are you sure? Maybe you just left it off and forgot.'

'No, Tom, I didn't,' she says sharply. She can tell that he doesn't believe her.

'Karen,' he says, 'you're under a lot of stress. Maybe you're just forgetting things. You know what the doctor said. I can hardly keep things straight these days myself. Yesterday I left my car keys in the office and had to go all the way back up to get them.'

'That's you,' she says, 'not me.' She looks at him and she can feel a hardness coming into her eyes. 'I can't afford not to notice details like this,' she says, her voice taking on a tone of underlying rage. 'Because for years, if I didn't do something *just right*, if things weren't *just so*, I'd get the living shit beat out of me. So I notice the little things. And I did not leave the stopper off that perfume bottle. *Someone has been in this house.*'

'Okay, calm down,' Tom says.

'Don't tell me to calm down!' she screams at him.

They stand in the small bathroom facing one another. She can see that he's as shocked as she is at her reaction. Her raw emotion has unsettled and appalled them both. They've never been this way with each other before. Then she notices the bathtub and hurries over to turn off the taps before the tub overflows.

225

She straightens up and looks at him. She's calmer now, but still frightened. 'I'm sorry, Tom. I didn't mean to yell at you. But someone must have been in here.'

'Karen,' Tom says. He's using a soothing tone, as if he's speaking to a child. 'Your former husband is dead. Who else would break into our house? Any ideas?'

When she says nothing, Tom asks, rather delicately, 'Do you want me to call the police?'

She can't tell for sure if he's being sarcastic – *Do you want me to call the police about an opened perfume bottle?* Or whether he's just exhausted and overwhelmed with everything that's happened. But there's something in his tone.

'No, don't call the police,' she says. When he stands there saying nothing further she says, 'Go, I'm going to have a bath.'

He leaves, and she locks the bathroom door behind him.

Chapter Thirty-two

BRIGID SITS AND watches out the window; she never tires of it. Every now and then she sniffs delicately at her wrist. She will stay up until Tom and Karen go to bed, until they are safely tucked in and all their lights are out.

Bob has been home briefly for dinner, but he's gone out again tonight for another function. That's every night this week. She wonders if it's really all work, or whether he's seeing someone on the side. She finds she doesn't really care. Still, she's simmering with rage beneath her cool, white skin – the cool, white skin that he hasn't touched in weeks, and they're supposed to be trying to have a baby. Sometimes she hates Bob. Sometimes she hates her life and everybody in it. Except there aren't that many people in her life any more. She's let a lot of things drop. Except for her knitting blog. And the Krupps.

Mostly, Brigid keeps an eye on Karen and Tom.

She would like . . . she would like to be someone else, in some other life. That's what she'd *really* like. She's slightly surprised to realize that what she wants most in the world isn't, after all, to be pregnant at last with Bob's baby. She's wanted that for so long that the wishing for it, the fantasizing about it, has become automatic. How refreshing to realize that she actually, earnestly, wants something else for a change; that she would actually like to be someone else, in another life entirely.

Someone with a handsome, caring husband, a husband who *pays attention*. Who comes home every night. Someone who would make her feel special and take her to Europe and kiss her at odd moments for no reason and look at her the way Tom looks at Karen. She puts her knitting down.

She hasn't been able to resist the pull of the Krupps' house. She can't help sneaking into their house across the street sometimes, and being there, alone, imagining herself living there with Tom. Lying in their bed. Going through Karen's things, going through Tom's things. Holding Tom's clothes to her face and smelling them – she even took an old T-shirt of Tom's from his drawer and hid it at home. Trying on Karen's clothes in front of her mirror. Using her lipstick, her perfume. Pretending that she's Tom's wife.

It's easy to do – she has a key. Tom had given her

one during their brief affair, and she'd secretly made a copy before she returned it. She can take the path alongside the Krupps' house that leads to the park beyond, and as long as there's no one looking, she can sneak through the unlocked gate and go in through the back door, with no one to see her do it.

She'd left the glass on the counter that day.

She's really never stopped wanting Tom. It's just a question of what she's willing to do to get him back.

This hits her rather hard and she holds her breath for a second.

Lately, she hasn't been able to stop thinking about what they were like together, back when they were lovers. They had some serious chemistry. And Tom was such a pleasure to seduce, so eager to try new things. So willing to follow her lead. How perfect it all was, before he broke it off with her and started seeing Karen instead.

He hadn't been comfortable with the fact that she was married, but he'd swallowed her flirtatious little lie and been happy to sleep with her anyway. That changed when he learned the truth – he dumped her. *God, how it hurt.* She'd made things difficult for him for a while – she couldn't help it, she felt so out of control. Bob had no idea what was going on, but he could see how upset and unhappy she was. He insisted she see someone. Eventually she adjusted. She'd even been able to agree with Tom – quite civilly, she thought – not to tell anyone about their affair. They've kept it secret from Karen all this time. Oh, all the times Brigid had wanted to tell her, over coffee, about what she and Tom had done together!

Now, Brigid recalls the electricity that went through her body the other night when she touched Tom's arm. She's sure he felt it, too, that intense sexual energy that they'd shared flaring up again – surely that's why he stepped away from her so quickly. He can't admit that he still has feelings for her. He's married now; he's too decent a man for that. But she's sure those feelings he had for her are still there.

She wonders if he's getting tired of Karen by now. She's picked up on the tension between them.

Brigid knows that Karen thinks of her as her best friend, even though Karen doesn't know how to be a very good friend sometimes. Karen has disappointed her again and again. It's hard to think of Karen the same way now, after everything that's happened. After all she's put Tom through. Especially since Brigid's realized that she might be able to get Tom for herself.

Karen's not her friend; she's her rival. She's always been her rival.

A whole world seems to be opening up before Brigid, a new future unfurling.

Brigid has sat in this spot by the window these last few days, avidly following the goings-on across the street. She knows Karen's in deep trouble. Maybe soon the police will arrest her for murder.

And then Tom will be all alone, and understandably shattered. He'll be doubting Karen and everything they had together. And Brigid will be there, helping him pick up the pieces. Nudging him in the right direction – away from Karen, toward *her*.

There will be more of that electricity between them, she's sure of it. And he won't be able to resist coming back to her. They were meant to be together.

Everything happens for a reason.

She'll leave Bob; he'll probably barely notice. And she'll move in across the street. She'll have everything she's ever wanted. Karen's beautifully decorated home. Her smart clothes – as luck would have it, they're the same size – her handsome, attentive husband. She suspects Tom has a good sperm count, too, unlike her useless husband.

Brigid's heart flutters at the prospect of her future, as she watches the lights across the street.

That night, Tom lies awake, unable to sleep. Karen is moving around fitfully in the bed.

It wasn't until that overwrought moment in the bathroom, with Karen screaming at him, that he really began to understand what she must have been through and what it must have done to her. For the

231

first time he realized that there are whole parts of her that he's never had any access to. Dark, angry parts of her, and a grim history that she'll never share fully with him. He now knows the broad outlines of how she'd lived, but he doesn't know all the ugly details. This sudden glimpse into her, into the darkness at the heart of her past, has shaken him badly. She really isn't the woman he thought she was. She's much tougher, much harder, and much more damaged than he ever suspected.

She's not the woman he fell in love with. The woman he fell in love with, Karen Fairfield, was a mirage.

He never knew Georgina Traynor. If he had, would he have fallen in love with her? Would he have been man enough to fall in love with a woman with her kind of baggage? Or would he have stayed the hell away?

He likes to think he would have fallen in love with her just the same, and taken her safely away from all that.

But the lies ... He's not sure he can get past the lies.

Yes, Karen had her – excellent – reasons for what she did. But she lied to him. Her wedding vows were a lie. And he's sure she would have *kept* lying to him if the police hadn't tripped her up. That's what's bothering him.

The question he keeps asking himself is: if she hadn't had the accident that night, if she'd managed to calm herself down and come home, would she have made up some story about a friend calling her with an emergency – a story he wouldn't have questioned? Would she have gone to bed with him that night and lain beside him, knowing that she'd shot a man dead – with him never being any the wiser? Because Tom doesn't believe that she wasn't capable of killing her former husband; he's sure now, after that outburst in the bathroom, that she *was* capable of it.

If things had gone just a little differently, he might have continued in his happy, ignorant bubble, unaware of her crime. But he can't ignore it now.

And the one other thing he can't forget. The gloves. She took the gloves with her.

Tom is certain that she intended to kill her former husband – or why take the gloves? There's no doubt in his mind about that. As far as the law is concerned, he's pretty sure she's guilty.

Whether he can live with that or not . . . the jury's still out.

Chapter Thirty-three

THE NEXT DAY, just before noon, Karen's alone in the house when she hears a firm knock at the front door. When she peeks out and sees the detectives, she knows the time has come. She has only a moment to pull herself together before she opens the door.

Rasbach stands on the front porch, looking more serious than she has yet seen him. That's how she knows – they've figured out who the dead man is.

'May we come in?' he asks, his tone surprisingly gentle.

She pulls open the door. She wants it to be over. She cannot bear the tension any longer.

'Is your husband home?' Rasbach asks. She shakes her head. 'Do you want to call him? We can wait.'

'No. That won't be necessary.' She feels calm, detached, as if none of this is really happening. It's like a dream, or as if it's happening to someone else. She's lost her opportunity to flee. It's too late now.

Rasbach says, 'Karen Krupp, you are under arrest for the murder of Robert Traynor. You have the right to remain silent. Anything you say can and will be used against you in a court of law. You have the right to an attorney . . .'

She holds her hands out in front of her as Jennings puts the handcuffs on her. Her legs suddenly go weak. She tells herself she will not faint, hears, as if from a distance, *Catch her.* She feels strong arms at her back – and then nothing.

Tom bolts out of the office and races to the police station. Jack Calvin has called him and told him that Karen is already there, under arrest. Calvin, too, is on his way.

Tom's knuckles are white from squeezing the steering wheel, and he's clenching his jaw, hard. His world is coming completely apart. He doesn't know what to do, how to act. He hopes Jack Calvin will be able to advise him.

He was expecting this, but it's still a shock. You don't exchange wedding vows expecting one day to hear that your wife is at the police station under arrest for murder.

He stops at a red light. He doesn't understand Karen; he doesn't understand why she did it. There were other options. She could have told him. They could have gone to the police. *Why didn't she go to the police?* She didn't have to go there that night and kill that son of a bitch.

The light changes and he pulls ahead impatiently with a jerk. He's angry at her. For lying to him, for bringing this madness down upon them unnecessarily. She's going to go to prison. He'll have to visit her there. He feels for a moment like he might throw up. He pulls over into a store's parking lot to wait for the feeling to pass.

Now he's grateful that they hadn't yet had children. Thank God, he thinks bitterly, for that.

Karen is sitting in an interview room, with her lawyer on her right side, waiting for the detectives to arrive. Before they were brought in here, Calvin told her what to expect.

'You have the right to remain silent, and you're going to use it,' Calvin said bluntly. 'We're going to listen to their questions, get a feel for what they know, or suspect. You're not going to say anything. That will come later, when you're ready to make a statement.'

She nodded nervously. 'Okay.'

'The state must prove its case against you. Your job is not to help them do that. Your job is to follow my instructions. If you listen to me, and do what I say, it all may work out.' And then he added, 'Although I can't promise anything, of course.'

She swallowed, her throat dry. 'They must have enough, or they wouldn't have charged me,' Karen said, her voice tense.

'There's a higher standard of proof at trial,' Calvin told her. 'Courage. Let's take it one step at a time.'

And then she was brought in here.

Her handcuffs have already been removed, perhaps because she's a woman, she thinks, or perhaps because of the nature of her alleged crime. She's probably not considered dangerous; they think she's a woman who killed her husband in cold blood, but surely they don't think she's likely to kill anyone else?

At the sound of the door opening, Karen starts nervously. Rasbach and Jennings enter. 'Can I get you anything?' Rasbach asks her politely. 'Water? Coffee?'

She shakes her head no.

After the necessary preliminaries, the videotaped interview begins.

Rasbach says, 'We know that Karen Krupp is a new identity for you, one that you adopted about three years ago.' He's sitting directly across from her, a buff folder closed on the table in front of him. The detective looks down at the file and opens it.

Karen immediately sees the photograph there of her as Georgina; she recognizes the picture. She knows he wants her to see it. She merely glances at it, and raises her eyes again.

He reviews the file silently for a moment, then looks up at her. 'We know that you are actually Georgina Traynor, and that you were married to Robert Traynor, the man shot to death last week. And we can put you at the scene of the murder.'

She says nothing. Beside her, Calvin sits quietly. He seems to be completely relaxed, but alert – not unlike the detective who sits diagonally across from him. She's grateful that she has Calvin here. If she were alone in this room with Rasbach, she might make a mistake. But Calvin is here to make sure that doesn't happen.

'I tell you what,' Rasbach says. 'I'll tell you what I think, and you can just nod if I'm on the right track.'

'She's not an imbecile,' Calvin says mildly.

'I'm well aware of that,' Rasbach answers curtly. 'Anyone who can successfully fake her own death is clearly not an imbecile.' He turns his gaze to Karen. 'Maybe we should talk about that first. My hat's off to you. You're obviously a very clever woman.'

He's trying to get her to talk by appealing to her ego, she thinks. It's not going to work. She'll talk when it suits her, when she's ready. She knows she's going to jail, because Calvin has told her that there's no bail on a charge of murder. The thought of jail petrifies her.

'Tell me how you did it,' Rasbach says.

She says nothing.

'Okay, then tell me *why* you did it. Why did you fake such an elaborate, convincing death, and start over as someone else?' When she still doesn't speak, he says, 'My guess is that you were running from your husband. My guess is that you were a battered wife, and you had to get away. He wouldn't let you leave. You couldn't just divorce him; he would come after you. So you faked your death. But then, after three years, he calls you up on the phone. You're in your kitchen, in your new life. You hear his voice. You're shocked, terrified – you panic.'

She lets him talk. She wants to hear what he has to say. What he thinks he knows.

'He asks you to meet him,' Rasbach continues. 'Perhaps he threatens you that if you don't, he will come after you and kill you. He knows your phone number; he no doubt knows where you live. So you agree to see him. You fly out of the house that night. You're so rattled that you don't think to leave a note for your husband, you don't bring your phone, or your purse, you don't even lock the door.' Rasbach sits back in his chair. She's watching him; their eyes are locked. He waits a long moment. 'Or *maybe* you were thinking more clearly than we've all been giving you credit for.' He pauses for effect. 'Maybe there's a reason you don't bring your phone or your purse – you don't want to risk leaving anything behind. Maybe you didn't bring your phone because you were afraid it could be used to locate you. Maybe you were thinking pretty clearly after all, because you brought a gun, a thirty-eight-calibre handgun – which we're still looking for, by the way – and you brought your rubber gloves with you.' He adds, 'All of which looks like premeditation to me.'

Rasbach leans forward and looks deeply into her eyes, his blue eyes piercing hers. She's frightened by his gaze, but is determined not to show it. Rasbach's ignoring her lawyer and the other detective, as if it's only the two of them in the room. She has to remind herself that she's not alone with this detective. But his eyes are mesmerizing.

Calvin breaks in. 'You're dreaming about the gun, and you have no idea whose gloves those are. You can't prove they belonged to my client.'

'I think I can,' Rasbach counters. He doesn't take his eyes off Karen to look, even briefly, at her lawyer. 'I think you took a gun, and those gloves, and drove down to that abandoned restaurant on Hoffman Street and parked in the little parking lot nearby. You went into the deserted restaurant, where Robert Traynor was waiting for you, and you shot him, in cold blood.'

Karen remains stubbornly silent and reminds herself that they don't have the weapon that killed him, and even if they find it, it can't possibly hurt her. She's confident about the gun. They can't prove that she had a gun when she went into that restaurant. They can only prove that she was there.

'What did you do with the gun?' Rasbach asks.

She feels a sudden stab of fear and quickly smothers it. He doesn't *know* about the gun, she thinks – he might guess, or assume, but that's all.

'It's more than possible,' Rasbach continues, 'even likely, that you owned a gun illegally. A woman as smart as you, a woman who faked her death, fooling all and sundry, a woman who began over with a new identity and didn't get caught until her husband found her . . . how do you think he found you, by the way?'

Her thighs tense under the table, but she will not be drawn into conversation with him.

Rasbach tilts his head at her. 'And then, after you shot him, *then* you panicked. You saw that you'd killed him. Did you drop the gun? Because you panicked? Or because you knew it couldn't be traced to you and didn't have your prints on it and it didn't matter? Or did you take it with you and toss it out the window somewhere?'

The detective pushes himself away from the table, and the sudden movement startles her and she flinches in her seat. He gets up and starts walking around the room, as if he's thinking it through as he speaks. But she's not fooled. This is all an act. He's an actor, just as she is. They are each other's audience. He's planned everything he's going to say.

'When you get to your car, you tear off the gloves and drop them there, in the parking lot. This is why I know you were panicking at this point, because why leave the gloves behind? There could be traces of your skin, your DNA, on the inside of the gloves.' He turns and looks at her intently.

She looks away. She can feel herself begin to tremble and tenses her body hard to stop it. She does not want him to see how frightened she is.

'And we both know how important those gloves are, don't we, Georgina?' He stops in front of her and looks down at her. She refuses to lift her head to look at him. 'Because if we get DNA off those gloves, they prove without a doubt that you were there. And because those gloves show *intention*.'

He pulls his chair out and sits down again, and waits until she raises her eyes to him. 'By then you were so panicked by what you'd done that you got in your car and drove as fast as you could to get away from there. Everyone agrees that you never go over the speed limit. Everybody goes over the speed limit sometimes, but not you. You never go through a red light. Why? Because you never want to get pulled over by the police. Because the number one rule for people who have taken on a new identity is: *Keep a low profile.*

And that's what you did, for years. Everyone we spoke to was shocked at the way you drove that night. It was *so out of character*. You know what? I'm wondering what your character is really like, *when you're not pretending to be someone else*.'

He's getting to her. She feels angry and threatened, but she must remain in control. She wonders why her lawyer doesn't say something. She knows she can't deny who she is. They can easily prove that she's Georgina Traynor. They know she faked her death and ran away and took on a false identity. These are things she will admit to. She might have to admit that she was there. But they cannot prove that she killed him. They have no weapon, no witness. They have motive, though, and that's what scares her. She had plenty of motive to kill her husband, and they all know it.

'So let's just say you panicked,' Rasbach continues. 'You got in the car, drove too fast, lost control, and hit a pole. Rather unfortunate. Because if you hadn't panicked, you would probably have gotten away with murder.'

She looks up at him now; she hates him at this moment.

'If you'd calmly driven home, put the gloves back in your kitchen, made up some story for your husband about where you'd been, then no one would ever have connected you to the dead body in that abandoned restaurant. We would eventually have figured out who he was. And we would have seen that his wife had predeceased him years earlier, but that's it. That would have been the end of it, as far as you're concerned. There wouldn't have been any red flags – no car accident, no tyre tracks, no gloves – to connect you to the crime. No one to look at you and find out that you're not who you say you are. You would have gone on with your nice, suburban life with your new, unsuspecting husband.'

She wants to slap his smug, superior face. Instead she drives her fingernails into her palms under the table, where he can't see.

'But the thing is, I can understand why you did what you did. I really can. You don't want to tell me what life with Robert Traynor was like, but I think it will come out at trial. If the state proves that you killed him, of course you will want everyone to know *why* you killed him. You will want to paint as monstrous a picture of the man as you possibly can. More power to you. He probably *was* a monster, to drive a nice woman like you to murder.'

She looks straight ahead at the wall in front of her, digging her fingernails into her palms.

'I think that's all, for now,' Rasbach says. The interview is over.

Chapter Thirty-four

BRIGID KNOWS WHAT'S happened. She saw the
two detectives arrive around lunchtime. She'd been
waiting – hoping – for such a development. She
watched them bring Karen out of the house in handcuffs. She could hardly contain her satisfaction.

She has been keeping a restless eye on the house all
day, waiting for Tom to come home so that she can
comfort him. He'll be alone now in that house, his life
all but destroyed. Brigid knows it's all over for Karen;
she will be convicted. She's sure of it. And then Tom
can begin again, with her. They'll be happy together,
happier than he ever was with Karen. And she will
never tear his life apart the way Karen has.

Someday, Tom will see that Karen being taken
away in handcuffs was the best thing that ever happened to him.

*

Tom returns home in a state of shock. His wife has been arrested for murder. And he's pretty sure she did it.

He wanders aimlessly into the kitchen and opens the fridge. He stands there, staring inside, suddenly remembering that other time he stood here, staring sightlessly into the refrigerator. The night Karen disappeared. The night this all began.

This is going to destroy their marriage. It's going to destroy their lives. And now his wife is caught up in the workings of the legal system. This is going to bankrupt him. He reaches in for a beer. He screws the cap off almost violently and then turns and hurls it across the room. The cap hits a cupboard and ricochets around the kitchen, ending up somewhere under the table. *What the fuck is he going to do?*

He paces the house angrily. There's nothing he can do. He can't believe it's come to this. And he's sure it's going to get worse in the days, weeks, and months ahead.

He doesn't bother making himself something to eat. He has no appetite for food. He finishes the first beer quickly and returns automatically to the fridge for another. He's never been tested like this before, and he doesn't like what he sees. He's weak, and he's a coward, and he knows it. He's been trying to be strong for Karen. But his wife is much stronger and braver than he is. She appears to be made of steel.

246

He stares in the mirror over the fireplace. He hardly recognizes himself. His hair is wild from nervously running his hands through it. He looks haggard, almost mean. He expected everything to be sunshine and kisses when he married Karen. It's as if life made him a promise the day that he married her, and now life has broken that promise. He feels intensely sorry for himself.

He steps out the sliding glass doors to the backyard and sits outside on the patio in the summer night, as darkness falls upon him.

Funny, he thinks now, three beers in, it hasn't occurred to him until this moment to remember what a hard time he had getting her to say yes. Of course it all makes sense now. *She was already married.*

The first time he asked her to marry him she laughed it off, as if he couldn't possibly mean it. Although he was careful not to show it, he'd been both taken aback and hurt. He wondered why she treated his proposal so flippantly; he was completely serious when he asked her. They were lying all bundled up on a scratchy wool blanket, looking at the stars. They'd gone to a little inn in the Catskills for the weekend to see the fall colours. He grabbed the blanket from the back of the car and found a private spot. They lay down together and he propped himself up on one elbow and gazed down at her. He can still remember the way the moonlight lit her face, and the happiness in her eyes. He asked, 'Will you marry me?'

And she laughed, as if he were making a joke.

He looks up at those same stars now, twinkling in the dark. How changed everything is.

He remembers how he hid his hurt and disappointment, both at the time and in the weeks following. He waited a bit, and then bought a big, expensive diamond ring – he wanted to show her that he was serious. He presented it to her on Valentine's Day over a glass of pricey champagne at her favourite restaurant. Perhaps that was a mistake, Valentine's Day. But it doesn't make any difference now. What she said, he recalls, as he sits in the dark on the patio with his beer in his hand, was, *Why can't we have a love story instead of a marriage?*

This is their love story, come crashing down around their ears.

Does he wish now that she'd never said yes, that she'd never agreed, finally, under his steady pressure, to get married? He doesn't know, and anyway it's too late to change anything.

And yet, these last two years have been the happiest of his life.

Until all this happened.

Tom sees something moving in the dark, at the side of the house. He freezes. He hasn't turned the light on in the back, not wanting to attract bugs to the light, so it's completely dark except for the stars. He can see someone approaching, but he can't tell who it is. It can't be the police. They've already arrested his wife. Surely they're not going to arrest him, too?

He thinks it might be Dan, come to check on him. Dan had called earlier, but Tom hadn't called him back, and he must be worried. All this runs like quicksilver through Tom's head as he gets to his feet. He puts the almost empty bottle of beer down on a side table and squints into the dark.

It's not Dan coming toward him in the dark, he sees with dismay – it's Brigid. He doesn't want to talk to Brigid. He wants to go back inside the house and close the door, but he can't exactly do that.

Brigid always makes him feel uncomfortable. He'd been so intimate with her, so unrestrained. There was something reckless and exciting about her that he found irresistible at first, and that touched something reckless in him. But she soon became too intense for him, too much; he felt that she might swallow him whole. He never knew what to expect from her; she was too emotional. When he broke it off with her he'd had quite a few anxious weeks – afraid that she would tell her husband about them and he would throw her out, and that she'd come banging on his door. Or later, that she would tell

Karen, embellishing what happened with lies, and destroy their promising new relationship. But she seemed to calm down. And then, quite unexpectedly, she'd become such good friends with his wife. There was nothing he could do about that.

'Hi, Brigid,' he says. He says it crisply, enunciating carefully. He's not drunk, after three fast beers on an empty stomach. He's what might be called 'happy', except that he's not happy at all. Tom realizes rather suddenly that he doesn't want to be alone. 'Would you like a drink?' he asks her.

She looks at him as if surprised. 'I knocked at the front, but nobody answered. I came over to talk to Karen,' Brigid says. 'Is she here?'

'No, I'm afraid not,' Tom says, and he can hear the bitterness in his own voice coming across loud and clear.

'What's wrong?' Brigid asks.

He sees her eyes taking in how wrecked he looks, sliding to the beer bottle on the side table.

Tom knows that it would be foolish to unburden himself to Brigid, but there's no one else right now. He realizes how terribly lonely he feels without Karen. He's never felt so lonely in his life.

He gestures toward the kitchen, just inside. 'Let me get you a drink. What will you have? A beer? Or I can mix you something, if you want.' She follows him into the house. He opens the cupboard, scanning the liquor bottles on the shelf to see what he has to offer her.

She's standing behind him. When he turns to ask her what she wants, she's staring at him with such avidity that it startles him. He turns back to look inside the cupboard. 'I have rum, vodka . . .'

'Can you make me a martini?' she asks.

He looks back at her stupidly. When did she get so fancy? He has no idea how to make a martini. He wasn't expecting her to ask for something so exotic. 'I don't know how.'

'I do,' she says smoothly, and comes up beside him and looks into the cupboard. She starts taking down bottles – vodka, vermouth. 'You must have a shaker around here somewhere,' she says, opening another cupboard and looking up high.

Her eyes seem to light immediately on a silver cocktail shaker – something he'd forgotten they even had. Another leftover wedding present. They never use it – he and Karen are unfussy, beer and wine drinkers, usually. He remembers how the two of them had needed a shot of whiskey the other night.

'Do you have any ice?' Brigid asks.

Tom turns to the freezer and pulls out the ice. While he's at it, he gets himself another beer. This will be his last one tonight, he promises himself, twisting off the cap and watching Brigid make herself a martini in his kitchen as if she owns the place. It feels strange, having her here, instead of Karen.

'So where's Karen?' she asks. She's finished with the shaker now. She's grabbed a proper martini glass from the cupboard – he'd forgotten about those, too – and pours herself a drink. She holds the glass close to her lips and takes a sip, looking coyly over the rim at him.

For a second Tom's confused. She's asking about Karen, who's in jail, but her tone is all wrong. She sounds more like she's flirting with him, the way she used to. Suddenly he regrets having asked her in for a drink. It's too dangerous.

'What's the matter?' she says, looking more the way she should, and he thinks that maybe he imagined it.

He shakes his head. 'Nothing,' he says. Then, 'Everything.'

'Tell me,' she says.

'Karen's been arrested.'

'Arrested!'

He nods. He must keep his feelings to himself. It wouldn't do to start getting too personal with Brigid. He shouldn't be telling her anything at all, but the beer has loosened his tongue. And what difference does it make? It will all be in the newspapers tomorrow.

'Arrested for what?' Brigid says.

He wonders if he looks as ghastly as he feels. 'Murder.'

One hand flutters to her mouth while the other puts her drink down on the counter beside her. Then Brigid turns her face away, as if she's overcome with emotion.

He stands awkwardly, watching her.

Finally she reaches up into the cupboard for another martini glass and pours what's left in the shaker into it. She holds it out to him.

He eyes it warily. And then he thinks, *What the hell*. He takes the glass from her, lifts it in a silent, cynical toast, and downs it in one go.

'Tom—'

The alcohol hits him hard and fast, making everything fuzzy, blurring lines. 'Maybe you should go,' he says. He tries to backpedal the seriousness of the situation; he just wants to get her out of here, before he says or does something he shouldn't. 'The police are grasping at straws. They don't have any other suspects and they're trying to hang it on her. But she's got a good lawyer.' He's speaking slowly, carefully, because, he realizes, he's drunk. 'They're going to realize she didn't do it. She told me she didn't do it, and I believe her.'

'Tom,' she says again.

He looks at her uneasily. He can see the outline of

253

her breasts beneath her top. He knows those breasts. For a moment he has a vivid memory of being in bed with her, what she was like. Very different from Karen. He forces the thought aside.

'There's something you should know.'

He doesn't like the warning tone he hears in her voice. He doesn't want to hear about any little confidences Karen might have shared with her friend across the street. And he doesn't want another woman, an attractive woman, with whom he shares an erotic history, offering him comfort when he's vulnerable like this. He can feel himself becoming aroused at having her so close. It must be the alcohol. His defences are down. 'I think you should go. Please,' Tom says, looking at the floor. He wants her to leave.

'You need to hear this,' she insists.

It's impossible to think in here; it's like being in the middle of a constant brawl. Karen curls into a fetal position on the uncomfortable cot inside her holding cell in the basement of the police station and tries to keep it together as the night wears interminably on. She's surrounded by drunks and prostitutes; the stench is unbearable. She tries to breathe only through her mouth. So far she has a cell to herself, but every time she hears footsteps, and shouts, as the cops bring in someone else, she's afraid that they will open her cell door and put them in here with her.

She thinks of Tom alone in their bed at home and tries not to cry. If only she were there with him, they could comfort each other. There's no comfort to be had here.

Chapter Thirty-five

TOM LOOKS UP at Brigid warily.

'That night, the night Karen had her accident,' Brigid begins, 'I was home, sitting at the window. It was around twenty after eight. I saw Karen come running out of the house.'

'I know all this,' Tom says sullenly.

'I watched her get into her car and tear away. And I thought – I thought maybe something was wrong.'

Tom's staring at her now, wondering where this is going.

'So I got in my car and I followed her.'

Tom feels as if his heart has stopped. He hadn't expected that. This is going to be worse than he thought. He wants to cover his ears and refuse to listen, but he just stands there and hears it all.

'She was driving a bit fast, but she had to stop at a couple of lights, and I was able to keep up with her, a ways behind. I was worried when I saw her run out of the house like that.' Brigid picks up her martini from the counter and takes a quick gulp, and then another, as if she needs courage for what she has to say next. 'I realized she was heading into a bad part of town. I couldn't think why. I was wondering what she was up to. It occurred to me that she might not like me following her – but she's a friend, and I was concerned. I just wanted to make sure she was all right. So I stayed with her, but far enough back so that she wouldn't see me. After a while she pulled into this little parking lot off the main road. I drove past while she was parking and then I did a U-turn and came back and parked across the street.'

Tom's watching her closely through eyes that refuse to focus; he's trying to tell if she's lying. He's so bad at telling when someone is lying, judging by his past performance at it. He fears that she's telling him the truth. He's thinking that Brigid is a witness, and it's making him sick with fear. She's going to put Karen away.

'I was almost afraid to get out of the car. But I was so worried about Karen. I saw her go behind a boarded-up restaurant. I got out of the car and walked closer. And then I heard shots. Three gun-shots.' She closes her eyes briefly, opens them again. 'I was petrified. It sounded like they came from inside the restaurant. Then I saw Karen come

257

bolting out of there and hightail it for her car. She was wearing these pink rubber gloves, which I thought was odd. She tore them off before she got in the car. I stood there in the dark, against the building – I'm sure she didn't see me – and watched her take off out of the parking lot. She was driving way too fast. I thought about going after her, but I knew I'd never catch up with her, going at that speed. So – I went into the restaurant that she came out of.' She pauses to catch her breath.

Tom's heart is beating wildly, and all he can think is, *She didn't actually see Karen pull the trigger.*

'I got to the door and I opened it and went inside. It was pretty dark, but I could see that there was a body, a man, dead on the floor.' She shudders. 'It was horrible. He'd been shot in the face, and the chest.'

Brigid walks up closer to him, until she's within arm's reach. 'Tom, she shot him. She *killed* that man.'

'No she didn't,' Tom says.

'Tom, I know this is hard for you to hear, but I was *there*.'

Tom says desperately, 'You didn't *see* her shoot him. You heard shots. You saw Karen run away. Maybe someone else was in that restaurant. Maybe she was just in the wrong place at the wrong time.' He knows how frantic he sounds, how foolish.

'Tom, I didn't see anybody else come out of the building. And she was carrying a gun when she went in there. I *saw* her.'

'You didn't say that you saw her carrying a gun when she went into the building.'

'Well, I did.'

'Did she have it when she left?'

'No.'

'Did you see the gun there, when you were in the restaurant?'

'I don't think so.'

'What do you mean, you don't think so?'

'I don't know, Tom! I didn't pay attention to the gun. It was dark. She must have left it there somewhere. I was too freaked out by the dead body, by what she'd done, to notice the gun.'

Jesus. Tom's thinking furiously. This is not good. This is very, very bad. He has to know what Brigid's going to do. His head is spinning with fear and alcohol. He says slowly, 'What are you going to do, Brigid?'

'What do you mean?'

'Are you going to tell the police what you saw?'

She looks at him and comes closer. Her eyes soften. She bites her lower lip. She reaches up and touches his face gently. He's frozen in place, confused, waiting for her answer.

She says, 'No, of course not. Karen's my *friend*.' And she kisses him deeply.

He reaches for her and succumbs helplessly to the comfort she's offering.

Karen hasn't slept at all. She has an arraignment this morning, and right now, her lawyer is sitting across from her in a small interview room trying to get her to drink strong coffee. But it tastes bitter and sour in her mouth and she pushes it away. Besides, she doesn't think she can keep anything down. She feels grimy, unwashed. Her head aches and her eyes burn. She wonders if this is how she's going to feel for the rest of her life. *Is she going to spend the rest of her life in prison?*

'Karen, you need to focus,' Calvin tells her urgently.

'Where's Tom?' she asks again. It's nine o'clock already. Her arraignment is this morning. Why isn't he here? His absence makes her feel abandoned. She doesn't think she can do this if he isn't by her side.

'I'm sure he'll be here,' Calvin says. 'Maybe he's caught in traffic.'

She reaches for the coffee, like a good client. Right now, everything depends on what her lawyer can do for her.

Calvin says, 'The evidence against you is all circumstantial, meaning there's no direct evidence – no gun with your prints, no trace evidence from you at the scene – and no witnesses tying you to the crime.

At least none that we know of so far. They may find some. The tyre track evidence isn't conclusive. The gloves are at the lab but they haven't gotten any DNA off them yet. The lab's a busy place, but they'll get to it. They'll probably find DNA. I'll fight getting that admitted every way I know how. But they may be able to prove that they were your gloves, in which case we've got a big problem.'

'I don't think I killed him,' she says stubbornly.

He waits a few beats. 'So we have to try to figure out who did – come up with a plausible alternative theory. Because even if you *did* kill him' – the lawyer speaks carefully, as if not wanting to upset her – 'they can't convict unless they can prove it beyond a reasonable doubt. It's our job to furnish that reasonable doubt. We have to come up with a credible theory of who might have killed him, other than you.'

'I don't know. Did he have a new wife? Because if he did, she probably wanted to kill him.' She laughs hollowly.

'No, he didn't.' Calvin presses her. 'You said before that he might have enemies.'

'I don't know. I haven't seen him in years. I thought he dealt with some questionable people, but I don't know who they were. I stayed out of the business. I didn't want any part of it.'

'I'm going to start having some people look into his business contacts, see if he'd pissed anybody off.'

She looks at the clock on the wall and wonders again where Tom is. She's starting to feel uneasy about Tom. Can she count on him? Maybe he doesn't believe her; maybe he thinks she's a murderer. Is he going to come?

'Did you see anyone else there?' Calvin asks. 'Think. Did you hear anything inside the restaurant? Could there have been someone there, hiding in the shadows?'

She tries to concentrate. 'I don't know. I can't remember everything. I don't remember being inside. There could have been somebody there.' She blinks her eyes. 'There must have been.'

Calvin takes a sip of his own coffee from a Styrofoam cup. 'You told me before that you felt that your husband had been in your house in the weeks leading up to the phone call.'

'Yes, I'm sure of it,' she says. She gives an involuntary shudder. 'When I think of it now – it still disturbs me. I wonder if I'll ever stop being afraid of him, even though I know he's . . .'

'Do you still have the photos on your phone? The ones you took of the house in the mornings before you went to work?'

'Yes, I think so.'

'Good. Those photos show that you were in a particular state of mind – that you thought you were being stalked by him in your own home. You were in

262

mortal fear. We need to preserve those photos – in case we need them.'

'But isn't that worse?' she asks, her voice catching. 'If I thought he'd found me, and was breaking into the house, stalking me, doesn't it make it look more likely that I killed him?'

'Yes,' the lawyer says. He pauses. 'But it also gives you a defence. If we can prove that he was in your house.' Calvin makes a note on his legal pad. 'We need to get fingerprints taken. I'll look into getting that done.'

She looks at him with dismay but says nothing. She knows how bad it looks. No one's going to believe her. Her own lawyer doesn't believe her. And she's not sure about her husband either.

She hears a noise outside in the corridor and looks up quickly. The door opens, and a guard ushers Tom into the interview room.

Karen feels immense relief. She wants to ask him what the hell took him so long, but one look at him stops her. He looks like hell. And *she's* the one who spent the night in a cell. She feels a surge of annoyance. She needs him to pull himself together; she can't do this on her own. She says nothing, but eyes him closely.

'Sorry, I overslept,' Tom says, flushing. 'I couldn't get to sleep, and then when I finally did . . .' He trails off.

'She'll be appearing in court soon,' Calvin tells him.

Tom nods, as if it's completely normal for his wife to be going to court on a murder charge.

Karen wants to shake him. He seems so . . . removed.

'Can we have a moment alone?' she asks, looking at Calvin.

The lawyer takes a quick glance at his watch and says, 'Sure, a few minutes.' He gets up with a scrape of his chair and exits, leaving the two of them alone.

Karen stands up and takes a step toward Tom. They eye one another. Karen breaks the silence first. 'You look like hell.'

'You don't look so good yourself.'

It breaks the tension, and they both smile a little.

'Tom,' Karen says, 'I don't think Calvin believes me.' She's testing him. She knows it doesn't really matter what her lawyer believes; his job is to defend her anyway. But she wants to hear Tom say that he believes her. She needs to hear it. 'I don't think I could have killed him, Tom, and if you don't believe me—'

He steps forward and takes her in his arms and holds her tight as she presses her face into his chest, stifling a sob. 'Shhhhhh . . . Of course I believe you.'

It's comforting to be held by him, to hear him say it. Even so, she begins to shake uncontrollably. Suddenly the enormity of what she's facing catches up with her.

Chapter Thirty-six

ACROSS THE STREET from 24 Dogwood Drive, the big picture window is empty. No one sits looking out today.

Brigid has things to do. Last night . . . last night was the beginning of a whole new life for her. She feels as if she might explode with happiness.

And if someone else has to suffer for her to be happy, if someone else has to go to jail for the rest of her life – well, that's the way the cookie crumbles. Life is a zero-sum game, after all.

Brigid thinks back to the day it all happened, the day that has changed everything. It started out like any other day on sleepy Dogwood Drive. She was doing a bit of housework, glancing outside occasionally, when she noticed a strange man poking around the Krupps' house. She turned off the vacuum cleaner and watched him. He mounted the front steps and looked in the window at the top of the door. But she noticed that he didn't knock or ring the bell. He seemed to know that no one was home. There was no car in the driveway. Then he walked around the back. Brigid's curiosity, and her indignation, were aroused. She wanted to know who he was and what he was doing there.

She grabbed her gardening gloves and went out to the bottom of her front yard to tackle the weeds and keep an eye on the man snooping around the Krupps' house. When he reappeared in the front, she stood up and watched him. He waved at her in a friendly way and then walked over to talk to her.

'Hi,' he said casually.

'Hello,' Brigid responded stiffly, not about to be won over by a pleasant smile and good looks. She didn't know who this guy was. Maybe he was an insurance adjustor or something, and had a perfectly acceptable reason for looking around the Krupps' property. But he didn't look like an insurance adjustor.

'Do you live here?' he asked, indicating her own house behind her.

'Yes,' she said.

'You must know the people across the street,' he said, tilting his head at the Krupps' house. She nodded cautiously. 'I'm an old friend,' he told her, 'of the wife.'

'Oh,' Brigid said, not sure she believed him. 'From where?'

He looked at her, all pleasantness fell away, and a mean sort of glint came into his eye. 'From another life.' And then he waved at her dismissively and walked briskly away.

The man's demeanour made her feel uneasy. Once he was gone she returned to the house, thinking about the odd exchange. It made Brigid wonder about Karen. She never seemed to talk about her life before she was with Tom, other than saying that she was from Wisconsin, and that she had no family. And another thing, Karen wasn't online at all. Nothing came up on her. She wasn't even on Facebook. Everybody's on Facebook.

Brigid remembered Karen's maiden name from when she and Tom were dating. Karen had changed her name to Krupp after the wedding. Brigid got on the computer and Googled Karen Fairfield, but she didn't get any hits. That wasn't too surprising. But the more she thought about the man, about his *from another life* comment, the more curious she became. That was how Brigid got drawn into the Internet sinkhole and started researching how people disappear and turn up in a new life as someone else. It wasn't long before she began to suspect – to convince herself – that Karen might not be who she said she was. That's when she called Tom at his office and arranged to meet him that same night. She wanted to tell him about the strange man, and her suspicions about Karen.

But that evening, when Brigid was about to leave to meet Tom at their old spot down by the river, she saw Karen peel out of the house in a desperate hurry. And because of the man's odd visit earlier in the day, Brigid followed her, instead. Tom could wait.

She saw what she saw. And now, everything is different.

She thinks about what happened with Tom the night before, and a languid warmth begins somewhere low and spreads throughout her body. How she's missed him! She hadn't even realized how much, until she kissed him again.

That kiss – sensuous and dark – was fraught with all sorts of delicious undercurrents and memories. His mouth felt and tasted just like she remembered. Pleasure travelled along her body in a current. That kiss left her breathless. They shared a past, and it was all revived in that kiss. When it was over, and he pulled away and looked at her, she could tell that he was as blown away by it as she was.

And then she'd taken him by the hand and led him upstairs to the bedroom, where they made love in Karen and Tom's bed. The same bed she and Tom used to make love in, before Karen moved in. That interloping bitch.

Brigid thinks about the lewd things she and Tom did together the night before and feels that glow again. She remembers how afterward, a feeling of great power and wickedness had come over her. She propped herself on her elbow, full breasts on display, and looked at Tom lying naked and vulnerable in the bed beside her. She walked her fingers slowly up his leg, and said, 'You don't want me to tell the police what I saw, do you?'

He'd looked at her in fear. 'No.'

There's no mistaking it, she thinks now, the connection they share. Tom loved her once, she's sure of it, and he will love her again. He will be in her thrall once more, like he was before. Tom knows now what Karen has done, that she's a murderer, because Brigid was there, and she told him.

Brigid has promised Tom that she isn't going to say anything to the police.

But Brigid has a plan.

There's no going back.

It's all going to be perfect.

Tom is shaken to his core by the arraignment. It was a circus in the courtroom, too noisy to hear anything, too much going on, and all of it happening so fast. He'd expected it to be a lot more solemn and easier to follow. Karen went up in front of the bench with Jack Calvin when her name was called. Tom sat in the courtroom, fairly far back, the only place he could get a seat. He could only see Karen from behind. The size of the courtroom and the tumult all around made her seem small and defeated. He had to strain to hear.

It was all over in a couple of minutes, and then she was being escorted out. He stood up. She glanced back at him, frightened, as they led her out of the courtroom. Tom sat back down in his seat, stunned, unsure of what to do. Calvin saw him and approached.

'You might as well go home,' he said. 'They're transporting her to the county jail. You can see her there later today.'

So Tom had gone home. He didn't know what else to do. Then he'd called in sick indefinitely. He knows that no one is going to believe he's sick, once the news gets out.

Now, he goes into the bedroom and stares at the rumpled sheets with horror. He should never have slept with Brigid again. How could he have let that happen?

He knows how – he was very lonely, and very drunk, and she was sympathetic. She could also be irresistibly sexy, and they had all that history. But then, afterward, she made it quite clear that sleeping with her had been the price of her silence.

Now he feels sick and scared. What if she's lying? What if Brigid hadn't been there at all? Either way, she's manipulating him to get back into his bed. What if she visits Karen in jail and tells her what he did? If he were to tell Karen that he slept with Brigid to protect her, would she believe him?

Tom suddenly rips the sheets off the bed in a rage and throws them in a ball on the floor. He'll put them in the laundry and wash any trace of Brigid from their bed.

But getting rid of Brigid – that might not be so simple.

Jack Calvin takes a quick flight to Las Vegas, Nevada, to visit the counselling centre for battered women that Karen used when she was married to Robert Traynor. He's already checked: it's still there. And there are people there who remember her. They're expecting him.

He's also hired a private investigator in Las Vegas to look into Robert Traynor's business associates. Maybe something will turn up there, but he's not particularly hopeful.

He lands and takes a cab into the city. He soon locates the Open Arms Women's Shelter and Counseling Center. The building is a bit run-down, but it's trying hard to be a happy, warm, and welcoming place. There are children's paintings up everywhere.

He goes to the information desk. Very soon the

director of the facility comes out to meet him and takes him back to her office.

'I'm Theresa Wolcak,' she says, offering him a seat.

'Jack Calvin,' he says. 'As I told you on the phone, I represent a woman, now living in New York State, who used to come here for counselling three or four years ago, it would be now. Georgina Traynor.'

She nods. 'May I see some identification?'

'Yes, of course.' He reaches for his ID. He also opens his briefcase and hands over a letter that identifies the writer as Georgina Traynor and gives her informed consent for information to be disclosed to her lawyer, Jack Calvin.

She pushes her glasses up higher on her nose and reads it. Then she nods briskly. 'Okay. How can I help?'

'My client, Georgina Traynor, has been charged with the murder of her husband, Robert Traynor.'

Theresa looks at him and nods tiredly. 'And now the law needs her to justify herself.'

'She's accused of killing a man. They need to see justice done. If what she says is true, I don't think a jury will have a very difficult time seeing it from her point of view, that she was frightened for her life.'

'The counsellor who saw your client most regularly is a woman named Stacy Howell. Let me get her for you.'

Soon Calvin and the counsellor are closeted together in a small private office. Stacy, a no-nonsense black woman with a soft voice, brings Georgina Traynor's file with her and opens up immediately when she's read the letter.

'I remember her, sure. You would think I wouldn't because I see so many, all with the same sad story, but I remember her. Georgina isn't that common a name. And I really liked her. I saw her for at least a year.'

'What was she like?'

'She was like all the other women who come here. Scared shitless. Sorry to be so blunt. But nobody seems to get what these women go through. The man she was married to was a real bastard. She felt trapped. She felt that if she told anyone but us what he did to her, nobody would believe her.'

'So what did you tell her? Did you tell her to leave him?'

'It's not that simple. We have women living here for their own protection. It's difficult to get the supports in place. The restraining orders don't seem to do much good.' She sighs in discouragement. 'I told her she had some leverage. He had a good business. I told her that if she wanted to she could leave him and get a restraining order and threaten to make it public. Shaming them sometimes works. But she was too afraid.'

Calvin nods.

'One day she didn't show up for her appointment. We heard that she'd jumped off the Hoover Dam Bridge. They didn't recover the body. I read about it in the paper.' She shakes her head sadly, remembering. 'I thought for sure that he'd killed her, that he'd tried to make it look like suicide.'

'Did you go to the police?'

'Of course I did. They looked into him, but he had an airtight alibi. He was working, lots of people saw him throughout the day. They dropped it.'

'He didn't kill her,' Calvin says, indicating the letter.

'No, she got away after all. Good for her.'

'But now she's facing a murder charge.'

'She killed him?' Stacy says with surprise. She puffs air sharply out her nose. 'He had it coming, the son of a bitch.' And then she looks at him in distress and says, 'What's going to happen to her?'

Chapter Thirty-seven

DETECTIVE RASBACH IS pretty certain that from here on out, the Krupp case is going to be fairly straightforward. It's like a puzzle, difficult at first, but once you have the outline, all the pieces start slipping neatly into place. It seems quite clear to him that Karen Krupp is a killer. He feels sorry for her, though. In different circumstances, he thinks, it's unlikely she would ever have killed anyone. If she'd never met Robert Traynor, for instance.

They know now how Traynor tracked her down. They've looked at his computer, which they had sent in from Vegas by the Las Vegas police. Traynor had been systematically searching websites of accounting and bookkeeping firms all over the US. He'd bookmarked a page on the website of Simpson & Merritt, Tom Krupp's employer. And there she was, in the background, at an office Christmas party, standing beside Tom Krupp, who had a profile on the same website.

It's so difficult to truly disappear, Rasbach thinks.

Rasbach wonders why Traynor went to such efforts to find her. He obviously hadn't been convinced by her suicide, perhaps because her body had never been recovered.

He believes he has a solid case to take to the district attorney. Although the physical evidence is not yet conclusive, the circumstances are compelling. Despite steady door-to-door work on the surrounding businesses and apartments in the area, they have not been able to find any witnesses to the crime.

Rasbach recalls his unproductive interview with Karen Krupp. She's clearly terrified. He feels sorry for Tom Krupp, too. He doesn't feel the least bit sorry for Robert Traynor.

Detective Jennings knocks on the open door and enters Rasbach's office. He's holding a paper bag with wrapped sandwiches in it. He offers one to Rasbach and sits down. 'Someone called in a tip in the Krupp case,' he says.

'A tip,' Rasbach says wryly. He glances down at the newspaper open on his desk.

A local housewife, Karen Krupp, has been arrested for the murder of a previously unidentified man in an abandoned restaurant on

276

Hoffman Street. That man has now been identified as Robert Traynor, of Las Vegas, Nevada. No other details are known at this time.

Karen and Tom Krupp aren't talking to the press, and the police made only a very basic statement after the arrest, giving the names of the people involved. No details. But it's not every day that an attractive, respectable suburban housewife is charged with murder. The press is going to be all over this. Nobody knows yet that Karen Krupp used to be someone else, that she faked her death, or that she'd previously been married to the victim.

'Yeah, I know,' Detective Jennings says, following Rasbach's gaze to the newspaper. 'Lots of crazies out there. The calls will probably start to come flooding in.'

'What did he say?'

'It was a she.'

'Did she leave a name?'

'Nope.'

'They never do,' Rasbach says.

Jennings finishes chewing a big bite of his sandwich and swallows. 'She said we should search the Krupp property for the murder weapon.'

Rasbach raises his eyebrows, waves his sandwich in the air. 'Karen Krupp shoots the guy, panics, and flees. The gun wasn't on the scene, and it wasn't in the car. So where's the gun? It would be nice if we had the gun, and if we could prove that it was the gun that killed him, and if we could connect that same gun to Karen Krupp. But if she still had the gun with her when she left the scene, she either stashed it somewhere nearby – not likely as she seems to have been in a full-blown panic, and we would have found it – or she threw it out the car window. And then, after getting out of the hospital, she went back to pick it up, or find it, and put it back in her house somewhere. I don't know, like maybe in her underwear drawer.' He starts unwrapping his sandwich. 'An incredibly stupid thing to do. And she's not stupid.'

'Yeah, not likely.'

'I don't think we're going to need any tips from the public to solve this one,' Rasbach says, and takes a bite of tuna salad on wholewheat.

Later that afternoon, Tom goes to visit Karen at the county jail.

He stands by his car in the parking lot for a minute, staring queasily at the big, hulking brick building. He doesn't want to go in there. But he thinks of Karen and screws up his courage. If she can survive in there, he can at least put on a brave front when he visits.

He makes his way through the front doors of the

prison, past the guards to the security desk. He must get used to all these barriers – doors and guards and procedures and searches – to get to talk to his wife. He wonders how she's doing. Will she be holding up well, or is she going to be a mess? When he asks her, will she tell him the truth, or will she try to protect him and tell him that she's managing just fine?

Finally he gets to see her, in a large room full of tables. He spots her at one and takes the seat across from her, under the watchful eyes of the guards at the front of the room. There are other visits going on around them, at other tables, but if they keep their voices low, they have enough privacy to talk.

'Karen—' he says, his voice breaking at the sight of her. Instantly his eyes sting with tears. He brushes them away, tries to smile through them.

Tears spill down her face. 'Tom!' She swallows. 'I'm so glad you came. I thought you might not.'

'Of course I came! I will always come see you, whenever I can, Karen, I promise,' Tom says desperately. 'Until we get you out of here.' He's overwhelmed with guilt and shame for what he did with Brigid, while Karen was in jail.

'I'm scared, Tom,' she says. She looks as if she hasn't slept at all. Her hair is unwashed. She seems to notice the way he's looking at her and says, 'I can't take a shower in here whenever I want, you know.'

'Is there anything I can do?' he asks hopelessly. He feels utterly powerless. 'Can I bring you anything?'

'I don't think you're allowed to.'

This almost makes him break down. He has to stifle a sob. He's always loved to bring her surprises – chocolates, flowers. He can't bear to think of her spartan future in here; she's always loved her little luxuries. She's not suited to prison. As if anyone is. 'I'll find out, okay?'

She tilts her head at him. 'Hey, cheer up. I'm going to get out of here. My lawyer says so.'

Tom doubts that Calvin would have made any such assurances to her, but he pretends that they all believe that she'll be out soon. They just have to hang tough. But there's something he has to tell her. 'Karen,' he says cautiously, his voice very low. 'I was talking to Brigid last night.'

'Brigid?' Karen repeats, surprised.

He hopes she doesn't notice the slight flush that he can feel colouring his face. His guilt. He glances down at the table for a moment, avoiding her eyes, then looks up again. 'Yes. She came over to talk to you. She didn't know that you'd been arrested.'

'Okay.'

'But she told me something.'

'What?' Karen says, her voice also low, but now wary.

'She said that the night of your accident, she saw

you go out the front door.' He looks right into his wife's lovely, lying eyes. He keeps his voice very quiet. 'She told me she followed you that night.'

Karen becomes suddenly alert. 'What?'

'She says she followed you, in her car, far enough behind you that you wouldn't notice her.' Karen remains perfectly still, and Tom's heart sinks as he watches complex emotions play across her face. *It's true,* he thinks, *what Brigid said.*

'What else did she say?'

'She said she followed you until you parked and then she parked across the street. She watched you go to the back of the restaurant. She heard gunshots. Three shots. And then she saw you run out of the building to your car. She says she saw you tear off the gloves and get in the car and speed away.'

His wife says nothing. She is clearly shocked by this news.

'Karen,' Tom whispers.

She still says nothing.

'*Karen!*' Tom says it urgently. He lowers his voice, instinctively looking around to be sure they aren't overheard. But no one else can hear them in the room's chatter. 'She was *there*!'

'Maybe she's lying.'

'I don't think so,' Tom says quietly. 'How would she know about the gloves?' Karen is quiet, her eyes wide. He can see a vein throb in her throat. Nobody knows about the gloves – except the police. Tom shakes his head. 'I think she was there. I think she saw you. She says you had a gun in your hand on the way in, and you ran out with just the gloves.'

'And what did she do then?' Karen asks, her hands gripping the edge of the table.

'She went into the restaurant and saw the body,' Tom says. He watches Karen go pale, and feels bile rising in his throat. 'She freaked out and got the hell out of there and went home.' He leans as close to her as he dares under the guard's watchful eye, disturbed by the story her face is telling him. 'Karen, tell me the truth. Do you *really* not remember?' He says it gently, coaxingly. He forgives her – if only she will tell him the truth. He can see by the look on her face how terrorized she must have been. Surely a jury will see it, too.

'*She's a witness,*' Karen says, as if she can hardly believe it.

'Did you kill him?' Tom presses, his voice so low it's almost inaudible. He looks around again. No one's paying any attention to them. 'You can tell me,' he says. 'Only me.'

She looks back at him and says, 'I don't remember. But I don't think I could shoot anyone.'

If only he could believe her. He sits back in his chair, full of despair. Maybe the jury will under- stand why she did what she did. Even so, she'll still

282

be in jail for years and years, Tom thinks bleakly. It's not fair, when it was all Robert Traynor's fault. If he hadn't come after her again, if he'd just left her alone, they wouldn't be sitting here right now, in a county jail, frightened and miserable.

Even if she can't admit the truth to him – maybe she can't even admit it to herself, maybe she's completely repressed it from her conscious mind – he thinks he still loves her, this different, terribly wronged, Karen. He can't let her go to prison for the rest of her life. Living without her through empty days, empty nights, thinking of her locked up in a cage – it's unimaginable.

'She's a witness,' Karen says again, pulling herself together and leaning toward him. 'Even if they're able to prove the gloves are mine, that still isn't proof that I killed him. It's only proof that I was there. I *was* there – but I—' She looks desperately at him. 'If I were able to kill him, I would have done it when I was married to him, don't you think? If Brigid says she heard shots and saw me running out right after, she must be lying!' Karen looks at him with fear in her eyes. 'Why would she lie?'

Tom shakes his head and says nothing. He doesn't think Brigid is lying; he thinks Karen is lying – or at best, she really doesn't know what happened. 'I don't think she's going to say anything,' Tom says finally.

'How can you be so sure?' Karen whispers back, anxiety in her voice.

'She's your friend,' he says uneasily.

'What kind of friend makes up a lie like that? Maybe she followed me, maybe she was there – but maybe it didn't happen the way she says it did.'

Tom looks at Karen unhappily. He leans forward again and says, 'We have to make sure they never find out that she was there. They have no reason to think she knows anything about it. They have no reason to call her as a witness. She's not going to say anything.'

'I hope you're right,' Karen says apprehensively. 'But I don't trust her any more.'

Tom doesn't trust Brigid either, but he does think she's telling the truth.

Chapter Thirty-eight

KAREN STARTS TO tremble when Tom leaves. As she watches him go, it's as if her last connection to the outside world is disappearing. In here, she fears her real self might just dissolve. Watching his retreating back she almost screams, *Don't leave me here!* But then a guard comes for her and she must hold it together, because if she doesn't, if she shows weakness, she will never survive in here.

It all may work out, Calvin has told her. But it's getting harder and harder to believe it. She's shocked that Brigid followed her that night. She suddenly remembers something she glimpsed from the corner of her eye, in the plaza, something familiar that didn't quite register at the time – *Brigid's car.* She remembers it now. Why can't she remember the rest? It's driving her mad.

Why did Brigid follow her? What possible reason

could she have had? It can only be because Brigid saw her tear out of the house so fast; she sensed drama and couldn't resist.

What incredibly bad luck for her that Brigid lives across the street.

Tom is on his way to his car when he gets a call from the office. His heart sinks. He doesn't want to deal with work. He's going to have to tell them that he needs some time off. He hasn't been to the office since Karen was arrested the day before, and he'd flown out when Jack Calvin called. And now the story is all over the papers.

He reluctantly takes the call.

'Tom,' James Merritt says. Merritt is a senior partner at Simpson & Merritt. Tom has never much cared for him.

'Yes?' Tom says impatiently.

'We need you to come into the office,' Merritt says in his smooth, commanding baritone.

'Now? I . . . I have some things I have to sort out—'

'Half an hour, in the boardroom.' The call is disconnected.

'*Fuck!*' Of course they know that Karen's been arrested for murder. That won't play well with the clients.

He drives home quickly to put on a suit and then

heads to the office. He parks in his usual spot and sits for a minute in the car, preparing himself. With a strong sense of foreboding, he climbs out of the car and strides into the building. He takes the elevator up to the boardroom on the twelfth floor, a room he rarely visits.

When he steps inside, he sees the partners all seated around the large, smooth table. The murmuring in the room stops suddenly in an unnerving way, and Tom knows that, of course, they were talking about him. About his wife.

'Have a seat, Tom,' Merritt says, directing him to an open chair.

Tom sits, looking around the room at the members of the firm gathered there. Some of them meet his eyes curiously, others don't.

'What's this about?' Tom asks boldly.

'We were hoping you would tell *us*,' Merritt says.

Tom is anxious. He's never really fitted in. He's not from the right background. He doesn't come from money, doesn't play golf in the right clubs. He's risen as far as he has because he's a damned good accountant. And he works like a fiend, never complaining. But they were probably never going to make him partner. And now this.

'If this is about my wife, I don't think it's any of your business,' Tom says.

'On the contrary, we *do* think it's our business,'

Merritt says. He gives Tom a cold look. 'We're sorry for your troubles,' he continues, not looking particularly sorry. He and the other partners look more appalled than anything. 'But we are naturally concerned about how it looks.' Merritt sweeps his eyes down the table at the other partners, most of whom are nodding silently.

Tom stares at each of them in turn, quietly furious.

'There's no question you're an excellent accountant, Tom,' Merritt says. 'But you must understand our position. We have to think of our clients, their sensibilities. I'm afraid we have to suspend you without pay, until such time as the charges against your wife are dropped.' He lets that sink in. 'Of course,' he adds, 'you're free to pursue opportunities elsewhere. We would be happy to give you a good reference.'

Tom blinks rapidly. They're firing him. He stands up and, without uttering a word, walks out of the boardroom, slamming the door resoundingly behind him.

He tears out of the parking lot in a fury. He needs money for Karen's legal bills, which are going to be enormous. And now he has no way to pay them.

Brigid sees Tom return home. She watches him get out of the car and slam the door, as if he's angry. He strides up the steps and disappears inside the house.

Her heart picks up speed. She wonders what's happened now.

The sooner he's rid of Karen, the sooner he has her as a fixture in his life, the happier he'll be. Brigid believes this with her whole heart.

It's so perfect that Karen is out of the way, in jail. When Tom visits her, Brigid thinks, how different she must be, with her unwashed hair and ugly prison clothes. Karen was always so attractive – she has those perfect features and that expensive pixie haircut that shows off her fine bone structure. She won't have that flattering cut for much longer. How fun it would be to visit her, Brigid imagines. She would like to visit Karen in jail and see the new, unattractive Karen for herself. How satisfying that would be. Brigid always sensed a certain entitlement in Karen. But now, Brigid is the one who's entitled to everything – including Tom. She will have all of Karen's nice things, including her husband. Soon Karen will understand that and she won't be able to do a damn thing about it.

Brigid will wait until later, until Bob has come home to grab supper and has gone out again. Really, the man just comes home to eat and sleep. And now she's glad, because it leaves her free to do as she pleases.

This afternoon, she had her hair cut short, in the same pixie style that Karen wears. And she had a mani-pedi. Brigid knows that Karen regularly treats herself to mani-pedis. Or at least she used to. She won't be doing that any more. Brigid smiles when she thinks that maybe Karen will be getting home-made tattoos in prison instead. She even knows which nail salon Karen went to, and who cut her hair, because Karen had told her. Now, Brigid regards herself in her bathroom mirror and likes what she sees. Gone is the shoulder-length brown hair with the boring middle part. The new short, flirty cut makes her look completely different. She loves it. As she sat in the stylist's chair and watched her hair fall to the floor in clumps, she could feel her old life, and her old self, falling away. She feels like a gorgeous butterfly emerging from a long sleep.

If she's going to slip into Karen Krupp's life, she's going to do it right. She will be everything Tom wants her to be, and more. She holds her hands out in front of her and admires her professionally done nails.

Soon she will go across the street and see Tom again. She quivers with excitement. He won't dare turn her away.

Chapter Thirty-nine

JENNINGS POPS HIS head in Rasbach's door again at the end of the day. Rasbach looks up. 'What is it?' Rasbach asks.

'We got another call about the Krupp case. From the same woman.'

'Already? What did she say this time?'

'She asked why we weren't searching the Krupps' property for the murder weapon.'

Rasbach sits back in his chair, while Jennings takes his usual seat in front of Rasbach's desk. 'So she knows we aren't there searching. She must be keeping an eye on the place. A neighbour, maybe.'

'Yup. I wouldn't have bothered you with it, but she said something else that rang some very loud bells.'

'What?' Rasbach says sharply.

'She asked me whether we got the gloves.'

Rasbach leans forward intently. 'Nobody knows

about the gloves.' Only the police, and Karen and Tom Krupp. There has been nothing in the newspapers about the gloves.

'This woman does.'

'We might have a witness,' Rasbach says, 'or at least somebody who knows something.' He feels a little thrill of adrenaline. 'There's no way Karen Krupp could have put the murder weapon back in her house,' Rasbach says. 'We talked about this earlier today. It wasn't in the car when she crashed, and if she'd hidden it, or thrown it out the window, we would have found it.'

'Maybe she wasn't the only one there,' Jennings suggests. 'Maybe someone else was there, and picked up the gun.'

Rasbach looks at him and nods. 'Yeah. We'd better get a warrant.'

One of the worst things for Tom is that he can no longer talk to Karen whenever he wants. He never realized how much he relied on hearing her voice throughout the day, and on the e-mails and texts they exchanged. She was always there. And now she isn't. He can only talk to her when she gets to use the phone at the jail, and he doesn't know when or how often that will be. And they won't be able to say much. He can only visit during visiting hours.

She has been *put away*. How apt that description is.

And he's here, alone in the house. Tom feels like he's going out of his mind – but it must be so much harder for her. Being trapped in there like an animal, with so many other people, people not like her. People who have done bad things. Karen hasn't really done anything wrong, has she, except protect herself? But even if she gets lucky and they are lenient with her, there will be years, probably, when she will suffer horribly in prison, even if she was justified in what she did.

And when she finally gets out . . . they will both be so changed.

Tom thinks uneasily about Brigid. He's afraid she'll be back. And he can't afford to piss her off.

He hopes that all she wanted was a one-night stand, for old times' sake, that she'll be happy with that, and go back to her husband. But as if his thoughts have drawn her, he hears a rap on the door. It makes him jump.

Too late, Tom realizes that he should have spent the night at a hotel. Or gone to stay with his brother. He shouldn't be here, where Brigid can find him. He should go stay with his brother for a while. That should stop her coming round. But he doesn't know if he dares, or if that will only infuriate Brigid into doing something to hurt him and Karen.

She'll have seen his car in the driveway. Reluctantly, he pulls the door open. He's startled – appalled – by her appearance. 'You've cut your hair,' he says before he can stop himself.

'Do you like it?' she asks coyly.

He's sickened. She's cut her hair to look exactly like Karen's. *What is wrong with her?* And her tone of voice is so off-putting, so inappropriate under the circumstances. He'd dislike her less if she came out and said, *Sleep with me or I'll tell the police about your wife*. But this pretending that they're lovers again, it's making him nauseated. He wants to slam the door in her face and put the deadbolt on. No one can take the place of Karen, no one. Especially not Brigid.

'What's wrong?' she asks.

'Nothing,' he says, recovering quickly. He's not sure how to handle her. Her moods change so quickly; he remembers that about her, how volatile she is. He doesn't want to sleep with her again. He doesn't want to touch her. He doesn't want anything to do with her. He wants her to leave.

'Then,' she says, walking into the living room and turning around to face him as he closes the door, 'why don't you get me something to drink?'

So, she wants a replay of the night before. He hasn't got the stomach for it. He doubts he can even perform to her satisfaction. Maybe that's his out. Maybe he won't be able to get it up and she'll laugh at him and scorn him and leave him alone. That would be fine by him. But what if it makes her angry, and she tells the police what she saw?

Tom feels the perspiration tickle the back of his neck. His heart is beating hard in his chest. He knows he's got himself into a mess. He can't tell Karen about this.

'Brigid,' he says, letting all the exhaustion and despair he's feeling find an outlet in his voice, 'I don't think I'm up to anything tonight. I'm exhausted.'

She looks at him, her eyes narrowing in disappointment.

'And – I'm really worried about Karen,' he adds. He immediately realizes that was the wrong thing to say, and silently curses himself for being an idiot.

'You need to stop worrying about Karen,' Brigid says, with an edge to her voice. 'She's in jail. There's nothing you can do for her. You know, and she knows, and I know that she killed a man. She's going to be convicted. She won't be out for a very long time.' She adds even more harshly, 'She deserves what's coming to her.'

Tom can't believe what he's hearing. And the sudden hatred on Brigid's face is alarming. 'Brigid – she's your *friend*,' Tom reminds her. 'How can you feel that way?' His heart is pounding; his voice has begun to sound pleading.

Brigid says, 'She stopped being my friend the day she killed that man and lied to you and ruined your

295

life. What kind of woman does that to the man she loves? You deserve so much better than that.'

She walks up close to him. She puts her hands around his neck. He tries not to pull his head back in disgust. He realizes now – looking at her with her hair cut just like Karen's – that she's delusional, unhinged. She's not thinking like a normal person.

'Brigid,' he says, looking her right in the eyes. 'I don't know what you're thinking . . .'

'Oh, I think you do,' she says in a breathless, sexy voice. He wants to recoil from her, but he doesn't dare.

He takes her hands and gently withdraws them from his neck. 'Brigid, maybe last night was a mistake . . .'

'Don't say that!' she cries. Her face is ugly, twisted with fury.

'But, Brigid,' Tom says desperately, 'we're both married – I'm married to Karen now, and I can't just abandon her, even if I wanted to. And you're married to Bob—'

'It doesn't matter,' Brigid protests. 'I love you, Tom. I've loved you all this time – ever since you broke it off with me and started to see Karen. I've been watching you from across the street. I feel so connected to you – don't you feel it? This thing with Karen – maybe it was meant to be. Don't you believe in fate? Maybe this was supposed to happen, so that you and I can be together.'

He looks at her, appalled. She can't mean it. But she does. He's dealing with a woman who is clearly crazy.

He feels so manipulated, he feels such rage at the power she holds over him and Karen and their happiness together that he could gladly put his hands around her throat and squeeze.

Chapter Forty

THE NEXT MORNING Tom is startled awake. He looks over to the other side of the bed, Karen's side. It's empty, of course. Karen's in jail. It always takes a second, every morning, to remember what has happened, to awaken fully to the nightmare that is his life now. And another second to remember the more recent, paralysing details. Brigid. She'd been in his bed again last night.

She's gone back across the street to her husband. Thank God for that.

He hears a loud thumping at his front door. He glances at the alarm clock on his bedside table. It's 9:26 A.M. Normally he would be at work by now, but he doesn't have a job to go to any more.

Tom quickly pulls on a robe and pads nervously down the carpeted stairs to see who's banging and looks out. It's Detective Rasbach. Of course. Who else ever comes to his door but that damned detective and the nutcase from across the street? This time, he has an entire team of people with him. Tom feels his head beginning to pound.

He opens the door. 'What do you want?' He can't keep the surliness out of his voice. This man, more than anyone else – other than Robert Traynor – has ruined his life. And he's embarrassed by his own unkempt appearance and the fact that he's wearing nothing but a bathrobe at 9:30 in the morning, while the detective is cleanly shaven, smartly dressed, and raring to go.

'I have a warrant to search the premises,' Rasbach says, offering him a piece of paper.

Tom snatches it from him and looks at it. He hands it back. 'Go ahead,' he says. This is an inconvenience, nothing more. There's nothing to find here. Tom has already looked.

'How long is this going to take?' he asks Rasbach as the detective enters the house and starts directing his team.

'That depends,' Rasbach says unhelpfully.

'I'm going to go upstairs and shower,' Tom says.

Rasbach nods and goes about his business.

Tom returns to the bedroom. He grabs his cell phone and calls Jack Calvin.

'What's up?' Calvin asks with his customary brusqueness.

'Rasbach's here, with a search warrant.' There's a brief silence on the other end of the line. 'What do I do?' Tom asks.

'There's nothing you can do,' the lawyer advises him. 'Let them search. But stick around and see if they find anything.'

'They're not going to find anything,' Tom insists.

'I got in late last night from Vegas. I'm heading over to the jail to see Karen later. Keep me apprised.' And then the lawyer ends the call.

Tom showers, shaves, and gets dressed in jeans and a fresh shirt. Only then does he go downstairs. Stubbornly, he sticks to his usual routine. He puts on a pot of coffee. Makes himself a toasted bagel and pours himself some juice, all the while watching the police tear his kitchen apart with their gloved hands. *Having fun?* he wants to sneer at them, but he doesn't. When they're done with the kitchen, he follows them around the house, carrying his mug of coffee, watching them. He's not nervous, for once. He knows there's nothing to find.

'What are you looking for?' Tom asks Rasbach curiously, as the morning wears on. Rasbach merely looks at him and doesn't answer.

Finally, they seem to be finished. They haven't found anything. Tom can't wait for them to leave. 'So, are we all done here?' Tom asks.

'Not quite. We still have to check the yard and the garage.'

Tom is annoyed at how public such a search will be. But once he steps outside he sees not only all the police cars parked in front of his house, but also the news vans, the reporters, and the curious who have gathered there. He realizes it doesn't make any difference; all privacy was lost the night Karen killed someone.

There's no way he's going to talk to the press.

Rasbach's team tackles the garage first. It's a two-car garage, normally empty this time of the year – they only park inside in the winter. For now, there's just the usual clutter of tools and garden items to be sifted through, the familiar smell of oil on cement. It can't take much longer; then he'll be free of them.

There's a female police officer crouching down near the workbench. She's going carefully through a toolbox with an upper, removable tray and a catchall at the bottom. Tom searched through that toolbox himself, when Karen was in the hospital.

'I've got something,' the female officer says.

Rasbach walks over and crouches down beside her. 'Okay, let's see it,' Rasbach tells her. He doesn't sound surprised.

Tom's curiosity is piqued, but he's also afraid. *What have they found?*

With her hand encased in a latex glove, using two fingers, the woman officer lifts out a handgun.

Tom feels the blood rushing from his head. He doesn't understand. 'What's that?' he says stupidly.

'My guess is that it's the murder weapon,' Rasbach says calmly, as the officer bags and marks the evidence.

The police wrap up their search once they've checked the yard. They found what they were looking for, Tom thinks hollowly. His mind reels with disbelief.

The minute they've left he packs an overnight bag and throws it in the car. He stands by the car door for a moment and looks across the street at Brigid's house. She's in the window, watching him. He feels a chill run down his spine.

Then he gets in the car and calls Jack Calvin. Calvin picks up the call. 'Calvin.'

'They found a gun!' Tom practically shouts at the lawyer. 'They found a gun in the garage! They think it's the murder weapon!'

'Calm down, Tom, please,' Calvin says. 'Where are you?'

'I just got in the car. I'm heading for your office.'

'I'm on my way to see Karen. Meet me at the jail, and we'll talk about it.'

Tom tries to calm himself as he heads in the direction of the jail. If the gun they found is the murder weapon – and he knows that tests can prove conclusively whether it is or not – it wasn't there when he searched the place after the accident. So if it's Karen's gun, how did it get there? She wouldn't hide it in the garage. She couldn't have. Which means someone else must have planted it there.

There's only one person he can think of who would do that. And he's sleeping with her.

Chapter Forty-one

THE CONSTANT NOISE around her all night in jail prevents Karen from sleeping. Even with her pillow over her head she can't keep the din out. She wonders how anyone ever gets used to it. She feels hollow-eyed and worn out when morning rolls around, and even worse as the day wears on.

She's so alone here, so scared – how quickly jail has crushed her spirits. She has to be tougher than this, if she's to survive. She reminds herself that she is a survivor. She's going to have to be realistic now, and tough. She's not going to be able to just walk away from this.

A female guard approaches her cell and says, 'You got company.'

Karen almost weeps with relief as she gets up off her cot and follows the woman, who ushers her into a room where Calvin and Tom are waiting. Karen hugs Tom fiercely, tears stinging her eyes. She feels his arms wrap around her and squeeze tight. He smells of the outside, not of the jail, and she breathes in deeply. She won't let him go. She's sobbing into his neck. Finally, Tom pulls away and looks at her. She can see the tears in his eyes, too. He looks awful.

Calvin clears his throat; he obviously wants to get down to business. 'We need to talk.'

Karen fixes her eyes on her lawyer anxiously as they all sit down. Her entire future seems to rest in the hands of this man. She reaches for Tom; she needs to draw strength from him. 'Did you go to Las Vegas? Did you visit the shelter?' Karen asks.

'Yes,' Calvin says. 'They confirmed that you went there for help with your husband's abuse for over a year.' He pauses. 'But there's been a new development.'

Karen glances anxiously at Tom. Tom squeezes her hand.

Calvin says, 'They executed a search warrant on your property this morning.'

Karen looks back and forth between her lawyer and her husband; both of them look tense. 'So?' she says.

'So, they found a gun,' Calvin says.

She's stunned. 'What? How's that possible?' Karen asks. She turns to Tom for confirmation.

'They think it's the murder weapon,' Calvin says.

'I've just spoken to Detective Rasbach. They're running tests.'

'That's impossible!' Karen says emphatically. She can feel panic rising within her, threatening to choke her.

Calvin leans forward and looks right into her eyes. 'Let's speak hypothetically for a minute. Is there any way, hypothetically, that the gun found in your garage this morning could be the murder weapon?'

She shakes her head. 'No. It can't be.'

'Then what the hell's going on here?' He shifts his gaze to Tom. 'Do you know?'

She watches Tom take a deep breath. Then he says, 'I might have an idea.' He looks at Karen, his expression one of foreboding. 'I think someone might have put it there.'

'And why would you think that?' the lawyer asks carefully.

'Because I know it wasn't there when I searched the house after the accident, when Karen was in the hospital. I tore the place apart, including the garage. And I looked in that toolbox, and there was no gun there.'

Karen stares at him in surprise. He searched the house while she was in the hospital. And he never told her.

Calvin says, 'But the gun was there today. So how did it get there? Karen?'

'I don't know,' she whispers. 'I didn't put it there.'

'Think about it,' Tom says to Calvin. 'Karen was in that car accident. They didn't find the gun in the car. She obviously didn't take it with her to the hospital. How is she supposed to have used the weapon and hidden it in her own garage afterward? And why the hell would she?'

They're all quiet for a moment.

'I can think of one possibility,' Tom says now. Karen looks at him, frightened, hardly breathing.

Calvin looks back at them tiredly. 'Really? And who would that be?'

'Our neighbour across the street, Brigid Cruikshank.'

They're going to have to tell him, Karen thinks.

Calvin looks mildly interested now. 'And why would this woman across the street plant a gun in your garage?'

Tom says, 'Because she's crazy.'

Karen looks from her husband to her lawyer and takes a deep breath. 'And because she was there.'

'What?' Calvin says, obviously startled.

Karen says, 'She told Tom that she followed me that night.'

'Why would she do that?' the lawyer asks suspiciously.

'I don't know,' Karen says.

'I know why,' Tom says suddenly, turning to her.

'She's obsessed with you, Karen, and even more obsessed with me. She sits in that living room window across the street and watches us all day long, watches everything we do, because she's in love with me. And she *hates* you, Karen.'

'What?' Karen is shocked.

'You don't know her,' Tom says tersely, 'not like I do.'

'What are you talking about? She doesn't hate me,' Karen protests. 'That's ridiculous. And you hardly know her at all.'

Tom shakes his head. 'No.'

'Tom, she's my *best friend.*'

'No, she isn't,' Tom says harshly. 'When she came over and told me that she followed you the night of the accident . . .' He hesitates.

She stares at him. She wonders anxiously what's coming, what he knows that she doesn't. What is it that he doesn't want to tell her?

Tom looks away, as if he can't meet her eyes. 'There's something you need to know, Karen. Before I met you, Brigid and I – we had an affair. It was a mistake. I broke it off just before I met you.' He looks at her, ashamed.

Karen stares back at him in disbelief, utterly still. For a moment she can't even speak. Finally she says, 'And you never thought to tell me?'

'It wasn't relevant to you and me,' he says, quietly desperate. 'It was over before we met.'

She continues to stare at him, thinking of all the times she spent with Brigid, not knowing that she'd slept with her husband. She feels sick.

Tom says, 'We agreed not to say anything about it because – it would have been awkward, for everyone.'

Karen stares at him with something akin to loathing. 'She's married, Tom.'

'I know, but she lied to me – she said they were separating, seeing other people. She's very manipulative – you have no idea.' Tom continues, 'That night that she came over and told me that she followed you – she – she came on to me, and told me that if . . . if I slept with her, she wouldn't tell the police that she was there, that she saw you that night – that she heard the shots and saw you run out of the building right after.'

Karen is stunned. 'You had sex with her – that night? With Brigid? While I was – in jail?' For a moment, she doesn't even think to pull her hand away from his, but then she does. Tom flushes to the roots of his hair. He hates that he's hurting her this way.

'I didn't want to! I did it to protect you!' Tom says. 'And now she has some crazy idea that she and I are meant for each other, and that now you're in jail, we can be together. She thinks it's fate. Don't you see? *She* must have planted the gun in our garage. She's trying to make sure you go to prison for murder!'

Karen tries to think, her heart racing. 'Brigid was there – she must have picked up the gun.'

Tom nods. 'That's what I'm saying.'

Karen says to Tom, thinking it through, 'Maybe Brigid left some prints at the murder scene. You said she told you she opened the door.' She turns to the lawyer. 'Are you going to have them look for Robert's prints inside our house?' Calvin nods. 'Maybe while they're at it, they'll find some of Brigid's, too. They must be there. And get them to compare them to any they might have found at the murder scene.'

Tom and Calvin are watching her intently.

She looks up at the two men staring at her. 'There's our reasonable doubt,' Karen says. 'I'm being framed by my crazy neighbour across the street. Because she's in love with my husband.'

Chapter Forty-two

FOR THE SECOND time that day, Detective Rasbach is at the Krupp residence.

How quickly things change, he thinks. Just yesterday he was telling himself that this case had become quite straightforward, that all the pieces of the puzzle were slipping nicely into place. But now he's feeling like the picture that's emerging isn't the same as the one on the box.

He was leery of the caller with the tip from the get-go. Someone with inside information, obviously, since she knew about the gloves. A possible witness. It could be someone who was there, who saw Karen Krupp peel off the gloves and flee. Someone who maybe saw her shoot the victim, and then went in afterward and picked up the gun. Who? He thought that maybe someone from the neighbourhood picked up the gun before the body was reported. But maybe it's not that simple.

If the gun has turned up in the Krupps' toolbox, someone else must have been at the crime scene and nabbed it. Someone who wants to see Karen Krupp go to prison. Because otherwise why not just leave the gun there, at the scene? Why pick it up at all, unless you have plans for it?

Rasbach sees Jack Calvin coming toward him from the kitchen, Tom Krupp right behind him. Rasbach respects Calvin; he's dealt with him in the past and he knows Calvin is a straight shooter. 'What's this about, exactly?'

Calvin says, 'My client believes that someone was stalking her for the last few weeks, coming into the house and going through her things when they were out. She thinks it was Robert Traynor. He'd obviously tracked her down. If we find Traynor's prints in the house, it's strong evidence of the danger she was in. It also explains her state of mind.'

Rasbach nods. 'Fair enough. We got his prints off the body. We'll have a look. If they're here, we'll find them.'

Calvin nods. 'And one other thing,' he says.

'What?'

'*Someone* was sneaking into the house. If it wasn't Traynor, we need to know who it was. My client did not put that gun in the toolbox. Someone else must have. We need to know who.' He pauses and then says carefully, 'We need to know if there are any

312

prints in this house that match any of those at the murder scene.'

Rasbach studies the lawyer – Calvin is trying to tell him something. He nods and says, 'Okay. Let's see what we get.'

Rasbach wants to know who might have been in the house, too. He feels like he's back at square one. He has a dead body, and a whole lot of questions with no answers.

Karen paces her cell, thinking about what's going on at home. Calvin has asked the police in to find proof of Robert being in their house. She's hoping that they find Robert's prints there, because that will support her position that she was a battered wife, stalked by a violent husband, in fear for her life. If she has to, she'll use this to reduce her time in prison. But now she's hoping for something else, something that will earn her a get-out-of-jail-free card.

Brigid. Brigid is going to be her ticket out of jail. Because Brigid might be crazy, she might be in love with her husband, but the most important thing about Brigid is that she is stupid. Brigid was so stupid she planted the murder weapon right in Karen's garage.

Karen could not have foreseen that Brigid would follow her that night. She could not have foreseen that Brigid would pick up the gun. Karen's still shocked by all that. But every cloud has a silver lining, and while Brigid is an actual witness who probably could have – with the weight of all the other evidence – put her away, she went about it entirely the wrong way. So heavy-handed. Planting the gun. Calling it in to the police. Pressuring Tom into sleeping with her.

Karen thinks about Brigid in her bed, having sex with her husband, while she was curled up on a wretched cot, in a wretched cell, in the basement of the police station, the noise and stench all around her. She thinks about how all this time, the two of them conspired to keep the secret of their past affair from her.

It infuriates her that Tom slept with Brigid again that night, but it's also the best thing that could have happened. Because Tom can tell the police how Brigid blackmailed him into sleeping with her, how she's in love with him and wants Karen out of the way. And to back him up, Brigid's fingerprints will be in her house, in places where they shouldn't be if she's just a friend of Karen's. They'll be in the bedroom.

It's very lucky that Karen hasn't told the police anything yet. Now she has a decision to make. Does she tell the truth – that she still can't remember anything after reaching the door of the restaurant? Or should she lie and say that she now remembers

314

everything? That she argued with Robert in the restaurant, and then fled for her life. That she didn't shoot him – he was alive when she left. And then the implication is there – that Brigid followed her and heard it all, and then must have killed him herself, after Karen fled, and kept the gun, thinking she could set Karen up for murder.

She doesn't need to prove that Brigid killed Robert – although that would be sweet. She wonders now how Brigid called the police about the gun; surely she wouldn't have called from her own phone? Wouldn't it be wonderful if she had? But it doesn't really matter. All they have to do is raise enough doubt, sow enough confusion, to get the charges against Karen dropped.

And Tom won't be sleeping with Brigid any more. She has nothing to hold over them now, because *they* are going to tell the police about Brigid being there that night. Karen knows that Tom has packed some things and is moving to his brother's for the time being. How angry Brigid will be that he's gone. How sad, how lonely, sitting at her window, looking across the street at their empty house.

Serves you right, Karen thinks.

Rasbach has put a rush on the fingerprints. By early the next morning, he's standing with the fingerprint expert looking at a full set of Robert Traynor's prints, and various prints that were lifted the day before from the Krupp house, as well as the prints recovered from the scene of the crime.

'There isn't a single print of the murder victim anywhere on the premises,' the expert tells him now. 'Nothing. He was never in that house. At least, not without gloves on. Traynor might have been in the house at some point, but we can't say that he was for sure.'

'That's going to disappoint Jack Calvin,' Rasbach muses.

'So was she imagining things,' Jennings asks, standing beside Rasbach, 'when she says someone was going through the house?'

The fingerprint expert shakes his head and says, 'Like I said, he could have worn gloves. But we found loads of prints of an unidentified person all over the house,' the expert says.

'Like where all over the house?' Rasbach asks.

'Everywhere. The living room, the kitchen, the bathrooms, the bedroom . . . I mean, it was like this person lived there. And whoever it was is very tactile, always touching and handling things. We even found this person's prints on the inside of Karen Krupp's underwear drawer. Inside the bathroom cupboards. On her perfume bottles. Inside the filing cabinets.'

'What about the garage?' Rasbach asks.

'No, nothing in the garage.'

'That's interesting,' Rasbach says.

'No. What's *really* interesting,' the technician says with a gleam in his eye, 'is that they match prints we found at the murder scene, on the back door of the restaurant. Whoever was going through the Krupps' house was also at the murder scene, at least at some point.'

'That *is* interesting,' Rasbach says.

'Nothing is showing up in the databanks. Whoever they belong to, they don't have a record.'

'I think we'll be able to narrow it down. Excellent work. Thank you,' Rasbach says, and motions for Jennings to follow him.

'She has a stalker, all right,' Rasbach says. 'It's just not who she thought it was.'

'Life is full of surprises,' Jennings says. He's oddly upbeat for a homicide detective.

'We need to talk to Karen Krupp again,' Rasbach says, 'and maybe this time she'll talk.'

Chapter Forty-three

'MY CLIENT IS ready to make a statement,' Calvin says.

Karen's seated with Calvin in an interview room at the jail. Tom isn't there. Rasbach sits across the table from them, with Jennings beside him. There's a video recorder in the room to capture her every word, her every movement, while she squirms under questioning.

Karen knows she has to be good. Her life depends on it.

After a few formalities, they begin.

'My name was Georgina Traynor,' she says. 'I was married to Robert Traynor, an antiques dealer in Las Vegas.' She tells them everything – about her life with him, how she escaped – all the ugly details. She tells them about thinking Robert had been in their

318

house, how frightened she was. She tells them about the night she got the phone call.

She drinks a sip of water because her voice is ragged. Reliving this is awful; she feels physically ill. 'I agreed to meet with him. I was terrified that he might hurt Tom.' She falters, but then continues. 'I had a gun that I'd bought when I left him, for protection in case he came after me. I kept it hidden in the furnace room. So when he called I got the gun and my rubber gloves from the kitchen, and went to meet him.'

She looks steadily at Detective Rasbach. 'For a long time, I couldn't remember what happened that night, I think because it was so traumatic. But I – I remember it all now.' She steadies herself with a deep breath before continuing. 'When I got there it was already dark. I went into the restaurant, and Robert was there, waiting for me. At first, he didn't seem angry, which surprised me. Maybe because he saw that I had a gun, he was more careful with me. But then he began threatening me, like he always did. He told me that I'd put him through a lot of trouble and expense to find me and that if he couldn't have me, nobody could. He said if I didn't leave with him he would find a way to kill both me and my new husband, and no one would ever figure it out, because I was already officially dead, and he had no connection to Tom. He said they would be the perfect murders, and I believed him.' She pauses. 'I was the one holding the gun, and he was threatening *me*. He knew I didn't have the guts to shoot him. He laughed.'

Rasbach is looking at her, expressionless. She can't tell what he's thinking; she can never tell what he's thinking.

'I didn't know what to do. I knew I couldn't shoot him. I panicked. I turned and ran. When I got to the car I dropped the gun and peeled off the gloves – I remember, I had the gun in my hand and the gloves on and I couldn't get the keys out of my pocket. So I dropped the gun and ripped the gloves off. And then I got in the car and took off as fast as I could, and drove too fast and went into that pole.' She looks Rasbach directly in the eyes. 'I swear to you, Robert was alive when I left him. He didn't chase after me. I thought he would – I kept expecting to be yanked back by my hair – but he let me go.' She adds, 'But he knew where Tom and I lived.' She shudders, as if reliving the fear.

'So how do you think your husband was killed?' Rasbach asks.

'I don't know for sure.'

'But you have an idea?'

'Yes.'

'Tell me.'

She doesn't look at Calvin. 'My neighbour, across the street. Brigid Cruikshank. She told Tom that she followed me that night, that she heard Robert and me in the restaurant.' She sees Rasbach's expression sharpen.

'Why would she follow you?'

'Because she's in love with my husband.' She thinks she's struck just the right note of indignation, bitterness, and hurt.

'And what do you think happened?'

'I think she picked up the gun where I dropped it in the parking lot and went into the building and shot Robert.' Her voice has lowered to a whisper.

'Why would she do that?' Rasbach asks, clearly sceptical.

'So that she could put me away for murder. She saw a perfect opportunity to get rid of me and take my husband away from me.' Rasbach looks unconvinced. His eyebrows have risen dramatically. She says, 'She and Tom had an affair, just before he met me. She wants him back, and she wants to get rid of me. Tom told me that she blackmailed him into having sex with her again – she told him that if he slept with her she wouldn't tell that she was there that night and that she saw me there, arguing with Robert. She must have heard everything we said.'

She sees the look Rasbach gives Jennings, as if he's finding all of this terribly far-fetched.

Karen's eyes dart from one detective to the other. 'She must have planted the gun in our garage. I didn't put it there. And if you look, you might find her fingerprints at the crime scene. Tom said she told him that she opened the door. You should check it.' Her voice is becoming a bit frantic. They don't seem to believe her.

'I see,' Rasbach says, as if he doesn't believe a word of it.

'She was there! You must be able to find witnesses who saw her drive down the street after me that night,' Karen says desperately. 'She must have been seen by the same people who saw me leaving the house and driving away. Have you asked any of them?'

'We'll look into it,' Rasbach says. 'Was Brigid a friend of yours?'

'She was.'

'Did you invite her over to your house, when you were friends?'

'Yes. Sometimes.'

'What would you do, when she was over?' Rasbach asks.

'We'd have coffee, usually in the kitchen or in the living room, and talk.' Now Karen is tired and wants to go back to her cell.

'Okay,' Rasbach says evenly. 'Let's go over it again.'

*

Rasbach sits back in his chair and regards Karen Krupp sitting across from him. She looks exhausted and a bit slovenly, but she meets his eyes readily enough, as if challenging him to find a hole in her story. He imagines that she's crafted it all quite carefully, almost as carefully as she crafted her escape. And while he's quite sympathetic about how she got away from her husband – he can understand why she did what she did – this story he's not ready to credit. It's the amnesia.

'A little strange, don't you think,' he says now, 'that you suddenly got your memory back. Right before our interview.'

Karen says, quite composed, 'If you talk to my doctor, you'll realize it's not strange at all. That's how it works. It comes back when it damn well pleases. Or not at all.'

'I've spoken to an amnesia expert,' he tells her, and watches for her reaction. She has none. She's quite good at this. 'And I find it rather pat, that you remember it all now. I mean, *today*.' He smiles. 'You couldn't remember anything a couple of days ago. It's a little convenient, that's all.'

She folds her arms across her chest and sits back in her chair. She says nothing.

'You see, I'm having a little trouble believing your version of events,' Rasbach says pleasantly. He waits for a moment to let her stew. The silence stretches out. 'The part I'm having difficulty with is that you say you met with Robert Traynor that night, he'd hunted you down after three long years, you wave a gun at him – and *he lets you go*.'

Karen stares stonily back at him.

'In my experience, angry, violent men who have been deceived don't exhibit such strong self-control,' Rasbach says. 'In fact, I'm surprised you got out of there alive, if everything you say is true.'

'I told you,' she says, her voice shaking slightly. 'I think he let me go because he knew where I lived. He knew who my husband was. He was planning to kill us both if I didn't do what he wanted – so he didn't have to kill me right then and there.'

Rasbach looks back at her doubtfully. 'But surely he wouldn't think that you'd just go home and wait for him to slaughter the two of you and get away with it. You're a clever woman. If he was going to kill you and Tom, wouldn't you have gone to the police?'

'I panicked. I told you. I just ran out of there, I wasn't thinking straight.'

'But my point is,' Rasbach says, leaning forward slightly, 'that Robert Traynor would *expect* you to go to the police. Or to disappear again. So *why on earth would he let you go?*'

Karen looks paler now, more nervous. 'I don't know. I don't know what he was thinking.'

'I don't think he would have let you go. I think he was dead when you ran out of there.' She meets his eyes steadily and doesn't waver. He changes tack. 'How long have you known about your husband's affair with your neighbour Brigid Cruikshank?'

'He just told me.'

Rasbach nods. 'Yes, he kept it a secret from you, didn't he? Why do you suppose he did that, if the affair was already over, as he said, when the two of you met?'

'Why don't you ask him?' she says, obviously stung by the question.

'I have. I want to hear what you think.'

She eyes him angrily. 'She told him that she and her husband were separating. He believed her. He wouldn't have slept with her otherwise.'

'So, why didn't he tell you early on? Do you think it might be because he was afraid you might not believe such a self-serving explanation?'

Karen gives him a sour look and he lets it go. 'Your marriage isn't exactly built on a foundation of total honesty,' Rasbach points out, 'but never mind.'

'You don't know anything about my marriage,' she says harshly.

She's getting a little rattled, he thinks. 'One more thing,' Rasbach says. 'I'm also having trouble imagining Brigid spontaneously picking up the gun you dropped in the parking lot, and then going into the restaurant and shooting Robert Traynor dead.'

'Why?' Karen counters. 'I don't have any trouble imagining it at all. She's off her head. She's obsessed with my husband. She wants me to go to jail. Talk to Tom. She's completely mad.'

'I will,' Rasbach says. 'And I'll talk to her, too.'

Rasbach and Jennings head back to the station from the county jail. The case, which had once seemed so straightforward, is now anything but. Rasbach no longer knows what to believe.

'Just playing devil's advocate here. What if she's right?' Jennings says. 'What if we get this woman Brigid's prints and they match the ones all over the Krupps' house and the ones at the crime scene? Maybe we've got the wrong one in jail.'

'Maybe. Whoever put the gun in the garage must have been at the murder scene. Maybe it was Brigid. Maybe it was someone else. Maybe Tom was at the murder scene. Maybe he's been having an affair with this woman across the street all along and that's why there are fingerprints all over the house.' Rasbach gazes contemplatively out the car window at the passing scenery.

Finally, he says, 'We should have the tests back on the weapon by now. Maybe it's not even the murder weapon, in which case, any crackpot in the city might have put it there and is trying to have some fun with us. Let's talk to the firearms examiner, and

326

get this Brigid woman fingerprinted and see what we actually have, in terms of evidence.'

When they get back to the station, Rasbach calls the firearms examiner, who confirms that the gun found in Karen Krupp's garage is definitely the gun that shot Robert Traynor.

'Well, that's one thing we know for sure,' Rasbach says. 'Let's go talk to Brigid Cruikshank.'

Chapter Forty-four

BRIGID GLOWERS AT the house across the street as
if that will bring him back.

Tom's car is gone. She hasn't seen it since yesterday. She watched the police arrive and go through
the house a second time, the day before, and was
puzzled. Hadn't they found the murder weapon? She
was pretty sure they had. She'd watched them go
through the garage from this very chair, and they
couldn't have missed it.

Finally they left, and soon after that she saw Tom
leave. Earlier that day, she'd seen him throw an overnight bag in his car. Then he stood by the car and
glared at her from across the street. Her heart had
shrivelled up inside her. Why was he leaving? Didn't
they have an understanding? Didn't he feel the way
she did, now that they were lovers again?

But he hadn't come back last night. He'd stayed

somewhere else, and she felt as if her whole world was falling apart. He was avoiding her. *What can she do to bring him back?*

She fights tears of frustration. He can't stay away forever with just one small suitcase. He'll have to start going back to work, he'll need his suits again. He'll have to return home, and she will be watching; he won't escape her. She'll make him see that he belongs with her. And she'll make sure that Karen never gets out of prison.

If she has to, she will testify against Karen, even if Tom doesn't like it, even if he hates her for it for a little while. Because as long as Karen exists in the world, Tom won't choose Brigid. This makes her angriest of all.

She sees a car come up the street and watches it park in front of her house. She knows that car. And she recognizes the two detectives getting out of it. What are they doing here? Her body tenses involuntarily.

The doorbell rings. Brigid, suddenly nervous, considers ignoring it, but they probably saw her in the window. Even if they didn't, they'll just come back. She gets up to answer the door. Just before she opens it, she rearranges her face into what she hopes is a composed smile. 'Yes?' she says.

'Good afternoon,' Detective Rasbach says and holds up his badge.

'I know who you are, detective,' she says. 'I remember you from the last time you were here.'

'May we come in?' he asks.

'Of course,' Brigid says, opening the door wide. She invites them to sit down in the living room. Jennings sits, but Rasbach wanders over to the big picture window and stands right behind Brigid's favourite chair, looking across at the Krupps' house.

'Nice view,' he says.

Then he comes and sits across from her. His sharp blue eyes are disconcerting. He must have noticed that she's changed her hair. She resists the urge to reach up and touch it. 'How can I help you?' she asks.

'We have a few questions,' Rasbach says, 'about your neighbour across the street – Karen Krupp. She's been arrested as part of an ongoing homicide investigation.'

Brigid crosses her legs and folds her hands tightly in her lap. 'I know. It's so shocking. I thought I knew her so well, but I had no idea what she's really like. I mean, I guess none of us did. I'm sure her husband didn't.'

'She hasn't been convicted yet,' Rasbach points out mildly.

She can feel herself flush slightly. 'No, of course not.' She recrosses her legs and volunteers, 'Karen told me – before she was arrested – that she thought she

330

must have witnessed something, a murder, and that you were trying to get her to remember what happened that night to help you in your investigation.' She looks directly at the handsome detective. 'But that isn't really true, is it?' When Rasbach doesn't answer, she glances back and forth at the two men conspiratorially. 'I knew something more was going on – the police have been coming and going over there a lot.' She leans forward from her seat on the sofa and hopes she conveys the appropriate concern when she asks, 'Who was that man? Do you know why she did it?'

'Right now, we're simply investigating all avenues,' Rasbach says smoothly. 'And we're hoping you can help us.'

'Of course,' she says, pulling back a little from him.

'Did Karen Krupp ever mention to you that she was afraid of someone, or worried about her safety?'

Brigid shakes her head. 'No.'

'Did she ever tell you that she had a gun?'

She gives them a look of surprise. 'No.'

'Did you ever see anyone suspicious around their property?'

Brigid shakes her head again and says, 'No, why?'

'The Krupps say that someone was coming into their house, over a period of several weeks. We think this may be tied to what happened that night. So we've taken fingerprints inside the house and since we know that you visited Karen there on occasion, we would like to get your prints to eliminate them from our list. Would you be willing to come down to the station and be fingerprinted? It would be very helpful.'

Brigid looks at him and thinks rapidly. She knows she wiped the gun clean – she even Googled how to do it properly – and she wore gloves when she hid it in the garage. She knows her prints aren't on the gun. And there's good reason for her prints to be in the Krupps' house; she's a friend. So she has nothing to worry about.

Except for one thing that's been bothering her lately. She's pretty sure she pushed open the door of the restaurant that night with her hand. But that's okay. Because if she has to, she can admit that she was there, and that she saw Karen kill that man. Tom will be angry, but Karen will be gone for good, and he'll come around, eventually. She doesn't see that she has much choice right now about the fingerprints. And if she has to admit that she was there – well, she hasn't said anything under oath about that night yet. She simply told them she wasn't home. She can change her story. She may have to tell the truth about what she saw. Rasbach is waiting for her answer.

'Okay,' she says. 'Now?'

'If you don't mind,' Rasbach says politely.

There's a sound near the front door and they all turn their heads suddenly in that direction. Bob Cruikshank comes unexpectedly into the living room, looking startled.

'What's going on?' he asks. 'Who are you?' he says to the detectives.

'What are you doing here?' Brigid asks, equally surprised. She doesn't want Bob here.

'I'm not feeling well,' her husband says. 'I came home to lie down.'

Rasbach stands up, flashes his badge, and says, 'I'm Detective Rasbach, and this is Detective Jennings. We're investigating a homicide, and came to ask your wife some questions.'

'What do you want with her?' he asks suspiciously. 'This is about that woman across the street, isn't it? They're friends, but I doubt Brigid can help you much.'

Brigid gives him a hostile look. She says, 'Maybe I'm not as useless as you think.'

At this he gives her a look of surprise, while the detectives silently observe the two of them.

'Let's go,' she says to the detectives and brushes past her husband.

She hears him call after her, 'Where are you going?'

She turns around and faces him and says, 'I'm going to be fingerprinted.' She enjoys the look of confusion on his face. *Let him think about that for a while.*

It's early evening when Rasbach gets the results from the lab about the fingerprints. He and Jennings are in Rasbach's office, chewing on a pizza, discussing the results, and where to go from here.

'Brigid Cruikshank was at the murder scene. Her prints are on the door,' Rasbach says. He's not at all surprised, because while waiting for the fingerprint results, he and Jennings had gone back to the suburb and interviewed the neighbours again, asking if they'd seen Brigid that night. And each of the two women who had seen Karen driving too fast down the street that night had also seen Brigid driving down the same street shortly after. So they can now be fairly certain that Brigid followed Karen Krupp.

'And her prints are all over the Krupps' house,' Jennings adds.

'Brigid is the stalker,' Rasbach says. 'She's the only one whose prints showed up in Karen's underwear drawer, for instance. Even Tom Krupp's prints weren't in his wife's underwear drawer.'

'So what was she doing, going through Karen Krupp's underwear?' Jennings muses. 'That's pretty creepy behaviour.'

'Brigid is most likely the one who picked up the gun and put it in the garage,' Rasbach says. 'Karen says that Brigid is in love with Tom and is trying to frame her for murder.' He takes a deep breath and exhales. 'What's really going on here?' Rasbach asks.

Jennings says, 'Maybe Brigid *is* in love with Tom. Maybe she's nuts. Maybe she did follow Karen, shoot Traynor, and then hide the gun in the garage.'

Rasbach says thoughtfully, 'They were both there. Either of them might have done it. They both had motive. We won't be able to prosecute either one of them, because each of them can point to the other.' He leans back in his chair, throws down a pizza crust in frustration. 'It's almost like they planned it together – the perfect murder.'

'Are we looking for collusion then, joint intention?' Jennings asks.

'I don't think we're going to be able to find it,' Rasbach says. He thinks for a minute. 'Because what's in it for Brigid? It's great for Karen. Robert, the threat, is gone for good. Karen gets off scot-free. All fine and dandy. But what's in it for Brigid? Brigid doesn't get anything.' Rasbach looks at Jennings. 'Would you do that for a friend?'

'No. I would not,' Jennings admits. Then he suggests, 'Maybe Brigid and Karen are more than friends. Maybe they're lovers and they planned this together to get rid of Robert. And Tom Krupp has no idea what's going on.'

Rasbach tilts his head at him. 'That's some pretty

creative thinking, Jennings.' Jennings shrugs good-naturedly. Rasbach runs his hand tiredly over his face, then he shakes his head. 'I don't think so.'

'Me neither.'

'I don't think they worked this out together. I think the two women are working at cross-purposes.' Rasbach sits back in his chair. 'We need to bring Brigid in for questioning. But let's bring Tom Krupp in first.'

Chapter Forty-five

TOM'S TENSE WHEN he comes in for questioning the next morning. He would rather be anywhere than in this interview room at the police station. The room is already warm, as if the air-conditioning is off, or broken. Have they done that on purpose, so they can see him sweat? Somehow Rasbach doesn't seem to notice the heat. Tom moves nervously in his seat as they get started.

'What is your relationship with Brigid Cruikshank?' Rasbach asks, not wasting any time.

Tom flushes. 'I've already told you.'

'Tell us again.'

He doesn't know if they have already spoken to Brigid or not, and what she might have told them. He worries that the way she tells it won't be the same as the way he does. He tells them again about their brief affair, and how he stopped it. 'I thought that was the end of it. I didn't think she still had any feelings for me. But after Karen was arrested, she came to our house and . . .' He pauses.

'And what?' Rasbach asks patiently.

'My wife told you all this.' Tom knows what Karen told the detectives the day before – every detail; Calvin has relayed it all to him. He also knows that Karen lied to her lawyer and the detectives about recovering all of her memory. He wishes she hadn't done that.

'We want to hear it from you,' Rasbach says.

Tom sighs deeply. 'Brigid told me that she followed Karen that night and that if I didn't have sex with her, she would tell the police that she was there, and . . .'

'And what?'

'And that she heard shots fired and saw Karen run out of the restaurant immediately after.'

Rasbach nods thoughtfully. 'I see. Did you have sex with her then, when she threatened you that way?'

'Yes,' Tom says. He knows he sounds sullen, ashamed; he knows he's twisting the truth. He lifts his head and looks the detective in the eye.

'So you believed her when she told you that Karen had committed murder,' the detective says.

'No! No, I did not,' Tom protests, flustered. 'I thought that she was making it up and that she would go to the police with all her lies, and that it would make it worse for Karen.' Tom squirms in his chair, feels the sweat beneath his shirt.

'Why do you think Brigid threatened you that way?' Rasbach asks.

'She's crazy,' Tom says. 'She's crazy, that's why! She sits in her window watching everything we do. She's obsessed with us, and she's in love with me. It's like something in her mind is twisted, and we're caught up in it somehow, like we're part of some fantasy she has.' He has no trouble saying any of this, because it's all too horribly true. Calvin has shared with him and Karen what the technicians found in the house; he knows about the fingerprints. Tom leans forward across the table and fixes his eyes on the detective. 'We all know now that she's been going into our house when we're not home. We all know what the fingerprints show. She must have been coming in for weeks, snooping through our house. *Lying down on our bed. Going through Karen's underwear.* And now she's even cut her hair just like Karen's. Tell me that's not crazy! Who does that?' Tom realizes he's been gesturing wildly with his arms; he leans back in his chair, trying to calm down.

Rasbach stares back at him, saying nothing.

'A few days ago,' Tom adds, 'Karen thought someone had taken the stopper off her perfume bottle and left it on the vanity. I thought she'd done it herself. But guess whose fingerprints were on that perfume stopper? Brigid's!'

'How do you think she got in?' Rasbach asks.

'Yeah, I've been thinking about that,' Tom says. 'I loaned her a spare set of keys when we were seeing each other. She returned them. But I'm thinking she must have made a copy before she gave them back.'

'And you never had your locks changed?'

'No. Why would I? I wasn't expecting any of this.' But he should have. Of course he should have changed the locks.

Rasbach continues to stare at him. 'Anything else?'

'Yes. She's the only one who could have planted the gun in our garage. She must have been there that night, like she says; she must have followed Karen. She must have picked up the gun.' Tom leans back in his chair again and folds his arms across his chest. 'So. Are you going to arrest her?'

'Arrest her for what, exactly?' Rasbach asks.

Tom glares back at him in disbelief. 'I don't know,' he says, with sarcasm, 'how about harassment, planting evidence . . .'

'I don't have any evidence that she planted the gun,' Rasbach says.

Tom feels a clutch of fear at his heart. 'Who else could it have been?' he asks, dismayed.

'I don't know. It might have been anyone. The calls came from a public telephone.'

Tom stares at Rasbach in disbelief, his anxiety mounting. *Fuck. If Rasbach doesn't believe Brigid planted the gun* . . . Tom feels his stomach tightening in fear as the detective watches him.

'I can probably,' Rasbach says, 'charge her with trespassing.' He stands up and says, 'I don't have any more questions at this time. You're free to go.'

Tom gets up slowly, trying to preserve his dignity.

'Pretty convenient, your wife getting her memory back all of a sudden,' Rasbach says casually.

Tom freezes, then forces himself to ignore the comment. He's not going to say anything.

'Oh, just one more thing,' Rasbach says. 'Why did Brigid want to meet you that night?'

Tom sits slowly back down. 'I asked her, that night, when I called her to see if she knew where Karen was. I asked her why she wanted to meet me, and why she stood me up. But she said to forget it, it wasn't important, that something had come up.' He pauses, remembering. 'I was so worried about Karen that I didn't push it. But later on . . .' He hesitates.

'Later on . . .' Rasbach prompts him.

Tom doesn't know if he should tell them this or not. But what if Brigid does? 'She told me that she'd wanted to meet me that night to tell me that she'd seen someone snooping around our house that morning.'

'Who?'

'I don't know for sure, but from the description, it sounded like Robert Traynor.'

Chapter Forty-six

BOB HAD BADGERED Brigid about coming with her to the station, but she hadn't let him. When she'd come home the evening before, after the fingerprinting, he was all over her. Why did they want her fingerprints? Was that normal police procedure? He looked at her like he was worried that she'd done something criminal. She let him stew for a bit before explaining that they only wanted her prints for exclusionary purposes.

But when the detectives telephoned this afternoon and asked her to come in to answer a few questions – Bob was still home, not feeling well – he asked her what the hell was going on. She said she was going down to the police station for questioning. He looked at her that way again, as if he were suddenly very worried about something. And he'd wanted to get dressed and come with her, but she'd told him no and taken the car without waiting for him. And now he's stuck at home, waiting and worrying. Brigid's enjoying this part of it. *Imagine, Bob taking an interest.* She smiles a cold smile. It's too late. She's already moved on.

She checks in at the front desk and is immediately taken into an interview room. The two detectives, Rasbach and Jennings, soon arrive. They tell her about the video camera. She likes the way they treat her – they are friendly but respectful, trying to put her at ease. As if she's doing them a favour. She *is* doing them a favour. They even bring her a coffee, which she accepts graciously. They are all friends here, with the same goal, surely. They want to catch a killer, and so does she.

'Brigid, what is your relationship with Karen Krupp?' Rasbach begins.

'We're neighbours and good friends,' Brigid says. 'We've been friends for about two years, since she married Tom and moved in with him across the street.'

Rasbach nods encouragement. 'And how do you feel about her husband, Tom Krupp?'

She blushes involuntarily; she's annoyed with herself for that. She reaches for her coffee. 'I like to think that we're friends, too,' she says, recovering her composure.

'Is that all you are, friends?' Rasbach asks pointedly.

Now she flushes in earnest. She's not sure what to say. Has Tom told them about their past affair? And that they've begun sleeping together again? Surely not. If he has, then he must no longer be afraid of her telling them that she saw Karen at the murder scene that night. Has Karen already made some kind of deal with the police? She says, 'Why are you asking me that?'

'Just answer the question, please,' Rasbach says firmly.

'I'm not going to answer that question,' Brigid says. She's not under arrest. She doesn't have to answer any of their questions. It worries her that Tom may have told the detectives about the two of them. She doesn't like losing the upper hand. She must go more carefully now, feeling her way.

The detective lets it go. 'Where were you August thirteenth, the night of Karen Krupp's accident, at around eight twenty P.M.?'

'I don't remember exactly.'

'Tom Krupp says that you called him that day, and arranged to meet him that evening at eight thirty, but you didn't show up.' She shifts in her seat, caught by surprise. 'What did you want to see him about?'

She looks from Rasbach to Jennings and back again. She doesn't want to get in trouble for not mentioning this before. 'I'd actually forgotten all about that, because of the accident. But yes, that morning, I saw a strange man snooping around the Krupps' house, looking in the windows. I called Tom at the office, and asked him to meet me that night.' She stops.

'And you felt you had to arrange a meeting in person about it, that evening?' Rasbach asks.

'There was more to it than that,' Brigid explains. 'The man spoke to me. He seemed – a little menacing. He said he knew Karen from another life. Those were his exact words. That's why I called Tom and asked him to meet me. I thought it was something he should know, and I didn't want to tell him over the phone.'

'But you didn't make it to your appointment with Tom Krupp that night. Why not?'

Brigid hesitates. She'd rather not tell them where she was that night. Better that they convict Karen without Brigid's eyewitness testimony. Better for her and Tom, and their future together. That's why she planted the gun.

Rasbach presses. 'When we came to your door after the accident, you told us you hadn't been at home that evening, so you hadn't seen Karen leave the house. Where were you?'

'I don't remember.'

'Really?' Rasbach says. 'We have two witnesses who saw you drive your car down the street, just a couple of minutes after Karen left, and turn in the same direction that she'd gone.'

She swallows.

'And we found your fingerprints and a palm print of yours on the door of the restaurant where the body was found.' Rasbach doesn't seem friendly any more.

Brigid is beginning to feel anxious.

'How do you explain that?' Rasbach presses.

She can't explain it – unless she tells the truth. She knew this might happen. 'Okay. I'll tell you the truth,' she says quickly, her eyes darting between the two detectives. 'Do I need to have a lawyer?'

'You're not under arrest. But you're certainly able to call one, if you'd like to.'

She shakes her head and licks her lips nervously. 'No, it's fine. I'd like to tell you what *really* happened.' She takes a deep breath and exhales. 'I *was* home that night. I was just about to leave to go meet Tom when I saw Karen take off out of the house. I thought it looked odd, like she might be in some kind of trouble, because she was in such a hurry, so I got in the car and decided to follow her, instead of meeting Tom. I'd seen that man around, in the morning. I thought she might need help, and she's a friend.' She pauses; the detectives are watching her closely. She twists her hands together under the table as she tells her story. 'I followed her to that awful part of town. She parked her car in a little lot by the restaurant and I parked in a plaza across the street. I saw her – she was wearing these pink rubber gloves and carrying a gun. She disappeared behind the restaurant. I was walking toward it when I heard three gunshots. Then I saw Karen run out of the building to her car. She pulled off the gloves and got in the car and sped away.'

'And what did you do?'

Brigid takes a deep breath. 'I went to the back door and then went inside. There was a man lying on the floor, dead.' She puts her hand up to her mouth, as if she might be sick. 'I couldn't believe it. I was horrified. I ran back to my car and went home.' She looks directly into the detective's sharp blue eyes. 'I was home for a while, wondering what to do, when Tom called and asked me if I knew where Karen was – and I said I didn't know.' She begins to cry. 'I didn't know what to tell him. I couldn't tell him that his wife had just murdered someone.' She lets the tears fall. Jennings slides a box of tissues in her direction, and she takes one gratefully.

'Why didn't you come to the police and tell them that you were there and what you knew? That you were a witness?' Rasbach stares at her with accusing eyes, unnerving her. 'Why didn't you tell us the truth when we questioned you?'

'She was a friend,' Brigid whispers. 'I know I should have come forward, but she was my friend.'

'Did you pick up the gun?'

'What?' She's getting more and more nervous.

'Did you pick up the gun that she dropped?'

She can't let them know that she planted the gun. 'No, I didn't see any gun. It was pretty dark, and I was upset. I just ran.'

'So you didn't pick up the gun and take it with you, and later plant it in the Krupps' garage?'

She colours and tries to look indignant, as she realizes that maybe she should have got a lawyer. 'No, I did not.' She raises her voice. 'Why would I do such a thing?'

'You didn't call the station, not once, but twice, and tell us to look for the murder weapon on the Krupps' property?'

'No, I did not.'

'So if we look at your phone records, we won't find a record of those calls?'

'No.'

'You're right, because those calls were made from a public telephone, which you know perfectly well, because you made them. We found your fingerprints on that public phone.'

She feels herself go completely bloodless. She can't think straight; she can't think her way out of this.

'Are you in love with Tom Krupp?'

She hesitates involuntarily, for a fraction of a second, startled by the question. 'No.'

'He says you are.'

'Does he?' She feels confused. 'What did he say?'

'He says that you're in love with him. He says that you tried to blackmail him, that you told him you followed Karen that night and saw what happened and that you wouldn't tell the police what you saw if he had sex with you. Is that true?'

Brigid is furious. How *dare* Tom tell them that, how dare he put it that way! Surely Tom wouldn't do that. It's this detective, twisting his words. She sits frozen still, and doesn't answer.

'Karen Krupp says that Robert Traynor was alive when she left him.'

'That's not true!' Brigid cries.

'Karen says that she dropped the gun and her gloves by the side of the car and took off. She says that you must have picked up the gun and gone back into the restaurant and shot Robert Traynor dead and then taken the gun home and later planted it in her garage.'

'What?' Brigid gasps, shocked.

'Because you want to see her go to jail, because you're in love with her husband.' Rasbach lowers himself down till his face is close to hers. 'We know all about your affair with Tom Krupp. He told us all about it – every detail.' He looks at her with his terribly direct blue eyes. 'And we know you've been sneaking into their house, going through their things. Your fingerprints are all over the house. We know you have a key.'

Brigid says, her spine rigid, 'That's bullshit. I would like to call a lawyer now.'

Chapter Forty-seven

RASBACH LETS BRIGID go, knowing that the first thing she'll do is scramble to find herself a lawyer, and they won't get anything more out of her. He and Jennings head back to Rasbach's office to discuss the case.

'What do you think?' Jennings asks him, as they sit down.

'I think this is really fucked up,' Rasbach says, letting his frustration show. They sit in silence for a minute. Finally, Rasbach asks, 'What did you think of Brigid?'

'I think she might have a screw loose, like the Krupps say.'

'But is she a murderer?'

Jennings tilts his head to one side. 'Maybe.'

'And that's the problem.' Rasbach sighs heavily and says, 'I still think Karen Krupp killed Traynor. I don't believe her story. The whole amnesia thing – and then suddenly remembering what happened? I don't buy it.'

'Me neither.'

'Interesting how Tom Krupp didn't have anything to say about that. I wonder what he really believes,' Rasbach says.

'I'd love to know, too,' Jennings says. 'The poor schmuck, he was waiting down by the river while all this was going down, without a clue.'

Rasbach nods. 'I don't believe that Karen ran away from Robert Traynor and dropped the gun, and that Brigid picked it up and went in and shot him. I can't see it. I don't think Traynor would let Karen get away, and I don't think Brigid thinks fast enough on her feet to figure it all out. I think Karen shot him, Brigid saw her do it, and *then* she smelled an opportunity and picked up the gun for later.'

Jennings nods thoughtfully.

Rasbach says, 'The district attorney's probably going to throw up her hands and drop the murder charge against Karen Krupp. She won't have much choice. She won't have a leg to stand on if there were two people there, both with a good motive – and we've got planted evidence.'

Jennings agrees. 'She's going to walk.'

'One of those two women killed Robert Traynor. I think it was Karen Krupp. But the only ones who really know for sure are Karen and Brigid.' He looks at Jennings and says, 'And it seems they're both in love with the same man. It's bound to get messy.'

'I'm sure as hell glad I'm not Tom Krupp,' Jennings says.

Susan Grimes is a competent DA. She's smart and practical, which is why Rasbach knows he's facing an uphill battle.

Rasbach has carefully laid out all of the evidence before her. Now he's standing by the window in her office, watching her as she sits back in the chair behind her large desk. Jennings is sitting across from her. It's the moment of truth.

'You've got to be kidding,' Susan Grimes says.

'Sadly, I am not,' Rasbach replies.

'You think Karen Krupp did it,' Grimes says.

'Yes, I do,' Rasbach says. 'I appreciate that it's going to be difficult to prove.'

'Difficult to prove? Try not worth bothering.' She sighs deeply, removes her glasses, and rubs her tired eyes. 'Krupp has the best motive – a very strong motive. We know she was there; we have physical evidence putting her there and the damning eyewitness testimony of the other woman. What's her name again?'

'Brigid Cruikshank,' Rasbach says.

'And she was clearly fleeing the scene.' Rasbach

nods. The DA tilts her head and continues. 'But we have Brigid's fingerprints on the door of the restaurant. The Krupps claim that Brigid is in love with Tom Krupp and trying to frame Karen Krupp for murder. What proof do they have of that?'

'Brigid isn't admitting to being in love with Tom Krupp; she hasn't even admitted to the earlier affair,' Rasbach says. 'So it's his word against hers. But her fingerprints are all over the Krupps' house. And there's the gun.'

'The gun,' the DA says. 'That's the real problem. The Krupps obviously didn't put it in their garage. And they can prove that Brigid called in the tip that it was there, because her fingerprints are on the pay phone.'

Rasbach nods. 'Yes.'

'And she was there, at the crime scene, so she *could* have picked up the gun.' She thinks for a long moment. 'If Brigid had just left well enough alone, if she'd just testified against her, we could have nailed Krupp. If only she hadn't planted the gun. It shows Brigid had motive.'

'That's the problem.'

She looks at Rasbach sharply. 'And you're sure there's no evidence that the two women hatched this plot together? They were friends at one time, weren't they?'

'Yes. But we can find no evidence of that.'

The DA shakes her head regretfully. 'Even the most incompetent attorney wouldn't have any difficulty raising reasonable doubt on this one,' she says. 'I'm sorry, we're going to have to drop it.'

'That's what I thought you'd say,' Rasbach says and looks moodily out the window.

Chapter Forty-eight

BEING HOME AGAIN feels strange and glorious after the discomforts of jail. Karen revels in the luxury of being alone, of having quiet, of not being constantly assaulted by hostile glares, bad smells, and god-awful food. The first few days back home again are like the best vacation Karen has ever had. She sleeps late, takes long, scented bubble baths, cooks her favourite meals. She loves her creature comforts; being deprived of them was torture.

And then there's the relief. She no longer has a murder charge hanging over her. She still has to deal with the reckless driving and the charges stemming from the fake ID, but those are relatively minor, considering. Jack Calvin is taking care of all that.

The relief is . . . amazing.

She no longer has to worry about Robert Traynor hunting her down and killing her.

She no longer has to worry about Tom somehow finding out about her false identity.

She doesn't have to worry about an intruder in her house. Because they know now who it was. And she won't be doing that any more. They've changed the locks. They've also installed a new security system that they'll keep on all the time, even when they're at home. It's an inconvenience and an annoyance, but it's something they have to do. Even with the restraining order they've obtained against Brigid.

Because who ever obeys a restraining order?

Things are good between her and Tom again. She was afraid at first that they wouldn't be able to get past everything that's happened. He hadn't liked her lying to the police, pretending to remember what happened that night.

'Why did you do that?' he asked her, when they were alone. 'If you don't remember, why didn't you just tell them the truth – *that you don't remember*?' He was visibly upset.

'I thought it would be better this way,' she told him. 'I thought it would help us.'

He glared at her. 'I don't like all the lies, Karen. I *hate* the lies.'

He'd been upset about that, but then the charges were dropped, and he seems to have put it behind them. She doesn't know what Tom *really* believes about who shot Robert Traynor. They don't talk about it. He knows she can't remember. He clearly believes that Brigid is unbalanced. He's afraid of Brigid. Karen thinks that if Tom does believe Karen shot her former husband, he understands why, and he's forgiven her. He's not afraid of *her*.

He seems to love Karen still, even if it's with a different, more cautious kind of love. When they came home together, when she first got out of jail, as soon as they'd crossed the threshold he closed the door firmly behind them and turned to her solemnly.

'I want us to make a fresh start,' he said. She'd never seen him look more serious. He reached out and held her by her arms, brought his face close to hers, and said, 'No more lies. Promise me, Karen.'

He was gripping her hard. She looked back at him intently. She said, 'I promise, Tom, no more lies. I swear.'

'Everything is out in the open now between us,' he said, 'and it's going to stay that way. For each of us. Always.'

'Yes, I promise, Tom,' she agreed, her eyes welling up.

'I promise too,' he said, and then he kissed her, hard and deep and long.

As she tidies up in the kitchen, Karen thinks about how angry Brigid must be, sitting across the street in her chair, watching them with her knitting in her lap. Things didn't go her way. Poor Brigid. And Karen has heard that Bob has left her. What a shock it must have been for Bob, to learn from the police that his wife had been stalking the couple across the street, letting herself into their home when they weren't there, playing house. That she was at the murder scene that night. That she might possibly be a killer, and that the police believe she planted a gun in the Krupps' garage. No wonder he left her. She's a nutcase. Perhaps he was afraid for his own life. Perhaps he should be. You just never know what Brigid might do.

Karen's done with Brigid, her former best friend. She's banished her from their life. Now she's going to enjoy herself. She's free, at last.

Brigid sits in her darkening, empty house. She's glaring across the street at the closed curtains of 24 Dogwood Drive. There's a soft glow of light behind the curtains, a warmth, a happiness there that she knows she will never attain, no matter how much she aspires to it, no matter how much she's willing to do to get it. Her knitting needles click violently – she's bitter, angry, and vengeful.

She thinks obsessively about everything that's happened. Something good *has* come out of it at least – Bob has left her. He was appalled when he found out what had been happening right under his nose. He hadn't been *paying attention*. Maybe if he'd been *paying attention*, none of this would have happened at all. But still, she's glad he's gone. Good riddance. She doesn't need his wariness, his contempt. She doesn't need his socks on the floor, his toothbrush by the sink; she doesn't need his mess, his demands, his presence in this house. As long as he keeps paying the bills, she's happy that he's gone.

She's glad to be alone, for now. If she can't have Tom, she doesn't want anybody. She will bide her time.

The weeks pass and the summer slips gradually into autumn. The leaves have turned orange and yellow and red, and the air is crisp, especially in the morning. Tom has found a new job with a rival accounting firm, and he is once again working downtown in a high-rise office building, doing excellent work as a senior accountant and wondering about his chances of making partner. Maybe next year he will make the time to take up golf.

Karen's happy again, for which Tom is grateful. And Tom is happy, or as happy as he can ever be, now that life has shown him just what it can do to you. Tom will never again live in a comfortable, unsuspecting bubble, thinking that nothing bad is ever going to happen. He knows better now. He worries sometimes that Brigid will confront him, that she'll come running out of her house with her hair all a mess, her expression wild, and try to put out his eyes with her knitting needles.

They're waiting for a sign to go up on the lawn across the street. Now that Bob has left her, Tom and Karen hope that he'll force Brigid to sell the house and move into something smaller, somewhere else. Tom has twice screwed up his courage and called Bob at work to ask him about their intentions regarding the house. But Bob refused to take his calls. He thinks about Bob sometimes, always with guilt and regret. If the Cruikshanks don't put their house up for sale, Tom and Karen may have to sell theirs. How can they live across the street from a crazy woman who's obsessed with him? It's unnerving. Tom would like to move, but nothing is selling right now and they would take a big loss. Better that the Cruikshanks sell, since they're divorcing anyway. So Tom and Karen are staying put for the time being.

It's not ideal.

Chapter Forty-nine

KAREN SEES TOM off to work and returns to the kitchen and finishes her cup of coffee. She's in a buoyant mood. She's taking the train into New York City today, to treat herself to a day of shopping.

She gathers up her purse and keys and a fall jacket and carefully arms the security system. She checks across the street. It's automatic now, the glance across to Brigid's house, to see if the coast is clear. She certainly doesn't want to run into Brigid.

Karen takes a city bus to the train station downtown. She's going to take the express to New York. She loves the train. One of her favourite things is to look out at the passing scenery as the train eats up the miles, and think and plan and dream. She likes to pretend that she could be going anywhere, be anyone. She's always been tempted by the road not taken.

She purchases her ticket and looks around, to make sure that Brigid isn't there, somewhere, lurking. She starts. That woman over by the magazines, could that be Brigid, in different clothes? Karen's entire body tenses. The woman turns, and Karen sees her profile. No, she's someone else entirely. Karen tries to relax.

Finally she's seated on the train, at the window. It's not busy today, and the seat beside her is empty. Karen puts her handbag on the empty seat, hoping no one comes along and wants to sit there. She wants to be alone.

Over the last few weeks her memory has completely returned, in pieces at first, and then in a flood. Now she can look back, push that grimy door open in her mind's eye, and watch everything unfold, the way it really happened. Dr Fulton was right; it did come back, it just took time.

Now, she watches the landscape speed by, and thinks about Tom, about how much she loves him, how trusting he is. She really doesn't deserve him.

It's so sweet that he believes everything she tells him. He's so protective – her knight in shining armour. She almost thinks that if Robert weren't already dead, Tom would go after him for her, he's so outraged by Robert's terrible ill treatment of her. But she's not a woman who needs a man's protection. She's never been that kind of woman. She's the kind of woman from whom men need to be protected. The thought makes her smile.

She loves Tom. She loves him so much that it surprises her a little. She hopes that she will love him this way for the rest of her life. But just because she loves him, and he loves her, it doesn't mean he *knows* her. What is love anyway, she thinks, but a grand illusion? We fall in love with an ideal, not a reality. Tom loves who he thinks she is. He's proven himself to be remarkably adaptable in that regard. She loves who she thinks he is. And that's the way it is the whole world over, she tells herself, watching out the train window, people falling in and out of love, as their perception of reality changes.

She is nobody's victim. She's not an abused or battered woman, and never has been. The idea almost makes her laugh. The day any man raises his hand to her will be the last day he'll try that ever again.

Robert had never been abusive. He'd been a decent enough man, not terribly good, but not terribly bad either. But she knew that he could be violent if someone got in the way of his money. He ran with those sort of people. And he obviously knew how to pick a lock. She had never been in love with him. Tom is the only man she has ever been in love with. No, Robert was an opportunity. Because of Robert, she has a safety deposit box with Chase Manhattan Bank in New York City with more than two million dollars cash in it. Her safety net. And now he will never be able to find her and demand it back. He's dead. She was always sure that if he found her again, he would kill her for it.

She remembers it all as she looks out the dirty window on her way into the city, how she met Robert in Vegas, at a casino. He was handsome and flashy – he had money and liked to spend it – whereas she had none. He was instantly taken with her. He told her that he dealt in antiques. That was true, but she soon realized that his antiques business provided him with an excellent cover for another role – part-time money launderer. Karen's no dummy. She lived with him for a while, watching how he did things. Sometimes he had a lot of cash to put in the safe at home, hidden behind an uninspired oil painting in the bedroom. He never told her the combination. She spent months trying to figure it out.

They got married in one of those god-awful chapels in Vegas where sad, desperate people get married, but she didn't care, she had a plan. He wanted to get married, so they got married. She's always been a long-term planner. That's how she's gotten as far as she has. It's only when she panics that things go wrong. She's learned that the hard way.

She lived with Robert as his wife for three years. She kept an eye on the patterns of cash going in and out of the safe. She finally discovered where he hid the record of the combination, which he changed every week. That's when she started going to the Open Arms in Las Vegas to build her story of being a battered wife. Because she knew then that she would be able to get the money out of the safe and that she would take it and leave him. She knew he wouldn't report the stolen cash – he couldn't. But she didn't want him coming after her for it. She carefully planned her apparent suicide and her resurrection as Karen Fairfield. She knew that if he did come after her, and wanted his money back, she would have to kill him, and if she were ever caught, she would have her carefully built defence of battered wife ready.

But it shouldn't have come to that. It *should* have been okay. She'd planned ahead for just such an eventuality. She acquired an unregistered gun that she was careful never to get her prints on. And she had her gloves. If she hadn't lost her cool that night, it would have been fine. Just like Detective Rasbach said – she would have gotten away with murder, with no one the wiser.

But she was more rattled than expected when she actually heard Robert's voice that night. And when it came to the moment she was face-to-face with him, and she had to kill him . . . it wasn't as easy as she thought it would be. It wasn't easy at all. She's never been a violent person. Greedy, yes, but not violent. He looked so surprised when she lifted the gun and pointed it at him. Her hand was shaking; they could both see it. He didn't think she had it in her. She couldn't do it. He laughed. She was about to lower the gun when he lunged for her, and in a panic – she hadn't meant to do it – she pulled the trigger. And then again, and again. She can still remember the kick of the gun in her hand, the explosion of gunshots to his chest and face, how sick it made her feel, the smell of the rubber gloves when she put her hand to her mouth to stop herself from retching.

If only she hadn't panicked! If she'd kept her head she could have driven away and dropped the gun in the river. She could have snuck the gloves back into the kitchen and told Tom some simple lie about where she'd been. The police would have found Robert, figured out who he was, and learned that his wife had died years before. But there would have been absolutely nothing to connect her – Karen Krupp – to Robert's death. If she hadn't panicked and dropped the gloves and had her stupid accident.

If Rasbach hadn't been so clever.

And if Brigid hadn't followed her. That's the second thing that almost did her in.

She hadn't seen that coming.

But it all worked out. She's actually grateful to Brigid. If Brigid hadn't wanted Tom so desperately, if

Brigid hadn't followed her, and planted the gun, Karen would still be in jail.

And now Tom will never know the truth, because Robert is dead.

Karen is perfectly happy. She's going into the city to check on her safety deposit box, and then she'll go shopping. She will buy Tom a little gift. Life is good. She loves Tom, and she hopes their love story lasts for ever. Maybe they will start trying in earnest for a baby.

She'll have to find some way to come into some money at some point, so that she and Tom can actually enjoy the money that she went through so much effort to get – or part of it, anyway.

She's sure she'll think of something.

Brigid, alone in her empty house, sits at the window and watches and waits. She bides her time. The only sound is the clicking of her busy knitting needles. She's so angry.

She knows Karen killed that man – Brigid was *there* – and yet she still got away with it. She got away with murder, even though Brigid told the truth about what she saw and heard that night. And Karen tried to turn it around on *her*, to make *her* look like the guilty one. *How dare she?*

And now Karen has everything she wants. Not only did she get away with murder, she still has Tom wrapped around her little finger. At least it looks that way. But perhaps not; it's hard to tell from here. Brigid wishes she could be a fly on the wall inside that house. But she thinks Tom still loves Karen, in spite of everything. How can he still love her, she wails to herself, her heart beating in anguish, after everything she's done, after all her lies? It's outrageous. *How can he not know that she's a murderer? How can he believe her?*

Brigid realizes that she blew it when she planted the gun. She should have left well enough alone. Her eyewitness account would have been enough. And now Karen has gotten away with murder, and humiliated her. Humiliated her in front of the police, her husband, their friends, everyone. Accusing *her* of murder, saying she planted the gun, that she stalked her inside the house. Charging her with trespassing, getting that ridiculous restraining order against her.

Karen obviously thinks Brigid's not as clever as she is. Well, they'll see about that.

Brigid isn't giving up, and she's not going away. She has a new plan. She'll make Karen pay.

And – she has a secret. Brigid smiles and looks down at the item that she's knitting with the utmost care: an impossibly small baby sweater in the softest ivory baby yarn she could find. She has lots of things to knit now. A matching bonnet and booties for the sweater on her lap. She's also just finished the butter yellow baby sweater that she'd been making for someone else but abandoned a few weeks ago because working on it made her angry.

It doesn't make her angry any more.

Brigid admires the adorable little sweater in her hands and her heart swells. She lifts her eyes to the house across the street.

Everything is going to be perfect.

Acknowledgements

I owe tremendous thanks to so many. It takes a lot of talented people to bring a thriller to market, and I am fortunate to have some of the best in the business to work with!

Thank you to Helen Heller – your insight, encouragement, smarts, and toughness are just what I need. I am in awe of you. Sincere thanks also to everyone at the Marsh Agency, for their excellent representation worldwide.

To my fabulous publishers I owe enormous gratitude. Huge thanks to Brian Tart, Pamela Dorman, and the first-rate team at Viking Penguin (US). Huge thanks also to Larry Finlay and Frankie Gray at Transworld UK and the top-notch team there. Sincere thanks to Kristin Cochrane, Amy Black, and Bhavna Chauhan, and the super team at Doubleday Canada. I am so fortunate to have such wonderful editing, marketing, and publicity teams on both sides of the Atlantic. Your enthusiasm, expertise, and commitment have blown me away.

Thanks to my first readers – Leslie Mutic, Sandra Ostler, Cathie Colombo, and Julia Lapena – your suggestions and opinions are always much appreciated.

Lastly, I could not do it at all without the whole-hearted support of my husband, Manuel, and my wildly enthusiastic and generous kids, Christopher and Julia, avid readers both.

Don't miss Shari Lapena's tantalising
new thriller

Read on for an exclusive look at the first
chapter now . . .

Friday, 4:45 P.M.

The road curves and twists unexpectedly as it leads higher and deeper into the Catskill Mountains, as if the further you get from civilization, the more uncertain the path. The shadows are deepening, the weather worsening. The Hudson River is there, appearing and disappearing from view. The forest that rises on either side of the road has a lurking quality, as if it might swallow you whole; it is the forest of fairy tales. The softly falling snow, however, lends it all a certain postcard charm.

Gwen Delaney grips the steering wheel tightly and squints through the windscreen. She's more one for grim fairy tales than picture postcards. The light is going; it will soon be dark. The snow coming down makes driving more difficult, more tiring. The flakes hit the glass in such profusion that she feels as though she's stuck in some kind of relentless video game. And the road is definitely becoming more slippery. She's grateful that she has good tyres on her little Fiat. Everything is turning into a white blur; it's hard to tell where the road ends and the ditch begins. She'll be glad when they get there. She's beginning to wish they'd chosen an inn a little less remote; this one is miles from anywhere.

Riley Shuter is silent in the passenger seat beside her, a ball of quiet tension; it's impossible not to pick up on it. Just being with her in the small car puts Gwen on edge. She hopes she hasn't made a mistake bringing her up here.

The whole point of this little escape, Gwen thinks, is to get Riley to relax a little, to take her mind off things.

Gwen bites her lip and stares hard at the road ahead. She's a city girl, born and bred; she's not used to country driving. It gets so dark up here. She's becoming anxious now – the drive has taken longer than planned. They shouldn't have stopped for coffee at that cute little antique place along the way.

She's not sure what she expected, suggesting this weekend getaway, other than a change of scenery, a chance to spend some quiet time together, with nothing to remind Riley that her life is in ruins. Perhaps that was naive.

Gwen has her own baggage, less recent, and she, too, carries it with her everywhere she goes. But she's decided she's going to put that behind her for this weekend at least. A small luxury hotel deep in the country, good food, no internet, pristine nature – it's exactly what they both need.

Riley watches nervously out of the car window, peering into the shadowy woods, trying not to imagine someone jumping in front of their car at any second, waving them down. She clenches her hands into fists inside the pockets of her down jacket. She reminds herself that she's not in Afghanistan anymore. She's home, safe, in New York State. Nothing bad can happen to her here.

Her career has changed her. Seeing what she has seen, Riley is so different that she hardly recognizes herself anymore. She glances furtively at Gwen. They'd been close once. She's not even sure why she agreed to come with her to this faraway country inn. She watches Gwen concentrating fiercely on the winding road up the slippery incline, heading into the mountains. 'Are you OK?' she asks suddenly.

'Me?' Gwen says. 'Yeah, I'm fine. We should be there soon.'

In journalism school, when they were both at NYU,

Gwen had been the steady, pragmatic one. But Riley was ambitious – she wanted to be where it was happening. Gwen had no taste for adventure. She'd always preferred books, and quiet. Out of journalism school, unable to find a decent job at a newspaper, Gwen had quickly parlayed her skills into a good corporate communications position and had never seemed to regret it. But Riley had headed to the war zones. And she'd managed to keep it together for a long time.

Why does she do this? Why does she keep thinking about it? She can feel herself starting to come apart. She tries to slow her breathing, the way she's been taught. To stop the images from coming back, from taking over.

David Paley parks his car in the shovelled parking area to the right of the hotel. He gets out of the car and stretches. The weather made the drive from New York City longer than expected, and now his muscles are stiff – a reminder that he's not quite as young as he used to be. Before grabbing his overnight bag from the back seat of his Mercedes, he stands for a moment in the thickly falling snow, looking at Mitchell's Inn.

It's a three-storey, graceful-looking structure of red brick and gingerbread trim, encircled by nearby forest. The front of the small hotel is open to view, with what must be a rather grand lawn underneath all the snow. Tall evergreens and mature trees bereft of leaves but draped in white seem to encroach on the building from a short distance away. In the front, an enormous tree in the middle of the lawn extends its thick branches in every direction. All is covered in a pure, muffling white snow. It feels quiet here, peaceful, and he feels his shoulders begin to relax.

There are large, rectangular windows spaced regularly across all three floors. Wide steps lead up to a wooden porch and double front doors decorated with boughs of evergreens. Although it is still daylight – barely – the lamps on either side of the doors are lit, and soft yellow light also spills from the windows on the ground floor, giving the building a warm, welcoming appearance. David stands still, willing the stresses of the day – and the week, and the years – to recede as the snow falls gently on his hair and tickles his lips. He feels like he's walking into an earlier, more gracious, more innocent time.

He will try not to think about work for an entire forty-eight hours. Everyone, no matter how busy, needs to recharge once in a while, even – perhaps especially – a top criminal attorney. It's rare for him to be able to fit in any downtime at all, much less an entire weekend. He's determined to enjoy it.

Friday, 5:00 P.M.

Lauren Day glances at the man next to her, Ian Beeton. He's driving his car expertly in rather challenging conditions, and making it all look easy. He has a disarming smile, and he turns it on her now. She smiles back. He's nice-looking, too, tall and spare, but it's the smile that first attracted her to him, his laid-back charm that makes him so appealing. Lauren rummages through her handbag for her lipstick. She finds it – a nice shade of red that brightens her face – and applies it carefully while looking in the mirror on the visor in front of her. The car skids a bit and she stops what she's doing, but Ian straightens the vehicle skilfully. The road winds more steeply now, and the car has an increasing tendency to swerve as it loses traction.

'Getting slippery,' she says.

'No worries. Nothing I can't handle,' he says and grins at her. She smiles back. She likes his self-confidence, too.

'Whoa – what's that?' she says suddenly. There's a dark

shape in front of them to the right. It's a dull day, and with the snow falling so heavily it's hard to see, but it looks like there's a car in the ditch.

She stares keenly out of the window as they pass by the vehicle, and Ian looks for somewhere to stop. 'I think there's someone in that car,' she says.

'Why don't they have the hazard lights on?' he mutters. He pulls over slowly to the side of the road, careful not to slide off the road himself. Lauren gets out of the warmth of the car and plunges into several inches of virgin snow, which immediately falls inside her boots, stinging her ankles. She can hear Ian getting out of the car, too, slamming the door.

'Hey!' she cries down to the motionless car. The driver's door opens slowly.

Lauren clambers down the incline carefully, sliding as she goes. The ground is uneven and she finds it hard to keep her balance. She reaches the car and grabs on to the door with her left hand for support as she peers into the front seat. 'You OK?' she asks.

The driver is a woman close to her own age – around thirty. She appears a bit shaken up, but the windscreen isn't cracked and she's wearing a seat belt. Lauren looks beyond the driver to the woman in the passenger seat. Her face is pale and sweating, and she's staring straight ahead, as if Lauren isn't even there. She looks like she's had a dreadful shock.

The driver glances quickly at her companion, and then turns back to Lauren gratefully. 'Yes, we're fine. We went off the road just a few minutes ago. We were wondering what to do next. Lucky for us you came along.'

Lauren feels Ian come up behind her and peer over her shoulder at the two women inside the car. He smiles his charming smile at them. 'Looks like you're going to need a tow.'

'Great,' the driver says.

'Where you headed?' Lauren asks.

'Mitchell's Inn,' she answers.

'Well, isn't that lucky,' Ian says. 'That's where we're going, too. Although I don't think there's much else out here. Why don't we give you a lift, and you can arrange from the hotel for someone to come get your car out?'

The woman smiles with relief and nods. She's obviously glad to be rescued. Lauren doesn't blame her. You could freeze to death out here all by yourself. But the woman with her doesn't react. She seems to be in her own world.

'You have any bags?' Lauren asks.

'Yes, in the back.' The driver gets out of the car and struggles through the deep snow to the back of the vehicle. Her passenger now seems to snap out of her trance and gets out on the other side. The driver opens the boot as the woman appears beside her. They each grab an over-night bag.

Ian reaches down and offers all three women a hand up to the road. Even with help, it's an awkward climb.

'Thanks so much,' the driver says. 'My name is Gwen, and this is Riley.'

'I'm Lauren and this is Ian,' she says. 'Let's get in the car. It's so cold.' She casts a furtive glance at the woman named Riley, who hasn't said a word. She wonders what's up with her. Something about her definitely seems off.

Available now